Undaunted

By Ronnie Douglas

Undaunted

COMING SOON

Unruly

Undaunted

Ronnie Douglas

wm

WILLIAM MORROW
An Imprint of HarperCollins*Publishers*

HarperCollins books may be purchased for educational, business, or sales promotional use. For information please e-mail the Special Markets Department at SPsales@harpercollins.com.

FIRST EDITION

Designed by Diahann Sturge

Library of Congress Cataloging-in-Publication Data has been applied for.

ISBN 978-0-06-238960-2

15 16 17 18 19   OV/RRD   10 9 8 7 6 5 4 3 2 1

To Cynthia and Jeanette, badass ladies and former motorcycle mamas. I'd hide a body for either of you without a moment's doubt or regret. Love you.

Undaunted

Chapter 1

THE SCREAM OF A HOUSE ALARM WOKE ME. AGAIN. IF anyone had said that the seniors' neighborhood in Williamsville, Tennessee, was a hotbed of crime, I'd have rolled my eyes. Unfortunately, three of the past eight nights had included alarms, sirens, or shouts, and I was starting to think that I'd moved into a *horrible* neighborhood.

The clock showed 4:48 A.M. as I stumbled to my feet, sheets tangled around me like they were actively trying to keep me in my nice, soft bed. It was too early to be awake. *Again.* I was glad no one was getting injured in these break-ins, but I was still irritated at the repeated disruptions of my sleep. I didn't understand why they'd started happening, and my grandmother's theories seemed to fluctuate between "bad luck" and "bad seeds."

As I opened my bedroom door, my grandmother stepped into the hallway.

"Are you okay?" I asked, more out of habit than worry. Grandma Maureen seemed impervious to harm even when she was caught off guard. It was one of the many reasons I wanted to be more like her when I eventually figured out how to grow up.

"Always," she said.

Her voice was as firm as it had been when she was terrifying classrooms full of high school students. Age hadn't worn her edges down. I sometimes thought that the popular culture images of sweet old grannies with knitting needles were her precise "what not to be" role models. If she ever hung a picture of one of those fictional grandmothers with a big red slash through it, I wouldn't be at all shocked.

"The sheriff needs to get off his oversized posterior," my grandmother announced. Her robe was already belted, and her house slippers poked out from under the hem.

"Did you already—?"

"Call him? Of course, dear." She patted my arm. "Go ahead and crawl back in bed. I have this under control."

I wanted to. I really did. Unfortunately, I am my grandmother's granddaughter. On the upside, that meant I was far more like her than like either of my nitwit parents. They weren't *bad* people. They just both seemed so caught up in their own drama that I wasn't entirely sure they'd noticed when I'd moved from Oregon to Tennessee last month. They'd obviously figured it out by now, but they weren't exactly dialed in on the parenting thing. They never had been.

Grandma Maureen had been my role model when I was a kid, and even though I'd turned twenty this past summer, I still thought she was the coolest woman I'd ever met. She was fierce and organized no matter what went on around her. I almost felt sorry for the sheriff.

Almost.

He'd done next to nothing about the rash of break-ins and weird vandalism in the neighborhood. Most of the neighbors were senior citizens. They all lived in tiny houses and on fixed incomes. There was no reason this neighborhood would be targeted. There were wealthier areas of town— not by much, but still . . . it made no sense to target the seniors. Were the thieves in dire need of walkers, hearing aids, and discount coupons? Did they supply black-market demand for geraniums? It didn't make sense.

"Put the kettle on if you're not going back to bed," Grandma Maureen ordered when she realized I was still standing in the hallway.

I shuffled to the kitchen to do as I was told. This whole thing was becoming a routine of late: alarms, middle-of-the-night conversations with the police, and the seniors in the kitchen drinking tea and discussing the latest event. It was getting ridiculous, but at least no one had gotten hurt. The increasing fear was that the vandalism and break-ins would escalate.

While my grandmother was outside gesticulating wildly at the sheriff, who looked more intimidated than usual, I poured the boiling water from the kettle into the well-used teapot. As I did so, I looked out the tiny window. In the street, illuminated by the one remaining streetlight, were two bikers. One looked to be around my mother's age, but the other appeared to be not much older than me. Both men wore the sort of black leather jackets with patches that I'd seen on most of the bikers around Williamsville. I didn't typically pay a lot of mind to bikers, but whenever I'd visited my grandmother over the years, I'd seen them, and I'd continued to see them regularly since I moved here. They'd always seemed polite or not particularly interested in me. In all they didn't make me nervous, but that didn't mean I loved the idea of them—or any stranger—around my grandmother, especially with all the crimes lately.

I put the teapot on the table, grabbed a sweater from one of the hooks by the door, and went outside. Just because she *could* take care of herself didn't mean she should *have to*. My companionship and support were among the few things I felt like I could contribute. She took me in, supported me, loved me, listened to me, and I mostly took up space and tried not to be a burden.

The sheriff looked at me as I approached, a question obvious in his gaze, but my grandmother didn't introduce us. Every other time he'd been called out to the neighborhood, I'd simply obeyed her and stayed in the house while she marched off to her neighbors' sides like a gray-haired general in a floral housecoat. Of course, every *other* time it was only police and seniors in the dark. The bikers changed things—and not just because they were bikers. Anyone watching my grandmother at this hour would've made me uncomfortable, and it was obvious that they were watching her specifically. I just didn't know why.

Grandma Maureen glanced my way briefly, but her attention quickly returned to the sheriff, who was saying, "Let us handle this, Miz Evans. Like I said last time—"

She cut him off. "Don't sass me, boy. You need to *listen*."

The sheriff closed his notebook with the sort of finality that made it abundantly clear that he thought that whatever else she had to say wasn't going to be relevant to his scribbled notes. He met her gaze and said, "The department is investigating. *Like I told you last time*, justice isn't always instantaneous."

One of the other neighbors—Beau, or maybe his name was Joe—snorted. I had met him last week, and his accent gave new meaning to the idea of a Southern drawl. I couldn't understand half his words, and the ones I could were laden with regionalisms and slang that seemed to mostly involve odd or graphic metaphors.

As the sheriff walked away, Beau-possibly-Joe announced, "Dumber than a sack of half-cracked bricks, that one is."

Grateful that I'd understood his words and meaning this time, I nodded. He was half-right. The sheriff seemed none too bright, but then again, I had started to wonder if it was dishonesty, not stupidity, making him so ineffectual.

"Beau!" Grandma Maureen called, unknowingly clearing up the name question for me.

When Beau looked her way, she gestured toward a cluster of senior citizens. "Tell the girls to meet me in the kitchen. Might as well have tea if we're already up."

Then my grandmother walked toward the bikers, who were leaning on their motorcycles watching everything. They gave her the sort of look that made me think they were watching approaching royalty. It was a mix between Southern gentlemanliness and the way a fighter acknowledges an equal.

"If I were the sheriff, I'd be sweating like a hussy in the Good Lord's house right now," Beau murmured from beside me.

When I looked his way, my confusion must've been obvious, because he added, "Miz Maureen has influential friends. She doesn't like to call on them, but she's about fed up waiting on the sheriff. That man couldn't find his ass with both hands and a map. Those boys there"—he nodded toward the street—"they get things done. Maybe not the way the law likes, but they get results."

"So they're not the ones doing this?"

Beau laughed. "Echo would dip a man in honey and stake him out for the bears to find if any one of them boys touched Miz Maureen." Beau inclined his head toward the bikers who were talking to her. "Your grandmother has the ear of one of the most powerful men in the state. She doesn't call on Echo for anything, so people forget that she *could* do so."

"Oh."

"Not a bad thing." Beau patted my hand. "Eddie Echo would steal the stars out from under the angels themselves if Miz Maureen so much as hinted that her yard wasn't bright enough."

I followed his gaze. I couldn't make out many details about the two men standing with my grandmother. They were both, obviously, riding Harleys. I didn't know enough about bikes to be more specific than that. One of the guys lifted his gaze and looked my way. Dark hair brushed the edge of a black leather jacket. Strong jaw, sharp cheekbones, and a mouth that looked made for sin, he was the sort of contrast in beauty and danger that made me think there had to be a trick of light. No man looked that good. Even as I argued with my own perception, I could tell that he was near my age, fit, and held himself with the kind of restrained energy that made sane girls look away and unhappy girls want to step a bit closer. I told myself that I was sane, that I was going to look away any moment now, that I didn't want to find an excuse to go check on Grandma Maureen.

I was lying.

"Ask your gran about Echo before you go staring at the likes of those boys." Beau paused and then added, "I'm going to head inside."

I glanced at him. "You go on ahead."

Beau and everyone else seemed to agree with me that she was tough, but she was also my *grandmother*. She was the only person I'd ever been able to count on in my life, and that meant that sometimes I tended to be a little overprotective of her. I didn't know that she needed me, but I felt better being able to see her.

"Apple didn't fall too far from the tree after all, did it?" Beau said, and then he grinned widely, showing off his teeth. I'd known him less than a week, and I already knew that the man was inordinately pleased to still have his "own chompers." He patted my cheek. "You're a lot like her, Aubrey Girl. Just talk to her before you go looking too long at bikers."

As much as I wanted to deny looking at them, I wasn't going to insult the grandfatherly man by doing so. Beau and a few of the others went into the house, and I admitted to myself that I also had a secondary motivation. The bikers who were talking to my grandmother intrigued me— especially the one who kept glancing my way. Men who looked like him didn't notice girls like me. Oh, they noticed my *body* easily enough. I had what were politely called "curves," so I'd spent years learning to hide them. Too much hip, too much bust. If there were ever a big call for throwback pinup girls, I'd be a shoo-in. Unfortunately, we lived in a world where stick-figure girls were considered more attractive by society at large. I just got the leers and catcalls. I had a body that invited a certain sort of thought, but I was a "good" girl. Men didn't pay me much attention when they realized that.

The biker looking at me wasn't catcalling, and for a rare

change, I didn't feel like I ought to tighten my robe to try to hide my body. Mostly, I felt like stepping forward to see if he looked as sin-pretty up close—but I wasn't stupid enough to do so. My brief spell of boy-craziness had been back at the start of high school. These days, I was anti-boyfriend. I wasn't going to throw that away because I was intrigued by the way the biker was watching me, even though I'd always had an odd fascination with motorcycles. I'd never even ridden one, but there was something about the sound of them as they roared by that had always drawn my attention.

I shook my head at the absurdity of telling *that* to my friends back in Oregon. Not surprisingly, Reed wasn't a hotbed of biker activity, and my father had always been a bit hostile about bikers. I was starting to wonder if the mysterious Mr. Echo was why. My grandmother obviously had some sort of connection to these bikers, and if Beau was to be believed, she had influence over them.

Grandma Maureen said something, and the biker who was staring my way turned back to her. They exchanged another few words, and then she turned away from them. As soon as she began walking away, both men started up their motorcycles. The sound of the engines growling in the once-more-silent street was intense enough that I couldn't help watching as the bikers took off in a roar of black and chrome. There was a raw beauty in that much power.

They were at the end of the street when I realized that my grandmother was at my side. "I'm safe with them, lovie. You didn't need to come outside."

I straightened my shoulders. "I was just surprised to see you chatting with bikers. Not that bikers are all bad, just . . . I worry about you."

"Hush. Those two were my students years back, and there's not a one of the boys wearing *that* jacket in Williamsville who would harm me—or you. Any of those boys make you uncomfortable, you tell them you're *my* granddaughter. You hear me?"

"Are you going to tell me why that would matter to them?" I paused and met her eyes. "Is one of them Echo? Beau said—"

"Beau talks too much." Grandma Maureen tucked her arm into the fold of mine and started toward the house. She didn't even pretend to acknowledge my other question, the more pressing one. Why did the local motorcycle club care about my grandmother? Instead, she said, "What say we pour that tea?"

I knew my grandmother well enough to know that she'd tell me if she thought I really ought to know, but I also knew that she was going to continue omitting whatever secret Beau had been talking about unless she couldn't avoid sharing it. For the time being, I decided that I would respect her desire to say nothing.

I owed Grandma Maureen everything. No matter how off course my life got, she'd always been there for me. Having everything I thought I could count on yanked away would've been crushing if not for my grandmother. All through high school, I'd worked hard for the grades and done the extracurriculars; I'd volunteered every free hour I had. I'd taken summer jobs that demonstrated a commitment to civic service or that diversified my application strengths. For the past five years, I'd done everything I was supposed to do.

I'd been *to the letter* perfect on every expectation, never stepping out of line. I'd spent four semesters at Reed College in gorgeous Portland, Oregon. The campus was picture perfect: beautiful buildings connected by meandering paths under stately trees where quirky students dedicated to knowledge studied and played in a campus that boasted a solid Honor Code, healthy dining, and a walking path to Trader Joe's.

Now I was in Williamsville, Tennessee, and I felt completely and utterly out of place. The only anchor I had in this world was my grandmother. I felt like everything I'd done was by the rules, and now I was starting over in a strange place where I didn't think I'd fit in at all. My parents had yanked the proverbial rug out from under me—Dad got caught embezzling, and instead of standing by him while they figured it out, my mother left him. My college fund was frozen . . . or maybe even seized by now. I wasn't sure, and they weren't telling me anything useful. Grandma Maureen had stepped in *again* to haul me to sanity, away from my parents, away from their fights and lawyers. I owed her everything, but she didn't ask for anything in return—which meant that I would swallow my questions about her biker connections.

I kept my silence as we walked to the house, but I slipped

my hand into hers and squeezed. Whatever came, I'd face it with her. I'd try to be the person she thought I was.

Several of the neighbors were in the kitchen when we went inside. It was an increasingly familiar scene to see them there, pouring tea and pondering crimes. I was impressed that they were refusing to be intimidated, but at the same time, it disappointed me that even at their advanced ages, they were having to deal with stress.

"Was that little Zion?" one of the women asked as we walked in.

"Not so little, Katie." Beau shook his head. "Boy's taken over as enforc—"

"Enough," Grandma Maureen interrupted in a stern voice. She shooed me toward the bedrooms. "Go on. Get a little more sleep. The excitement's over, and you don't need to sit listening to us go on about it all yet again."

I leaned in and kissed her cheek. Pushing her on a topic she obviously didn't want to discuss in front of me wasn't worth the stress it would cause her, no matter how curious I was.

"Good night, all," I said.

Then I shuffled off to the bedroom where I'd slept since I moved into my grandmother's house. It was filled with my clothes and books, but it wasn't truly mine. There was nowhere that was *mine* now. My home was gone, and now my dorm room was gone. I was adrift.

It was temporary. I reminded myself of that fact regularly, but it didn't make me feel any less lonely or lost. It simply helped me try to stay on my path—despite the all-too-recent reminder that doing so wasn't guaranteed to get me where I wanted to be. If staying on my path was all it took, I'd be in Oregon. I'd be with my friends. I'd be at Reed.

So I was working on a new path. That was what I'd done when things were a mess after my first year of high school. It had kept life orderly for the next three years of high school and the first two years of college. Everything had crashed recently, but that was temporary too. I just needed to sort out the new version of The Plan. I hadn't even had a real career plan—a secret I more or less hid from my high school and college friends. I was good at literature, good with words, and that was the closest thing I had to a focus. Reed didn't require declaring a major at entry. In fact, they were opposed to it. That meant I could answer with a vague "I love lit" reply when people prompted me, and that was enough. I wasn't sure I was cut out for teaching . . . or research . . . or writing . . . or law school. I didn't know. What I did know was that I needed to hold a 4.0, or as close to it as possible, so when I figured out what precisely I was doing after finishing my BA in English, I'd have choices.

I crawled under the covers and went over my latest version of The Plan. I needed to get back on schedule. So I had a strategy, a *good strategy* to do so. I needed to stay enrolled in classes and find a job. It would keep me super busy, but that was okay. I didn't fit in here, so it wasn't like I had anything to do with my time other than be with my grandmother, and she had a life of her own. I'd keep dating off the schedule too. That had worked well for years; there was no reason it shouldn't stay off *this* iteration of The Plan too.

Unfortunately, I still felt like I had a big sign flashing OUTSIDER over my head when I went anywhere in Williamsville, and I was just as tense as I always had been in unfamiliar places. Simply *deciding* to be bold wasn't having the results I wanted, so I returned to my tried-and-true solution when I felt adrift: make a plan, implement the plan.

However, implementing my plan was complicated by the troubles in my grandmother's neighborhood. Sheriff Patterson dismissed most of the complaints—when he actually bothered to show up to hear them—but that didn't mean the seniors were being quiet about their displeasure. Grandma Maureen was organizing a neighborhood watch, and she was lobbying for an article in whatever newspaper in Tennessee would take her calls.

Between the seniors' meetings and getting settled into Grandma's house, I hadn't explored Williamsville any further. Tomorrow, I would put my plan into motion: be bolder, get a job, start classes. I needed to get my new life on track, and I needed to do it before I did something stupid.

Chapter 2

AVOIDING STUPIDITY SOUNDED SO EASY, BUT THE SAD truth was that there was a pretty clear reason that I had to have The Plan. I was easily distracted by the desire to let my mind go quiet. It wasn't something I had ever quite mastered, but I knew it was possible. For a brief blink when I was fourteen, kissing had been amazingly effective at helping me reach that peace, but that led to other problems. Kissing led to dating; dating led to trouble. Now, I sought places, art, music, or exercise to help me reach those quiet moments when my worries all curled up for a nap.

"Your mother means well," Grandma Maureen repeated. She had already been getting ready for another meeting with the neighbors when my mother had called, and now

I was sitting on the edge of her bed thinking about how much easier life had been when I was a little girl. I used to love watching my mother dress up to go out to dinner or the theater with my father. It wasn't so long ago that they were happy. Now, my father was embarrassed about getting caught embezzling, and my mother was furious that he'd lied to her. They were so busy dealing with legal drama and divorce that I was all but forgotten.

"If she meant well, she'd stop fighting with Dad." I took a deep, shuddering breath before adding, "And *he*'d stop fighting with her. I swear that between the two of them they're like a natural damn disaster."

"Language, lovie." Grandma Maureen smoothed out her skirt even as her eyes lifted to meet mine in the mirror. "You need to let them be who they are, and you just be you. At the end of it all, that's how we live real lives: concentrate on being *you*."

I sighed. She was probably right. She almost always seemed to know just what to do. That's how I wanted to be, but just then, I also wanted to smack my parents. They couldn't go a week without one of them calling me about the other. I skipped as many calls as I could, but sometimes guilt prevailed—or maybe I was still hoping they wanted to talk *to* me, not at me. I'd had to give up my dream school and move to a state so unlike my home that it might as well be a foreign country, and I had no money for anything remotely close to the life I'd been living. They weren't supporting me—which was fine—but I wasn't eligible for any grants *or* loans for school either because they'd claimed me as a dependent on their taxes last year. Aid packages were based on the last year of income, and theirs was too high. That hadn't mattered when I'd had a college fund, but without that, I was out of luck. If they would agree not to claim me on their taxes next year, I might stand a chance at getting loans, but that left me drifting for the next two semesters.

"Why don't I drop you off down at the fair?" Grandma Maureen suggested, pulling me out of the nonstop grumbling in my mind lately. "I need the car, but I could drop you along the way."

I didn't have the heart to tell her that a small-town fair was not going to fix my mood. Being bitchy—especially to her—wasn't going to serve any purpose, and she certainly didn't deserve it. I forced a smile and said, "Let me change first."

Grandma Maureen nodded, and I went to my room to change into something a bit more rural, but still nice enough to wear out in public. My jeans were fine, but finding shoes to wear to a fair was challenging. Boots or tennis shoes, that was the critical choice for my evening. I shoved my feet into a pair of battered black Doc Marten's. They were Portland boots more than Tennessee boots, more grunge than country, but they weren't so out of place that people would stare.

"Maybe you'll meet someone," Grandma Maureen said as she steered her boat of a car toward the fairgrounds.

"I don't want to meet anyone," I told her.

"Spending all your time with old folks isn't very exciting, lovie." Grandma Maureen glanced my way. "Getting out would do you good. I'm not your mother, but—"

"You're a better mom than she ever was," I interjected.

"Hush. She means well. Your dad made some mistakes, and your parents are having a rocky spell." Grandma Maureen pursed her lips. "You can't let it ruin your outlook, though. Go out and make friends. I expect you to talk to someone tonight, you hear?"

"Yes, ma'am," I murmured meekly.

She nodded once, satisfied with my acquiescence. My grandmother was all about making the best of it, no matter what "it" was. She didn't come right out and say that she wasn't expecting my life to go back to normal anytime soon, but the vague nature of her plans made me well aware that she—and probably my parents—saw my move to Tennessee as indicative of an intent to settle in here. It wasn't part of The Plan, but I didn't hate it. I didn't really hate *anywhere*. I just felt more comfortable in some places than others.

About thirty minutes after my grandmother dropped me off, it was exceedingly clear that the fair wasn't on the comfortable-places list. There were families, couples, and groups of friends at the fair, but there was no one but me walking around alone and looking pitiful.

So when a boy in worn jeans and a T-shirt advertising some band I hadn't heard of walked up to me and said

"Hey," I wasn't as quick to ignore him as I usually would be—even though his gaze dropped to my bra line quickly and obviously.

"I'm Quincy."

"Aubrey."

"Are you waiting on someone?" he asked, looking around us as if people would magically materialize.

"Nope." I folded my arms over my stomach, not quite over my chest like I wanted. If I was going to be friendly and flirty, that wasn't the right move. Instead, I smiled and told him, "I'm new here."

"Well, then . . . These are John and Allan and their girls." ~~FUCK FACE~~

He motioned toward the two guys with him, both of whom appeared to be the same sort of nondescript pleasantly attractive guy he was. He was more built than they were, but none of them were out of shape.

"We're going out past the lights and crack a bottle or three." He patted his backpack. "My date had to bail. What say you come with me instead?"

It was possibly the least flattering invitation I'd ever received, but I was alone and bored and frustrated. I shrugged. "Why not?" SHUT THE FUCK UP ☺

"Good answer, beautiful. Just keep saying that." Quincy smiled in a way that I suspected I was supposed to find sexy.

Despite that, he was sort of cute and I was blue, so I resisted the urge to roll my eyes and joined the small group. Quincy's hand caught mine, and I followed him into the shadows. Maybe it would be fun. I remembered kissing in the shadows as being fun.

We could still hear the music when Quincy motioned for everyone to stop. There were two weathered picnic tables, both partially hidden by trees, and a grill that looked like at least a decade had passed since it had been rust-free.

"Ladies first," Quincy announced, filling a red plastic cup of something that smelled more like paint thinner than a drink.

I took it, but I wasn't quite ready to swallow the noxious stuff. A few moments later, everyone had a cup.

"Bottoms up," John—or possibly Allan—said.

Everyone else drank, and after a brief pause, so did I. My eyes watered, my throat burned, and I was fairly certain that my stomach lining was getting a big searing hole. I cleared my throat to keep from coughing and held my cup out.

"Good, huh?" Quincy poured another splash into my cup. "Tennessee moonshine. Bet they don't have that out in California or wherever."

I didn't bother correcting him. I just nodded and tossed back the nastiness in my cup. I wasn't here to make friends, not really. I was here to feel a little bit numb, and unless the poison in my cup killed me, numbness wasn't too far off.

A few cups of moonshine later, I was drunk, but still not having fun. All I really knew about Quincy was that he worked contracting, framing houses right now, but he had plans for a bigger role in the future. It wasn't the sort of thing I could imagine doing, but he sounded passionate about it. That was his most interesting trait, but he grew less and less interesting the more he drank. He wasn't a great kisser either.

"Come on," he insisted.

I shoved him as hard as I could, not that he moved far as a result. Shoving anyone wasn't particularly effective when I was sober. Drunk? My best effort was enough to push Quincy a few inches.

His arm was still around my waist, keeping me near him—not that I'd have moved far anyhow. The tree behind me was as much a prop to keep me from swaying as a barrier that trapped me against a guy I'd met just a few hours ago, a guy who wasn't any better at kissing than Groping Dave in ninth grade.

"Don't be like that," Quincy said, but he wasn't able to excite me, even as uninhibited as I was at the moment. He'd tried, but it did about as much for me as my annual gynecology exam. Hell, if Dr. Anderson weren't pushing seventy, he might have had better luck than Quincy. I told myself that later, when I wasn't falling-over drunk, I might need to think about that more carefully. Sometimes I thought the problem might be me. Maybe I just wasn't wired for lust like I'd thought I was five years ago.

Apparently, I wasn't exactly wired for drinking either.

Quincy was working on my nerves. It wasn't that he'd really done anything wrong, but he sure as hell wasn't doing anything right. He was supposed to be a good distraction, a way to let myself get lost for a little while. Instead, he was boring me.

I stared out at the lights of the midway while Quincy muttered compliments I didn't care to hear. The lights seemed so far away from our impromptu party—not that going over to them was any more appealing. I looked past Quincy at the other girls. *They* looked happy. I still wasn't—and I didn't care enough to fake anything. Worse yet, I wasn't sure *how* to fake it.

"Want to go home," I said.

I shook my head briefly, trying to shake my hair out of my face. It was at that irritating length where it seemed impossible to contain—or maybe that was partly because of the drinking too. Honestly, I couldn't be sure of a whole lot just then. What I knew for certain was that I wasn't where I wanted to be.

I laughed at that realization, startling Quincy. I wasn't *anywhere* I wanted to be: not in the right town, not with the right people; nothing about my life was what I wanted, what I'd planned.

Quincy must have misunderstood my laughter. "Sorry. Didn't mean to tickle you." He moved away from my ear and kissed my throat.

"Home," I repeated in a stronger voice.

"You don't want to go home yet. Stay here with me."

My mind wandered again. Forming words, especially anything near coherent ones, seemed ridiculously difficult.

My brain, however, felt like I'd been chugging espresso. Random thoughts swirled around my mind—about being stuck in this lame little town, about my friends on the other side of the country, about what I was doing in the dark with a drunk guy whose last name I didn't know.

He wasn't even my type, not that I *had* a type. I didn't date. Not now. Not ever, really. Hookups in my freshman year of high school and occasional nights out with guy friends didn't count. If I hadn't felt like the world was crumbling around me, I wouldn't be here at all, pushed up against a tree and trying to figure out how to leave. I didn't even belong in Williamsville, which meant that there weren't any friends I could call to come get me. That left calling my grandmother or finding out if there was a taxi service here.

I tried to focus on my words and said, "I'm sorry. I need to find a tax—"

Quincy kissed me again, cutting off my words. It was a decent kiss this time, not as clumsy as his last few. His kisses were okay, but they sure as hell weren't enough to make me change my mind about anything.

"Audrey—" he started.

"Au*brey*, not Audrey," I muttered.

"Sure, baby. I knew that."

This time, I shoved him harder. He didn't even know my *first* name. What was I doing here?

"Let go," I slurred.

He didn't.

"I said, *let go*," I repeated, much louder and clearer this time. I jerked my head to the side when he leaned in to kiss me again. Even if I couldn't push him away, I could at least dodge him.

But then Quincy was gone so suddenly that I stumbled.

I half slid, half fell to the ground, my butt hitting the dirt hard and my back still against the tree. Standing in front of Quincy was a dark-haired [Renaissance angel] in jeans, a T-shirt, and a leather jacket. For a brief moment, the angel looked at me, and I was glad I was already on the ground. If I ever *did* have a type, I wanted him to be it. He looked familiar enough that I could swear I'd seen him before—or maybe I just wished I had. [He studied me like I was some sort of maiden he'd pulled from the claws of a dragon.] *THIS SENTENCE IS DISGUSTING*

If I were sober, I'd be offended.

If I were back home in Portland, I'd be outraged.

I wasn't. I was drunk and in the middle of nowhere, in a town so small I was fairly sure that they had to date outside the town limits to avoid marrying relatives. I was far from offended or outraged. I was . . . intrigued.

I realized as I watched the angel that he and Quincy were arguing. Words blurred into trading punches, which was strangely attractive. Quincy wasn't as drunk as I was, but from the looks of it, he was drunker than I'd thought—or a remarkably uncoordinated fighter.

I was vaguely aware of other people coming toward us, but I couldn't look away from the fists. Maybe fighting helped people feel better. Drinking hadn't. Kissing Quincy hadn't. I wanted to feel better, but all I'd achieved with alcohol and a stranger was a little numbness. I felt untethered—which was not okay. I was better than this, stronger than this. I might not feel like it right now, but I would. First, though, I needed to get out of here, away from both the uncoordinated Quincy and the delicious-looking angel with the wolf on his jacket.

I pushed myself to my feet, using the tree for support.

"Your dad will have a fit if he finds you fighting again," one of the guys said as he tugged Quincy away from the angel.

"Screw my dad," Quincy snapped. He jerked his arm away from his friend and held a hand out to me. "Come on, Audrey. You need to come with me."

"*Aubrey. Aw. Bree,*" I corrected again. Maybe if I said it slowly, he'd finally get my name right.

"Right." Quincy shook his hand at me like I was a pet he was calling to him. Any remaining attractiveness he might've had evaporated at that.

"I'm staying here." I patted the tree. "You go on."

"Whatever," Quincy muttered before turning and stomping away with his friends.

I watched him go and sighed. "Idiot."

"Then what in the hell were you doing with him?"

I blinked, focusing my eyes on the man frowning at me, the angel who had punched Quincy. He was awfully pretty, even though he was scowling at me now.

"Oh," I managed to say. *"You're* still here."

He stared at me, and I had the sudden urge to shoo him away too. Boys were trouble. I *knew* that. This one . . . well, this one looked like trouble far, far out of my league. I would bet that his kisses were the sort to make me forget everything, though. He was so outside The Plan that he needed to vanish. Right. Now.

"Go on then," I added. "I'm fine."

He shook his head and squatted down in front of me. "Liar."

"I'll *be* fine," I told him, correcting myself, hoping that he would take me at my word.

He didn't budge an inch. He was definitely trouble, and like most of my trouble these days, he wasn't going away.

Chapter 3

TIME TICKED BY AWKWARDLY AS I STARED AT THE MAN IN front of me. Now that he was crouching, I could see more details. He was tall, built, and no older than twenty-six. His weathered jeans weren't snug, but they fit well enough to make it very clear that there was no fat hidden on him. It didn't make sense, but he also looked familiar. I didn't know where from, but I could swear I'd seen him before.

"I'm . . . Zion," he said. "You're Aubrey, I gather."

"I am." I squinted at him, trying to decide if he was any less attractive if I didn't stare at him quite as full-on. He didn't get any less gorgeous, but he did seem increasingly familiar. I just wasn't sure why. "How do you know my name?"

"You corrected Quincy," Zion said.

Great, he fought like violence was beautiful, looked like he'd been modeled on Renaissance paintings and listened when people spoke. Where was he when I was looking for a distraction earlier? → BITCH, SAY IT AGAIN

"Thanks. He was insis . . . insistingt . . . *pushy,* but not . . ." My skill with words—which was usually pretty good—was apparently still a bit absentee. I cleared my throat nervously and added, "Paint thinner–flavored booze, bad for the vocab'lary."

"Are you here with someone?" Zion asked. "Someone you could call or we could find?"

"Nope." I folded my arms over my chest, not thinking about the friends I'd summarily cut out of my life when my father made the news. "Don't know anyone here. I don't *belong* in Tennessee, you know? Was second-year Reedie . . . in Portland. That's where I belong."

"That's a college?"

"Uh-huh. Reed." I sighed and squinted at him. "This isn't Portland."

"Tennessee is a long way from Oregon."

"Exactly!"

When he stared at me, I tried to figure out what to do next. My brain was too fuzzy to stay focused on much of anything, and truthfully, I wasn't great at social skills even when I was sober. People always seemed to be doing and saying a lot more than the actual words they used, and sometimes it left me at a complete loss.

After a few quiet moments, Zion scooped up my bright red jacket from where it had fallen when Quincy was pawing me. "Let me take you home."

"To Portland?"

"No," he said, dragging the word out a little. "Wherever you're staying here in Williamsville."

I pushed away from the tree and lurched into him. He was warmer than the tree, but just as firm. I tilted my head and looked up at him as he pulled me to my feet. My chest was smashed against his, and he wrapped his arms around my waist to steady me. I could feel what I suspected was a gun strapped to his side under his jacket. I'd never been that close to a gun before, and for a moment, it made me nervous. He had rescued me, but the gun had me considering stepping backward.

"You seem like a bad man. Why are you helping me?" I asked.

"A bad man?" His lips quirked in the hint of a smile, making my nerves switch from fear back to intrigue. "How old are you?"

"Legal. Twenty." I felt more impulsive than I had in years as I suggested, "I bet *you* could make me feel better."

He sighed and helped me into my jacket like I was a small child instead of an adult who had just propositioned him. Maybe he didn't understand. Maybe he wasn't interested. Maybe I'd been too vague.

"I mean it. Quincy wasn't very good at kissing. I think you might be better," I explained carefully.

"Probably, but no." Zion swept my legs out from under me and lifted me into his arms. "If you weren't falling-down drunk? Yes. You're wasted, though. I don't mess with girls who aren't able to say yes."

"I'd say yes."

"Then say it when you're sober." Zion carried me across the edge of the fairgrounds like I weighed nothing. No one had ever carried me like this. I might be what people politely called petite, but I wasn't exactly starved-waif-looking.

The flashes of light from the hanging bulbs we passed gave me glimpses of his face—which was even prettier in the light. Sharp cheekbones, strong jaw, dark hair, and startling blue eyes; he was unnaturally beautiful. Of course he wasn't going to accept a proposition from *me*! I wasn't exciting enough for someone who probably had his pick of women.

"Where should I take you?"

I rested my head against his shoulder. "Maureen Evans' house. My grandma."

He paused for a minute, stopping midstep, and looked down at me. "You're Mrs. E.'s granddaughter? . . . If I'd have known *that*, I'd have hit him harder."

"Why?"

He shook his head and kept walking until he reached a parking lot.

When we stepped into the light, a loud motorcycle came toward us. Zion's arms tightened around me, but he didn't say anything. The other man stopped his bike right in front of us. He cut off the engine, but stayed astride the massive machine. He looked like the antithesis of Zion—light blond hair and dark eyes.

"What's up?"

"Disagreement with Quincy," Zion said, still not lowering my feet to the ground. "I clarified matters."

"Did he hurt her?"

"No!" I blinked at him, trying to focus my eyes. I should tell Zion to put me down, that I was able to walk, but there was something wonderful about being carried. If he wasn't putting me down, I wasn't arguing.

"I'm Noah."

"Aubrey," I offered. I tried to hold out my hand to shake his, but I couldn't reach him and Zion didn't move any closer to Noah. Then I looked from one to the other. "You two look like the angels in the paintings in my old art class."

Noah laughed. "Never been called an angel before. Maybe a—"

"Did you need something?" Zion asked, his voice suddenly terse.

For a moment, I thought he meant me, but then Noah answered. "Just checking in." He paused, glanced at me, and then added, "Do you want me to take her? You don't need to get involved in something with the sheriff's son."

Zion's arms tightened again. "I got her."

For a moment, they were silent, and I knew that there was a lot more in their conversation than the words I'd heard, but even if I'd been sober, I wasn't sure I'd have understood.

INTERESTING

Subtext often escaped me, and guy subtext was all sorts of baffling. According to my friends back in Oregon, I'd rejected guys without even realizing that they were interested. Overt statements were a lot more my speed. OH YES.

"Later, then," Noah said, and then he started his motorcycle again and sped out of the lot.

I noticed when he turned away that *he* didn't have any pictures on the back of his jacket. Vaguely, it occurred to me that there was a reason this mattered, but my brain was filled with enough liquor to make my thoughts foggy. Better to concentrate on the man rescuing me than secrets hidden on leather jackets.

"Sheriff?" I asked as another detail filtered into my liquor-slowed mind.

"Quincy's father is the sheriff," Zion clarified as he carried me across the lot.

"Sheriff's an idiot," I muttered.

Zion grinned. "He is."

If I'd known Quincy was the sheriff's son, I'd never have spoken to him in the first place. My opinion of Sheriff Patterson couldn't get much lower, and I wasn't impressed by Quincy either. Zion, however, made me feel safe. Biker. Fighter. Beautiful. He was appealing in a lot of ways. I sighed against his throat, not quite brave enough to pull him closer so I could reach his lips. I wanted to, though. I wanted a lot of things, and he looked like the sort of man who could give them to me.

The Plan hadn't worked. What was the point of following rules anyhow? I'd done everything I was supposed to for years. I was still without a home, tuition, or even a car. If not for my grandmother taking me in, I'd be . . . whatever came after fucked.

I wanted to be numb, to forget, to take control.

"I'm not that drunk," I told Zion in a light tone. Feeling a little braver, I kissed the skin along his collarbone.

He shifted his hold on me. "I'm going to put you down if you keep that up."

"Don't you ever just want to forget everything?" I asked. "To do something that would make you stop thinking, stop worrying?"

He stopped walking and peered into my face for a moment. In a very gentle voice, he asked, "Are you okay?"

"Not really," I admitted—and immediately regretted it. I didn't fall apart. I fractured a little, but I always pulled it together. I shoved my feelings under and briefly explained, "It's been a lousy month, but I'm not usually like this."

I don't know why I cared, but it suddenly seemed important that he understand that I was stronger than this. "I don't drink. I don't go off acting stupid. I'm just—"

"It's fine, Aubrey. We all have bad days or months." He lowered my feet to the ground and steadied me. "Can you stay awake and hold on to me? That's all I need you to do."

When he stepped back, I realized we were standing at the end of a row of motorcycles. Several of them had wolves painted on the tanks, just like on his jacket. One of the motorcycles was obviously his. I thought back to the bikers who had stood in the street watching the house, watching *me*, and I realized suddenly that he was one of them. Beau had even mentioned him. Here was an opportunity to ask about Echo, to find out what Grandma Maureen had to do with bikers, but . . . I suddenly didn't want to know. There was more than enough in my head to sort out.

"You were at the house," I said. "The other night. You were there talking to my grandmother."

"I was."

"Why?"

He reached behind me and grabbed a helmet from a motorcycle. "You need to put this on."

"So you're not going to answer?"

"Not my place to answer that," he said with a shrug.

I took the helmet and put it on my head, but I didn't know how to hook the strap. I fumbled with it for a few seconds, feeling like a clumsy child. Guys like him were probably used to women who could put on a motorcycle helmet gracefully even if they were a lot drunker than I was.

"Hold still." He reached out, fastened the strap, and stepped back.

"Where's your helmet?"

He tapped my head with one finger. "Right here."

"But—"

"I don't usually carry passengers, Aubrey. This is the only helmet I have here, and you're not in any shape to argue about wearing it." Then he threw his leg over his bike and looked back at me. "Climb on."

I hesitated. I'd never been on a motorcycle. The simple physics of it made sense, but the lack of a nice solid frame around the passenger and driver seemed dangerous. Car accidents could be horrible. Motorcycle accidents . . . I couldn't even fathom the risks a person took just getting on a bike. "Maybe there's a taxi or something."

Zion motioned me forward. "All you need to do is stay awake and hold on to me."

"What if I weigh too much?" I asked quietly, my face feeling like it was glowing hot enough to light the darkness.

"You don't." He looked me up and down slowly. "Even a little."

Fear was making me increasingly sober. I simply wasn't the sort of girl who rode on motorcycles. Ever. I looked at him, frozen. He said the right things. He rescued me. I was still afraid.

⊃ THE FUCK YOU GET RED FROM?

"You're safe, (Red," he said in a softer voice. "I'll take you to Grandmother's house."

He watched me, obviously waiting for something.

The best my drunken brain could offer was "The Big Bad Wolf eats Red." *TERRIBLE ATTEMPTS @ SYMBOLISM*

He paused, grinned, and patted the tiny seat behind him. "You're too drunk for that too."

I blinked at him. Then his words sank in, and I gasped. I hadn't meant *that*, but now that he'd planted the idea in my mind, I couldn't speak.

"You're safe with me," he promised, and then he patted the seat again.

20 PAGES AGO YOU WERE ALL ON ABOUT HOW YOU WERE IN LOVE W/THEM

I wanted to tell him that I didn't want to be *safe*, but I yanked my mind out of the gutter and climbed onto the motorcycle. Pretending I was calm, I wrapped my arms around his waist and tried not to shiver. I shouldn't like the way he talked, but I did. I liked the whole package: the rescue, the insinuations, the motorcycle.

Maybe alcohol and fumbled petting with Quincy had just skewed my judgment so severely that Zion seemed more tempting than he actually was. I wasn't sure. I also didn't think it mattered. By tomorrow, I would be too sober to think about kisses or any of the other things he might be good at doing.

He pulled my arms tighter around him, holding my hands together on his very taut stomach. It was a little embarrassing that being on the back of his Harley was doing far more for my libido than Quincy—and every other man before him—had.

"Hold on, Red." IS THIS BITCH A GINGER? DID I MISS SOMETHING?

THE RIDE HOME was blissful. There was no worry, no stress. Being on the motorcycle, or maybe being wrapped around Zion, gave me the sort of peace I'd tried to find in my ill-conceived attempt at hooking up with a stranger and drinking too much. I hadn't found that quiet place in my head through either of those things, but being on the back of a Harley-Davidson had delivered it. Nothing I'd ever done—including having sex—had left me feeling so connected to another person. I had to keep my body aware of his, and the road felt like it had so much more definition than I'd ever felt before. Every bump and dip was noticeable. The air felt so much more present, and the vibration of the engine resonated through me. It was like I had extra senses; my entire body was aware of the machine and the man between my legs. It was very easy to understand why bikers never seemed to be at a loss for women. Even if Zion *weren't* stunning, a simple ride on his bike would make him seem so. Since he was gorgeous . . . well, I was far too aware that I wasn't exciting or beautiful enough for a man like him.

When he stopped in front of the house a short while later, I sighed.

"You okay?"

I nodded. "I could stay right here forever."

He didn't laugh or make me feel stupid for my awkward admission. "First ride?"

"Yeah." I realized then that I still had my arms around him. Reluctantly, I let go.

"You tell me if you decide you want more."

"Rides, or . . ." I couldn't even finish the sentence, though. As I was sobering up, I was becoming mortified by the whole evening. Grandma Maureen had pretty much explained that the bikers would take care of me because of her, and here I was misunderstanding Zion's actions. I slid the rest of the way off the Harley and stepped to the side.

He looked up at me. "Whatever you want, Red. I'm here."

I shook my head. "Thank you for being so nice—and giving me a ride and, um, hitting Quincy."

Frowning, Zion started to get off the bike.

I put a hand on his shoulder. "I'm good. You don't need to hang around here. I've probably already ruined your night and—"

"Red," he cut me off. "I could've had my cousin bring you home or called a taxi. I *chose* to do this."

Mutely, I nodded.

He climbed off the bike with the sort of grace dancers would envy and gestured for me to precede him. He paused and teased, "Unless you want me to carry you?"

Still silent, I shook my head and walked toward the house. It was darkened, which meant my grandmother was either out somewhere or in her room sleeping already. Both were equally likely with her. She didn't bother with the television.

At the door, I stopped and turned back to Zion.

"I'll see you around," he said. TF DID THAT COMEFROM

Impulsively, I stepped forward and wrapped my arms around him in a hug, careful to avoid the gun at his side. At first, he tensed, and I wondered if I'd just been colossally stupid to hug him. Then he relaxed and squeezed me back.

"Thank you," I said, my voice muffled by his chest.

Then I let go, twisted out of his arms, and fumbled with the door. Zion stayed silent behind me until I had it open and stepped inside. I saw his confused expression when I turned to close the door. I didn't know what to say or do, though, so I just gave him a tight smile and looked down. Zion was a blink in my life, a few minutes of being treated like a princess in need of a knight to rescue her and a fabulous—and far too short—ride on his Harley. I knew that.

Still, I stood at the door and watched him walk away before I went to bed.

THIS REMINDS ME OF A BAD WATTPAD STORY

Chapter 4

FOR THE NEXT TWO WEEKS, I LOOKED AT THE STREET EVERY time I heard a Harley. It was never Zion, but there were more and more motorcycles on my block . . . or maybe I just noticed them more. Every so often I caught my grandmother looking up too, and I started to realize that the reason she had influence over Echo wasn't that mysterious. There was a look on Grandma Maureen's face a few times that I'd never seen there before. Echo was someone she used to love—or maybe still did. That was enough to keep me from asking questions about Echo or mentioning Zion.

Embarrassingly, though, I couldn't get Zion out of my mind. It was foolish. He wasn't in The Plan. I shouldn't even be thinking about him, but I was. I was watching for

FUCK YOUR PLAN

him too, but although I saw jackets and beautiful bikes with wolves on them, I didn't see *him*. I told myself that it was for the best. I wasn't sure what I'd do if I did see him again. This was why I had banned dating: it was distracting. I could give some shrink-talk on the fact that I used kissing to fill a gap for affection, or I could say it was about proving I was more than my brain, but the truth was—despite what my high school therapist had said—I just liked it. I liked boys. I liked kissing. I liked the way it made me feel, powerful and beautiful. What I didn't like was the way it made me forget everything else *after* the kisses ended. A few good kisses and I turned into the girl who kept checking to be sure the phone ringer was turned on. With Zion, it hadn't even taken a kiss. I would not, absolutely *should not*, let it get to the point of a kiss. He would consume me. I knew it, and I wasn't ever going to let that happen. Safe, calm, easy; that was the path I'd picked.

Today was the day I'd be able to start trying to focus on something else enough to stop thinking about him. This was it, the first day of classes at Williamsville Community College, but I felt like a failure, like everything I'd dreamed and planned was now out of reach. Worse yet, I felt like a fraud, like I'd been playing at being smart and having it together when really I was just as messed up as my parents. As I parked the car, I steeled myself. Fake confidence in place, I started to walk from the lot toward the tiny campus.

A few squat buildings were situated in a haphazard fashion in front of me. My first class of the day was on the other side of the road, and the footpath that led to it wound through an oversize pipe that had been used to create a tunnel from the lot to the buildings. The tunnel itself was decorated with graffiti and littered with refuse and cigarette butts. My first class was in the not very originally titled East Building, which reminded me of any number of corporate offices. It didn't scream "center of academic enlightenment" in any conceivable way. I paused and stared at it, not ready to enter but not seeing any other choices. This was where I was—not Reed, but at a small, ugly campus.

"Are you lost?"

I turned and saw motorcycle boots. Embarrassingly, those boots were enough to excite me. I lifted my gaze to the speaker, still hoping to see Zion despite my repeated self-lectures on the topic, but it wasn't him. His cousin Noah was standing with a motorcycle helmet in one hand and a cigarette in the other.

He stopped and waved the hand with the cigarette in front of my face. "Can you hear me, Aubrey?"

My heart stuttered. Noah looked more dangerous than angelic now that I was sober. It immediately made me wonder what I'd think if I saw Zion. In my memory, they'd both been softer somehow, but the man in front of me was a little intimidating. Would Zion be too?

Despite my twinge of nerves, I glanced at the cigarette in Noah's hand and said, "That's disgusting."

"Sorry." He lifted it to his lips, took a long drag, and then dropped it to the ground. "It *is* Aubrey, right? My cousin said you were Mrs. Evans' granddaughter."

"I am."

"Will you tell her I said hello?" Noah asked, sounding almost sheepish and suddenly a lot less intimidating. "I wouldn't have passed English without her encouragement. I'm good with numbers, but books aren't my thing."

"I'll tell her." I looked at him and tried to reconcile the images of biker and teacher's pet. It wasn't working for me. Admittedly, my grandmother had a weakness for troublemakers—and apparently for bikers. She was a fierce woman, even in her sixties, but she was also devoted to her students. I could certainly picture her being a favorite with someone like Noah.

"Sorry. You *do* remember me, don't you? Noah," he reminded me, as if I'd honestly be able to forget someone that sin-pretty "You were a bit drunk."

My face flamed at the memory and I explained, "I don't usually drink, and . . . I really *don't* drink or say the things I think I said to you and Zion."

Noah smiled again before he said, "I didn't mind. No one's ever called me an angel before."

I refused to let myself get any more embarrassed. I was here for at least the semester, probably more. From the looks of it, Noah was a student here too. I couldn't be embarrassed every time I saw him. That meant putting my one stupid night behind me. I'd been drunk a total of twice in my life. Even if *he* didn't know I was telling the truth about not being like that, I did.

Noah motioned for me to move, and once we started walking again, he prompted, "So you're . . ."

"Attending Williamsville," I said, but quickly added, "but only temporarily. I'm headed back to Reed, back to Oregon, as soon as I can."

"Let me show you around," Noah offered. "Give you the locals' tour."

"I don't know if that's a good idea," I hedged, feeling oddly guilty at the mere idea of going anywhere with Noah. It's not that I really thought I'd see Zion again, but it seemed . . . almost unfaithful to get on someone else's motorcycle.

Before I could come up with anything to say that wasn't either rude or idiotic sounding, Noah opened the door to the East Building and said, "If you want a ride home or wherever, I'll be done after this class. My bike's usually the only Harley in the lot."

Then he turned right and vanished down an overcrowded hallway, leaving me alone in a sea of strangers.

I stared after him. Williamsville was a peculiar place. I'd gone most of my life without being asked out, and in the past two weeks, I'd had Quincy invite me to drink with him, Zion defend me from the consequences of that decision, and Noah ask to show me around town. It was flattering, but only one of the three truly interested me so far. Quincy didn't tempt me. Sure, he was cute, but our brief hookup had been an exceedingly bad idea. Noah was

[handwritten marginalia: YOU AREN'T HOPPING ON THIS DICK]

[handwritten marginalia: → YOU MEAN HUMAN DECENCY?]

44

tempting, sexy, and charming, but . . . he wasn't the biker I thought about every day lately.

I realized then that Noah had said his was usually the *only* Harley . . . So that probably meant Zion wasn't a student here. I wondered what he did, where he worked—and if Noah would tell him that I was a student here. I *shouldn't* wonder, though.

Resolutely, I pushed thoughts of Zion out of my mind and went to find my classroom. This was precisely why I didn't date: a five-minute conversation in which Zion wasn't even overtly mentioned, and I was already distracted.

THIS BITCH BOY CRAZY

ONCE I FOUND the right classroom, I fixed my confident expression in place, took a deep breath, and went inside. It wasn't like I'd had all that many great friends at Reed, but I'd lived in the dorms on campus. It was like its own small town. After a few days, I knew people, and after two years there, I'd felt like I belonged. Before that, I'd been at the same high school for four years, and everyone knew me. Here, I was new and alone. I felt utterly lost.

I'd lived in a couple places before moving to Portland to attend Reed, but Portland was the sort of place that made sense. It had a giant independent bookstore that took up a full city block, thrift stores everywhere, and a vibrant music scene. The weather was gray drudge too often, but that just gave me an excuse for buying cool boots and jackets. It worked.

Williamsville was *nothing* like that. Sure, there were a couple of bookstores, and a few thrift stores, but both the music and the boots were more country than city. It was a foreign land in so many ways. *YOU'RE JUST WHINEY*

The instructor arrived, greeted a couple of students by name, and launched into an introductory lecture that seemed to focus more on rules than anything else. It wasn't particularly encouraging. I tried to remind myself that this was a gen ed course—I'd only registered for classes that I could transfer to fulfill requirements elsewhere—but even those classes were awesome at Reed. College wasn't supposed to be about the requirements; it was supposed to be about learning—and about the *experience*. *I'D LIKE TO HIT YOU*

"Are you okay?" whispered a girl next to me in a Rosie the Riveter T-shirt.

I glanced around to see whom she was talking to.

"Yep. I mean you," the girl confirmed. "You look like you're going to puke or something."

"I'm fine. Thanks, though."

The girl shrugged and turned her attention to the front of the room, where the importance of punctuality was being stressed.

I glanced down at the course syllabus for one of the two courses I was taking and read, HISTORY 215, SURVEY OF EUROPEAN HISTORY. It was a class that would transfer to fulfill a gen ed requirement, and the class size wasn't impossible like it would be if I went to the state university, but I wasn't going to be ending up anywhere else until I sorted out my finances. I focused my attention on the instructor, who was called Mr. Gamble, according to the handout on the desk.

By the time class was over, I was beyond convinced that I could handle these couple of courses *and* a full-time job. My only requirement for my off hours was the little bit of studying I had and to be home when I could so Grandma Maureen wasn't left alone as much. She was a tough woman, but the crime in her area was stressful for her. I wanted to be there for her and *not* be a burden on her.

"You looked like you were plotting Gamble's death," said the girl in the Rosie shirt as I was gathering my things at the end of class.

"He's different from the sort of professors I've had before," I offered as diplomatically as I could.

"So they didn't suck?"

Surprised, I laughed at her blunt assessment. "No. They really didn't."

"He's a tool," she said. "I wouldn't take any of his classes by choice, but I need this one, and he's the only one teaching it. I'm Ellen, by the way."

"Aubrey." I held out my hand.

After a moment, Ellen grasped my fingers and shook. "I feel like I'm in a job interview all of a sudden."

I stiffened for a moment, unsure whether or not I felt insulted.

"Relax."

"I'm not much for relaxing lately," I admitted with a small

laugh. "New girl. Not where I want to be. Not impressed with the classes . . ."

"Aside from being new, you just described everyone I know at WCC." Ellen shoved the last of her things into what looked like a handmade bag. I glanced at her multi-fabric skirt and realized it was handmade too.

"Come on," Ellen said.

I followed her for a minute before I said, "Not to be rude, but you don't look like you belong here."

She laughed. "Born and bred, babe. You'll find variety here just like in . . ." She looked at me expectantly.

"Portland, Oregon," I filled in as we headed out to the tiny quad.

"So you're a tree-hugging, pot-smoking Kurt Cobain lover?" She paused and gave me a once-over. My jeans and blouse certainly didn't match that description.

"Point taken," I said, abashed. "For what it's worth, I *do* like Nirvana, but I'm not so much with the pot."

"Stereotypes aren't always *entirely* wrong," Ellen said with a nod. "I, for example, am going to be a fashion designer despite being in Williamsville right now, *but* I like the blues, modern country like Jason Aldean, and classics like Reba."

For a moment, I almost admitted I had no idea who they were, but then I remembered a television show. "She was on a TV show, right? Reba?"

Ellen laughed and patted my arm. "She was a singer first, babe. Hell of a voice, strong woman, and straight-up country." She bumped her shoulder into mine and lowered her voice. "Don't look now, but one of our local boys is looking at you like you're the finest thing in town." *THIS GIVES ME*

"Noah? We met briefly." *VAMPIRE DIARIES VIBES.*

When she turned and met my gaze, her brow was raised. "Put a pin in that because we'll be talking about it later." She not-so-subtly steered me toward the tiny cafeteria. "I didn't mean Noah Dash. I meant Quincy."

"Ugh."

"You know *two* of the resident troublemakers already?"

Reluctantly, I nodded. "Noah's cousin Zion sort of rescued me from Quincy after I'd had a little too much to drink. I don't drink as a rule—" → *WE GET IT YOU DONT DRINK STFU!*

"And that's the top three."

Before she could say anything else, we were interrupted by Quincy. He seemed less appealing after our drunken encounter, but even now, I had to admit that he was cute, in that small-town-farm-boy way. He wasn't a farm boy, but he had that same sort of build that came from working outside. I remembered that before we'd gotten terribly drunk he had told me he worked for a contractor, which explained the muscles.

"Aubrey," he said. "I got it right that time, didn't I?"

"You did."

"Good." Quincy glanced at Ellen and nodded. Then he returned his attention to me. "I didn't know you were a student here. Let me show you around."

I grabbed Ellen's wrist when she started to walk away. She paused, but said nothing.

"Thanks, but Ellen already offered." I didn't mention that

Noah had too, or that spending time with the sheriff's kid wasn't on my to-do list.

Quincy looked at Ellen and then back at me. "Then I'll see you around. We can grab lunch or something."

I made a noncommittal noise. Saying I wasn't *ever* going to be free for lunch with him sounded ruder than I wanted to be, even though it was true. I settled on saying, "Good luck in your classes, Quincy."

And then I walked away with Ellen.

We hadn't gone very far before she looked at me and laughed. "You looked absolutely mortified. I take it there was no love match there?"

"None." I glanced back to make sure Quincy wasn't near enough to hear. "He's not a bad guy, but he's . . . not for me. We drank. We had sloppy kisses. He got pushy . . . and Zion showed up and punched him."

Ellen sat down on the grass but made a keep-going gesture with her hand, and I dropped to the ground next to her and filled her in on my brief adventure with cheap booze, bad choices, and fighting boys.

Afterward, she looked at me and whistled, "I don't know whether to envy or pity you. Killer is . . . trouble, but he doesn't bother with competition. Dash and Quincy, on the other hand, *hate* one another. They compete on everything, always have, and you, Miss Portland, are liable to be the newest contest. That is, unless Killer woos you before they can."

"Killer?"

THIS IS SO BADLY CLICHE *REAL FUCKIN ORIGINAL*

"Sorry. *Zion*," she clarified. "No one calls him that. Not since . . . I don't know, middle school, maybe? His name is Killer now. Honestly, I'm not sure most people even remember his original name."

"Whatever his name is, it doesn't matter." I shook my head, not daring to admit that I had thought of him a lot since that night. As if it would help me remind myself, I said aloud, "I don't date."

"Ever?"

"Ever," I confirmed.

"So you're a . . ."

"A what?" I knew the question, hated it, but I wasn't going to dodge it.

"A virgin?"

"Nope." I sat back and shook my head. "I handled that in high school. A bunch of us figured it was best to just pull the Band-Aid off. We got a few bottles of booze, picked partners, and got it out of the way before college."

Ellen's mouth gaped open.

I kept talking. "People make a big deal about it, and we decided not to let hormones get in the way of the schedule, so we all agreed to help one another out after prom."

"Like an orgy?" she whispered.

"Noooo. Like we all got hotel rooms, like most couples, but we paired up with friends. It's no big deal." I shook my head. "It's not a distraction now, and although it was pleasant, I don't see any need to repeat it until I'm ready for a relationship."

Ellen stared at me, and I wondered if I'd been too honest too soon. I'd said as much to people at Reed, but they'd mostly nodded in agreement. Ellen wasn't nodding. She echoed, "'Pleasant'?"

"Sure," I said. "Now that I know the truth, I don't think about wanting to do it the way I might if I didn't know that it's not that exciting."

I silently admitted that I was thinking about it lately, but that would fade. Zion was probably not that interesting in reality. I just had a fantasy image of him because of the way he'd rescued me.

"Maybe you just need more practice, babe, because if you do it right, it's a lot more than pleasant." Ellen flashed me a wide grin. "And both Killer and Dash are known for doing it verrrry right."

My traitorous mind flashed back to flirting with Zion and then to Noah's invitation for a ride home. Before I could shove all of those thoughts away again, I felt a flash of the sort of desire that served absolutely no purpose in my plan. I shook my head to chase away that thought before it could take hold.

"Nope. I'm not interested. Like I said, I don't date. I'll have a serious relationship no sooner than grad school. Right now, I have to get a job, save some money, and transfer back to Reed. If I decide to go past my BA, I'll need to get a fellowship or an assistantship to pay for grad school. Then after my master's degree or maybe even my PhD, I can find a spouse. That gives me time to get settled in a relation-

52

ship and probably a professorial career, so we can buy our starter house before we have our kids when I'm thirty-two or thirty-three."

Ellen stared at me in silence. Her mouth opened and closed. She still didn't say anything, though. When I delivered that plan at Reed, people commented, either sharing their own projected trajectory or asking questions. Ellen did neither. STOP FUCKING COMPARING TO REED

I added, "I hit a snag when I had to leave Reed temporarily, but that's reparable. Following The Plan will make everything manageable."

Finally, she spoke, saying only, "Damn. That's . . . detailed."

"Thanks." The Plan was reliable. Having things sorted out made decisions easier. Any time there was confusion about the right choice, it was easy to figure out. The right one was the one that supported The Plan.

"So no boys, but you need a job?" Ellen opened a notebook, tore out a piece of paper, and scribbled down a number and address. "I can help with that. In the spirit of new friends or . . . maybe a little awe of your scary planning skills, here you go." She held out the paper. "My cousin said that they're hiring over at Wolves."

Wolves? What was with this town and wolves? I made a mental note to see if they were indigenous here or something. It didn't match what I remembered, but I hadn't spent much time pondering Tennessee.

"What's Wolves?" I asked, not taking the paper. As much

as I needed to find a job, I couldn't take one where I had no qualification—not that I had many marketable skills. I had two years of college, not exactly the stuff of high-paying wages.

Instead of answering, Ellen waggled the paper at me. "They need a waitress or barmaid. Just tell them Bitty's girl sent you over."

Aside from the sheer oddity of the phrase "Bitty's girl," I figured that this wasn't an unusual way to go about things. Small towns often run on the idea of "who you know." I suspected that larger towns and cities did too, but in microcosmic ways.

"Thanks," I said, accepting the address as we stood.

Ellen nodded as she came to her feet.

We walked out to the parking lot in comfortable silence. I glanced at Noah's Harley, grateful that I was leaving before he saw me. I wasn't quite ready to deal with his invitation—or Quincy's looks as he saw me on campus, or the way all I really wanted was to see Zion. What I needed to do was ignore all of it and stay focused. Work was the next step.

"You'll call me," she more or less ordered. She pointed to the hand still holding her note. "*My* number is on there too. You call. Then we go grab lunch or study or something."

"You're a little scary yourself," I said.

"Yeah. You plan. I push." She grinned. "We should start a revolution."

I laughed. I'd never met anyone quite like her. In high

school, I picked friends who were studious or driven. We had exam review sessions or went to art films. My Reed friends were the same kind of people, but the cultivatedly quirky sort. Sometimes it felt like everyone was trying to out-blasé the rest or demonstrate more eco-social-political awareness. I'd never fit in. I played at it, but I never felt like I belonged. Ellen made me hope that maybe I could.

Then I looked at her as she sashayed across the lot, singing out loud and doing a little pirouette to face me again. "Go get a job. Call me or text me when you do . . . and later too."

"Yes, ma'am." *OOF*

She waved an arm over her head in what I took for affirmation and then spun away again.

I shook my head and climbed into my grandmother's boat of a car. It seemed ridiculously large to me, but I didn't have any other option. I needed to drive to get to campus, and hopefully to a job, and I didn't have a car of my own. I was lucky that Grandma Maureen let me borrow hers. Maybe I should take some of my money to buy a car, something used but mine. I hated the idea of spending any money, but I also had to be practical.

First, though, I needed to get the job.

I drove to the address Ellen had given me. I hadn't ever applied for a job for the sole purpose of earning money, but I didn't have a choice anymore. My days of campus jobs or internships to add to my appeal for eventual grad school apps were behind me. I needed to work to earn *money*, not prestige. I parked my grandmother's enormous car in front of a dim little place called Wolves & Whiskey. There were three motorcycles and one pickup truck in the lot. A few neon lights advertised beers, and a sign listed upcoming bands. It was apparently more of a bar than a restaurant. I wasn't too arrogant to turn down a job selling beer. I didn't know if I'd be any good at it, but I was more than willing to learn.

I squared my shoulders and walked gingerly across the lot, dodging an oil-slicked spot and several divots in the asphalt.

The door let out a loud creak as I jerked it open, and for a moment, I felt like I'd walked into the middle of a cautionary tale or some old-fashioned after-school special. The six men sitting inside were all giving me varying degrees of a once-over. Two older men in leather jackets sat at a scarred wooden table. They neither smiled nor glared; in all, their attention was brief, assessing, and then gone.

The guy shooting pool was another story altogether. He was shedding his jacket as I walked in, and I stared at the sight. It wasn't the gun holstered at his side that drew my attention. It was the body. He was sinewy and tensed for motion, and he filled out his jeans like a billboard model. What was it with this town and gorgeous men? I wasn't sure if it was in the water or what, but as much as I felt like an outsider here, I certainly couldn't complain about the view.

Then he turned to look at me, and I gasped.

Zion.

He didn't speak, but the look he gave me was as predatory as that of a tiger at the zoo sizing up a potential meal. I all but felt the weight of his gaze as he slowly took me in from toes to top. I couldn't look away from him or move.

The bartender, whose arms were tattoo-covered and whose face bore a long but faded scar, called out, "Come on in, little bit." He shot a look at Zion. "And you put those eyes back in your head, Killer. You're going to scare her away."

"I don't scare easy," I said, my gaze drifting back to Zion.

His lips quirked like he was trying not to smile, but then he turned back to the pool table without saying a word. After watching for him everywhere without even a glimpse, I'd walked into my first job interview to find him. I stared a moment longer, as if I could get my fill of looking, and then jerked my attention away.

The four men sitting at the bar itself gave me a mix of friendly greetings and smiles. One burly man whose arms seemed as wide as my legs patted a stool next to him. "Come on, shug. I'll keep the children at bay."

"I think I can handle them." I wasn't used to this kind of place, and I sure as hell wasn't used to the heat in Zion's gaze, but that wasn't going to make me back down. I pointedly didn't look his way again as I stepped farther into the bar and said, "I'm looking for the manager. Um, I'm supposed to tell you that Bitty's girl sent me."

"Karl!" the bartender yelled. "New barmaid for you." Then he glanced my way and added, "Grab a seat."

With a resolve I'd come to rely on more and more since my parents' massive case of idiocy, I strolled across the dimly lit bar to wait next to the massive man with his glass of beer and bowl of bar snacks. He flashed me a wide smile that put me at ease instantly.

"I'm Billy," he said. "That's Killer." He pointed at Zion, who didn't look up from the pool table. He made his shot as if no one were there, as if no one had spoken his name, and I tried to ignore the bereft feeling that came over me when he didn't look my way. Apparently, my deciding not to stare didn't equate to my being okay with *him* not noticing *me*.

"Bartender's called Mike," Billy continued. He pointed at the other three men sitting a few stools away. "These idiots aren't worth knowing."

I didn't ask about the two bikers at the table. They were speaking in low voices, and of the people there, they were the only ones who didn't seem to pay me any mind. One wore a jacket that looked a lot like Zion's; it had several patches on the back. I could make out a top bar, curved like the top section of a circle, with the words *Southern Wolves* in it; a howling wolf in the middle of the circle; *1%* on one side; *MC* on the other.

Billy noticed my furtive glance at them. "They're good people, shug. The only ones allowed to carry in here are Killer and his boss. The rest check their weapons or leave 'em at home. And the only colors allowed in here are the Wolves', so no worries about trouble."

The idea of a weapons check was both unsettling and

comforting at once. The other detail was a little more clari-fying. *Colors.* That was the term for club affiliation. I'd heard it before around my grandmother's neighborhood, and as I stood in the bar, I realized that the emblems on the jackets were exactly that: *MC* stood for motorcycle club; I wasn't sure what the *1%* meant, but I made a mental note to look it up.

Then an old man, presumably Karl, came out of a door in the side of the room. He had the sort of massive beard that called Santa Claus to mind, but he was wiry and fit. A black bandanna covered his head, and a long gray braid snaked down past the middle of his back. He was dressed like the rest of them: jeans, heavy black boots, and a shirt. Instead of a leather jacket, he had a vest over his long-sleeved shirt. His sleeves were rolled up, exposing faded tattoos on both forearms. Amid the art was another wolf image.

"Have you ever stepped foot inside a bar before?" he asked me, his tone pretty clearly stating that he knew the answer already.

"No. I'm only twenty."

"Law says you only need to be eighteen to bartend in Tennessee." Karl peered at me and asked, "Know anything about bikes?"

"No."

"Bikers?"

At this point, I realized that everyone in the room—except Zion—was watching us. I wasn't sure that mentioning that one of the bikers there had given me a ride was a good idea.

Zion certainly wasn't volunteering it. I paused, my temper slipping a little despite my best efforts. "Did your last waitress work on motorcycles or something?"

The old man grinned. "Nope. She minded the till, carried the drinks, cleared the tables, and scolded the boys."

"Right. Well, I can do all that." I folded my arms over my chest. "Probably better than she did."

"Might be." He nodded. "Hard to tell, though. I need a bartender, not just a waitress."

I wasn't going to backtrack. I saw the men at the table studying me. One of them winked and nodded once. It didn't feel flirtatious.

"I can learn," I insisted.

"Maybe." He met my gaze with a look that was somewhere between assessing and confrontational. "You'll need to collect any firearms or knives bigger than a pocketknife. The boys know it, and if anyone refuses, the bouncer will toss them out."

"Oh."

"It's like a coat check," Karl explained.

"So no one in the bar is to be armed?"

"Killer, the bouncers, and anyone Killer says is fine." He continued watching me as he spoke. "He or I'll tell you any other exceptions if they come up. Can you handle that?"

I thought about it. I'd never handled anything more dangerous than a kitchen knife, so the idea of a weapons check was unsettling. On the other hand, the fact that the people drinking in the bar would be *un*armed was comforting.

"I've never touched a gun, but if you show me how to do it, I'm sure I can manage."

"Sounds reasonable," he said with a single nod at me. "Are you sure you want to work here? I'm sure there are other places—"

"Hire me conditionally," I interrupted. "If I don't work out in thirty days, you can hire someone else."

Karl stared at me for what felt like minutes, and then he grinned and held out his hand. "You got a pair on you, don't you? You'll need them around here. Job's yours."

After I shook his hand, I felt like doing a victory dance. It wasn't the sort of job that would do much for my resume, but it would put more cash in my pocket. I had a few friends who'd talked about bartending. It paid well, according to them.

"You won't regret it, sir," I promised.

"Uncle Karl," he corrected, and then he motioned for me to follow him toward the room he'd come out of. "Let's get you sorted out."

Foolishly, I allowed my attention to drift briefly to Zion. The same biker who had winked at me quirked a brow at that and gave Zion a questioning look. I dropped my gaze and followed Uncle Karl. I wasn't here to flirt. I was here to collect tips to put in my "get back to Oregon" fund. That was all.

Chapter 5

AFTER HAVING SPENT A GOOD MANY HOURS WRITING OFF his encounter with Red as typical, just an average night that meant nothing, Zion felt like he'd taken a punch to the gut when she walked into the bar. He'd been prepared to see her a lot of places, but not at the bar. College girls didn't walk into the kinds of places where the Wolves spent their downtime, not unless they were looking for a short vacation in a world where they'd never stay. *He* didn't call it slumming, but he was well aware that many of them did. The bar saw its share of pretty college girls who wanted a few tastes of the forbidden before they settled into their well-manicured lives.

Red didn't seem like them. She'd seemed like she was

real, or maybe that was the booze, or maybe it was because he knew her grandmother—and *she* didn't look down on bikers. He didn't know. What he did know was that it didn't matter now. Red was about to be forbidden to him. There were rules about bartenders: it was fine to take them out once or twice, but if a barmaid was involved with one of the Wolves, she wasn't allowed to work at the bar. It had caused too much conflict in the club over the years, so Uncle Karl had a blanket policy these days. Anyone who was property of a Wolf, or even rode with him exclusively for a short while, wasn't able to work at the bar. *WHAT KIND OF BULL...*

Zion's gaze drifted to the door to Uncle Karl's office. He knew that Red was in there right now filling out the papers to work here. He wasn't sure whether he felt cursed or happy to see her at Wolves & Whiskey. With the way she'd been plaguing his mind, seeing her once or twice wouldn't be enough. He'd never attempted friendship with a girl, and he wasn't interested in starting to do so with *her*.

The pool cue didn't waver as he lined up the next shot. His attention didn't falter. He was on the clock, here in case Echo needed anything. Even if Zion weren't working, *she* wasn't meant for him. Those offers, those little sighs, the way she'd curled into his arms—that was the drink. It wasn't real. He'd told himself as much several times when he'd come damn near to riding out to her house. Ignoring that spark of interest had been a lot easier when she wasn't here in his bar.

"What do you think, Killer?" Billy called.

Zion shook his head and kept his mouth shut. What he thought wasn't something he'd be saying. The Wolves and the hangers-on were all well used to him taking the barmaids out once or twice. It wasn't quite a catch-and-release system, but it was pretty close. He didn't do commitments, and the bar's rules were clear enough that the "third time" excuse was handy. He didn't need to make up a reason to retreat, and the girls saved face. It was a win-win . . . and it was nowhere near what he'd considered when he thought about Red.

Steadily, as if he weren't bothered at all that she was here, Zion put his cue back in the wall rack and walked over to the bar. He tapped it, and Mike poured him a double shot of Jack without a word. There was more than one reason he was a good bartender.

"You'll explain who she shouldn't trust," Zion said after throwing the drink back.

"You're usually top of that list."

Zion lifted a brow. "I'd never hurt a woman."

"Different list," Mike said easily. "There's the ones she can't trust to keep her safe, and then there's those who sleep with all the girls."

"She's not the type of girl to do that," Zion said with more of a snarl than he'd intended.

"And you know this from seeing her walk in?"

There was no point in answering that. Mike would see soon enough that Red was special. They all would. A flare of jealousy filled Zion at that realization. They'd see, and

GROSS

someone would take a run at her. Several someones, inevitably.

"She's under my protection," he told Mike quietly. "Anyone hassles her, you tell me."

The bartender's eyes widened.

"I don't have any (claim) She's free to flirt all she wants, but if anyone hurts her or disrespects her, they'll answer to me. Make it known."

"I'll pass the word," Mike said. He didn't press Zion for any answers, but his curiosity was written clearly on his face.

Zion ignored those unspoken questions. The Southern Wolves' president was his boss, his *only* boss, and the only person who could demand answers of him. Zion didn't answer to anyone else, and he never wanted to. He was good at what he did, and he had a lot of freedom in his life. Most people gave him plenty of space. Zion was the person Echo let off the leash when someone else needed to answer questions; he was the one who sent messages and warnings. If being under Zion's protection wasn't enough to keep Red safe in the Wolves' den, nothing was.

The one member of his family undaunted by Zion's temper or position was the man now walking into the bar, his cousin Noah. They were as close as brothers and had been raised as if they were.

"Killer," Noah said, heading toward Uncle Karl's office, a backpack slung over his shoulder.

"Thought you had classes."

"Just one today. I'm done," Noah said. "I saw that girl from the fair on campus. She's something."

Noah grinned in a way that made Zion grit his teeth. He said nothing, though. This was neither the time nor the place.

Oblivious, Noah said, "I'm going to check in with Uncle K—"

"He's busy," Zion snapped.

He didn't want Noah in there with Red. It was stupid. He'd just finished telling Mike that he had no claim, but telling himself wasn't working out quite as well. He gestured to the pool table he'd vacated a few minutes ago and told Noah, "Rack 'em."

Behind him he heard Mike barely cover a laugh with a sudden cough.

Let him laugh, Zion thought. He wasn't subtle to begin with, but after what he'd as much as admitted to Mike already, he didn't feel the need to be too vague. The words he hadn't said were pretty fucking clear. He wanted Red. He was willing to defend her honor.

"Let me drop this in Uncle Karl's office first," Noah said, gesturing toward his bag.

"What? Your books aren't safe enough out here?"

His cousin flipped him off and kept walking.

Zion walked back to the table without a word.

Noah barely lowered his voice as he asked Mike, "What crawled up his ass?"

After a glance at Zion, Mike shrugged. Zion pretended he

couldn't hear or see either of them. He pulled out a pack of cigarettes and shook one out. Unlike a lot of places, the bar wasn't a smoking-free zone.

"Something happen?" Noah prompted Mike.

Mike shrugged again.

Noah shook his head, and then he walked over to Uncle Karl's door and opened it.

Zion didn't follow. Not here. Not yet. Noah *knew* that Zion had seen her first, had talked to her, was still thinking about her. They hadn't had some womanly heart-to-heart or anything, but they'd talked enough that Zion's interest in Aubrey wasn't a secret . . . but neither was the bar policy on taking up with any of the girls who worked at Wolves & Whiskey. Noah knew Zion was interested, knew he was hoping to see her again, and yet there he was talking about her like she was available. Maybe he hadn't understood that Zion wasn't sure if this one was the catch-and-release sort. That hesitation was why Zion hadn't marched up to Aubrey's door. He needed to think. Wanting to see a girl for a reason other than just sex wasn't his normal impulse, but there was something about her that made him want to talk to her too. She'd been drunk as hell the last time he'd seen her, but she'd still held her ground. She'd been closemouthed despite the rotgut liquor she'd had, and she'd looked at him like she saw a gentleman, not a criminal. All told, she was intriguing. Zion was weighing what to do about her.

But now that she had been hired, she was off-limits to him—and *not* to Noah.

IS HE NOT A WOLF?

In their whole lives, they'd never let a girl truly come between them, but she wasn't like other girls. Zion glanced over at Uncle Karl's door. He packed his cigarette, tapping the tip on the edge of the table to tamp down any loose tobacco, and lit it. The ritual of it was comforting, almost as much as the soothing feel of taking a long drag. He kept saying he was going to quit, but today wasn't going to be the day that happened.

"Double Jack," he said from halfway across the bar. It was quiet enough that Mike heard him even though Zion hadn't raised his voice. "And turn on some fucking music. It's like a church in here."

Then he returned his attention to the pool table while he waited for his drink.

Chapter 6

'D FILLED OUT ALL THE NECESSARY PAPERWORK WHILE
Uncle Karl made small talk. He seemed nice, maybe a
bit more grandfatherly than I'd expected of a bar owner,
but that wasn't such a bad thing. He stressed that most of
the patrons were regulars, but this wasn't a "private club."
I wasn't sure what the difference was, but it seemed important to him that I understood that detail.

I nodded.

Someone tapped Uncle Karl's door lightly before pushing
it open.

Seeing Noah step inside the tiny office probably shouldn't
have surprised me. Zion was there, and they were cousins—
and both motorcycle riders—so it was logical for him to

be here too. It just hadn't occurred to me. The world felt smaller here in Williamsville to begin with, but add in the bikers, and it seemed to shrink even more.

Noah stopped just inside the door and dropped his bag on the floor next to Uncle Karl's massive metal desk. "Sorry to interrupt—" he started. Then he noticed me. "Aubrey?"

"Hi." I looked down at my hands where they were folded in my lap. Not one but *both* of the bikers I'd met were here now. I felt even less comfortable with Noah after his attempt to ask me out when we'd met on campus. I pushed away a stray thought about Zion's reaction to that invitation.

Uncle Karl looked from Noah to me. "You know Dash?"

"I met him when—"

"School," Noah interrupted quickly. "I met her at school."

"All these years, and you still lie badly, son." Uncle Karl leaned back in his chair, folded his arms over his chest, and leveled a fierce look at Noah. "Try again, boy."

"She was stranded at the fair, and Killer gave her a ride. I saw them there."

"And?"

"Then I saw her at school," Noah said. "We talked. I offered her a ride. She didn't show."

"I didn't say I would," I interjected.

Uncle Karl stared at him skeptically but said nothing. He looked at me. "So you met Killer before today too? Any reason you didn't share that fact?"

At that, I felt worse. It hadn't seemed like the sort of thing to open an interview with, but now it looked bad—like I was hiding things. That hadn't been my intention, but I could see how it would seem that way. I looked at Uncle Karl and explained, "It was a ride. I got drunk at the fair because I was having a lousy day, and he rescued me. It doesn't paint me in the best light. I don't drink, though. I mean, that was the second time in my whole life and—"

"Breathe," Uncle Karl said.

Nervously, I nodded. "I'm sorry."

"Not you who should've spoken up," he said. The look he sent toward the closed door and then to Noah made me revise my assessment of him from grandfatherly man to aging badass. I wouldn't want to have anyone look at me with the irritation in his eyes.

"Noah and Zion were both perfect gentlemen when I met them and then today when I saw Noah on campus," I said in a quiet voice, half-afraid that I was about to lose the job I'd just taken but not willing to let the boys take blame for doing something wrong. I took a gulp of air before adding, "I need this job. I'm sorry if I made a mis—"

Noah cut in again. "You didn't, but there are people who are going to be off-limits if you work here. Killer doesn't do the knight thing, so that and his silence out there . . ." He shrugged and then looked at Uncle Karl. "You *did* tell her that rule, right?"

"I was getting to it," Uncle Karl snapped.

"I want this job," I told them both. "That's why I'm here."

Uncle Karl looked at me skeptically and said, "If you take up with any of the Wolves, you'll need to quit. Wolves have particular expectations of our women, possessive, and it makes working here a bad idea. You can flirt all you want, but if you're exclusive with anyone in the club, you can't work here. Three-date maximum with any of the boys wearing club colors. It's pretty straightforward, but if you have questions on it, you ask me."

I met first Noah's and then Uncle Karl's eyes as I said, "Here's the thing: I'm here to try to make a little money. I have to pay tuition and not be a burden to my grandmother." I paused and squirmed a little nervously, trying not to be rude but needing them to understand. "Maybe you're used to girls looking for a husband or boyfriend or something, but that's not on my schedule. I can smile, talk, and serve up drinks, but I have no intention of getting tied down to anyone here."

"That so?" Uncle Karl asked in a curiously flat tone.

"It's not that I object to bikers," I added quickly in case I'd offended him. "I just don't date at all."

"At all?" Noah echoed.

I nodded once.

Grinning now, Uncle Karl pushed his chair back. "Well, you'll be a breath of fresh air around here. Come on, then. Let's get you a few bar T-shirts. Then Mike can show you the way we do things. We'll start you out on tables and shadowing him behind the bar."

"Now?"

He gave me a challenging look. "Unless you got somewhere else you need to be tonight."

"No. Tonight works. I just need to call and tell my grandma where I'll be so she doesn't hold dinner for me."

Uncle Karl nodded once and then looked at Noah. "Talk to Killer."

Then he turned back to me and, in case I hadn't caught what they'd been saying already, he stressed, "Killer's a Southern Wolf, Aubrey, and"—he held up a hand as I opened my mouth to object— "I know you said you weren't looking, but the boy could charm the panties off a nun."

I folded my arms over my chest. "Fortunately for all of us, then, I'm not a nun."

Uncle Karl looked at me and shook his head. "Killer's a good boy." He inclined his head toward Noah. *"Both* of my boys are, but if either one of them gives you trouble, just tell me and I'll step in."

"Thank you, but I think I can handle them just fine. I've yet to meet a boy able to charm me out of my panties."

Noah's attention snapped to me again. "Ever?"

"Sorry, Noah. You missed the interview part of the meeting," I said lightly.

Uncle Karl guffawed.

I rolled my eyes and walked to the door. People focused far too much on sex. I didn't get it. Never had. Never would. At least that was what I was telling myself, despite those

strange moments the night I met Zion. I was mostly convinced that the whole lust thing was just a mix of alcohol
and circumstance. Now that I was employed at the bar, I
couldn't test that theory—no matter how much I wanted to
every time I even thought about Zion.

Chapter 7

AS I STOOD JUST OUTSIDE UNCLE KARL'S OFFICE WITH Noah, I immediately sought out Zion with my eyes. I didn't mean to, but I couldn't seem to *not* look. I felt a jolt when I saw that he was watching us surreptitiously, and I had to admit that he was even better-looking than in all the fantasies I'd had since we'd met. I wanted to apologize—for talking to Noah, for taking the job, and for being so drunk that he'd needed to help me. I wanted to tell him that I was glad I could talk to him. Now that I worked here, I could even flirt with him, and it was all safe. I smiled widely at the thought. This was perfect. I could enjoy the intense way he watched me without having to risk any consequences, and obviously, he wouldn't object. This was his bar, his MC, so they weren't *my* rules.

Zion met my eyes and quirked one brow, much like the older biker had when he'd caught me looking at Zion earlier.

"Aubrey?"

I jerked my attention away from Zion and looked up at Noah. Unlike the others, Noah was wearing a jacket without an insignia on it.

"Are you a Wolf too?"

"No," Noah said quietly. "My dad was . . . He was their president, actually, and Uncle Karl raised me. I'm not a Wolf, though."

I thought about what Uncle Karl had said, and then I clarified, "So you wouldn't be forbidden for me to date, but Zion is."

Noah nodded again. "Killer will understand you agreeing to go out with me."

"I *wasn't* agreeing to go out with you," I clarified in an even lower whisper.

"Yet." He grinned at me.

I shook my head, but I couldn't help smiling at him too. I wasn't immune to his charms. If I'd met Noah first, who knows?

I walked over to the biker I *had* met first. Without his jacket in the way, I could see tattoos on his biceps. I could also see the muscles I'd felt when he carried me to his Harley and when I'd been pressed up against him as he took me home. Zion had the build of a fighter, lean and muscular, with the ability to look like he was considering eating a person's still-warm heart.

I'm not sure I'd have ever spoken to him if not for his helping me with Quincy. Even now, I found him intimidating. I reminded myself that he'd been sweet, gentle almost, when I'd met him.

"Hi." I held out my hand. "I'm not sure we did this part properly the other night. I'm Aubrey. They say your name is Killer."

"Zion," he corrected. "You should still call me Zion."

He took my hand in his, but instead of shaking, he lifted it and kissed the air above my knuckles. His eyes held mine the entire time, and I felt my pulse race. All that touched my skin was the warm brush of his breath, but it felt far more intimate than almost anything I'd ever experienced.

"Aubrey is starting work here tonight," Noah said from behind me. He'd obviously followed. "She's a student over at WCC too."

"I know that," Zion said in a voice that was a lot less friendly than Noah's.

The two men stared at each other, and I felt like there was an entire conversation going on that I couldn't hear. The rest of the men in the bar were watching us, and I wondered just what they expected.

"Are you working tonight, Dash?" Zion asked finally, his voice oddly calm.

"No. Just dropping in to see if Uncle Karl needed anything before I go over to the house. You?"

"You both work here? Doing what?" I asked.

"Dash here is a bouncer when he's not at school," Zion

said with a chill I couldn't miss. "I don't work *here,* but I spend a lot of time here off the clock, so if you ever need anything . . ."

"There are plenty of people around to ask," Noah finished. He stepped closer to his cousin. "Killer, here, is like a big brother to the barmaids. *Many* of the Wolves are. We protect our own."

" 'We'?" Zion scoffed, stepping forward too so they were close enough that it looked like a fight was about to happen. Zion's arms hung loosely at his sides, but his expression as he stared at his cousin was far from friendly. "You're not using that word right, cuz. I'm sure you've already told Red that detail. You don't have the same rules, so don't act like you have a right to claim the privilege of being one of *us.* All or nothing. You keep choosing nothing."

The look Noah gave him was filled with even more fury. "I've been a member of this family my whole life—"

"Dash's father was a Wolf," Zion cut in, glancing at me. "But he doesn't know if we're worth—"

"Killer! Dash!" Uncle Karl yelled.

The two men straightened up, but they didn't step back or look away from each other for a moment. Then Zion reached into his jacket. When he pulled out his hand, he was holding a pen and a business card. He wrote something on the card.

"If you ever need anything"—Zion held out the card with the extra digits scrawled on it—"I'll be here . . . and I meant what I said the other night. Just say the word, Red."

I tensed. My belief when I'd walked out of Uncle Karl's office had been that Zion was going to be safe now. As he stood there propositioning me without anyone else knowing what he meant, I realized that I had been so incredibly wrong. There was nothing safe about him.

And there was no way to lie to myself. I was almost criminally tempted by him. I'd considered this moment since I woke up the morning after meeting him, but the rules of my new—and much-needed—job meant that the most I could have with him was three dates. I wasn't the sort of girl to have a one-night stand . . . or a three-night stand, for that matter. Zion was firmly off-limits if I intended to keep this job, and I needed the money too much to pick a "what if" with a man over a reliable way to handle the cost of being newly on my own.

I straightened my shoulders and said, "You don't know me. I could be a bitch."

Zion flashed me the smile that he'd surely used to remove those nuns' panties. "I know enough to want to know a lot more."

Despite every bit of common sense I knew I had, I silently took the card he was holding out. Zion was deadly when he really turned on the charm, and right now, he was aiming it at me. All my fantasies of the past two weeks weren't even close to right. He was more tempting, more dangerous than I remembered.

He held my gaze for a moment, and then he turned and walked away without another word.

"Aubrey?"

I pulled my attention away from the doorway where Zion had just exited and looked at Noah. "What?"

He let out a sigh and dragged his hand through his hair before saying, "Killer's actually a great guy. I'd trust him with my life."

"So . . . what was"—I waved my hand in the general direction of where they'd been standing—"*that* about, then?"

"That was me trying to keep him from seducing you," Noah said. He looked down at me. "You seem like a nice girl, Aubrey. Killer's my family, and he'd do anything for the Wolves, but despite him stepping in with Quincy the other night, he's not someone you should trust."

Although I had no practical room to argue, I *did* trust Zion. He'd had more than one opportunity to take advantage of me the night we'd met, but he hadn't—even when I'd all but thrown myself at him. He might be trouble in a lot of ways, but he'd made me feel safe that night. Today . . . *safe* wasn't what I felt, but I didn't think I knew the words for the tangled mess inside me. What I did know was that I instinctively trusted him.

After a moment, I shook my head and walked toward the bartender. "Mike, right?"

The bartender nodded.

"Karl says you're supposed to train me how to do"—I gestured at the bar—"what you do."

"Handle drunks and sell booze?"

"I guess." I smiled.

"Well, come on back then." Mike lifted the bar flap and gestured for me to come back. "Let's get you trained up right. You've already dealt with the worst of the young'uns, and you seem to be faring fine. Put your stuff in the back room, and come out when you're ready to work."

I went through the door he pointed toward and found myself in a cramped room accessible only to those behind the bar. It was more of a glorified closet than an actual room, but it had a pair of well-worn chairs that I assumed were for breaks. I tucked my bag into an empty space on a shelf before I fired off the promised text to Ellen and made a quick call to Grandma Maureen.

When I rejoined Mike, I took a moment to survey the bar. I hadn't spent any actual time in bars, and there was something surreal about starting to work in one. I could enjoy conversations with interesting people, but not have to drink *or* seem like I wanted to be picked up. In fact, Uncle Karl's rules protected me from the latter worry. Aside from keeping me from exploring the pull I felt toward Zion, the terms of my new job seemed sort of perfect to me.

"Ready?" Mike prompted.

I pulled my attention away from the wide, mostly empty bar and walked over to stand beside Mike.

Once I was at his side, he explained, "Dash doesn't usually bother the girls, but Killer beds most of the barmaids eventually. I swear half of them take the job just to get one of those boys to notice."

I folded my arms over my chest and leveled a gaze at him.

"I had no idea they were here. One of the girls at school sent me in for a job. I'm here to *work,* not get laid."

"All right, then," Mike said. He started opening the coolers that lined the area behind the bar. "We sort the beers by domestic and import. Coldest in the front, so when you stock, you fill from the back. When you sell, you pull from the front."

He went on like that, and I steadily got a sense of which drinks were where, which liquors were most popular, and the way the register worked.

A FEW HOURS later, I was exhausted but proud of myself—and at ease in my new job. In the short time I'd been there, I'd seen hugs, arm clasps, shoulder pounds, and a woman lifted into a hug and spun around like she was a small child. I hadn't come to the bar looking for more than a job, but there was a warmth there that felt very much like family already. I hadn't realized how much I craved that kind of easy affection until now.

Uncle Karl walked me out to the car, waited while I found my keys, and then told me, "Someone will walk you out every night. If I'm not here, you can trust Killer, Dash, Mike, or Billy. Most nights, one of us will be around. Soon enough, you'll get to know a few others who are trustworthy enough. Till then, I'll be sure one of us is here."

He paused and looked at me like he was searching for some answer on my face. His hand came down on my shoulder, stopping me as I was about to get into the car. "If you need to talk about anything that happens at the bar or with one of the Wolves, you come to me, you hear?"

"Thank you." Impulsively, I hugged him.

"You'll be just fine," Uncle Karl said with a pleased look as he stepped back from my hug.

"I think so now," I agreed. "Thank you for giving me a shot."

"You're Maureen's granddaughter. If there wasn't a job for you with us, we'd have helped you find something. We take care of our own."

I paused a moment before asking the question I'd been pondering. I was pretty sure I knew the answer, but I wanted confirmation. "I don't suppose you'd tell me why you include me and my grandma in that category? I haven't seen a Harley jacket in the house, and unless I'm mistaken, women can't be Wolves."

"You're not wrong." Uncle Karl shook his head. "Maureen is still family, though. She'll tell you what she thinks you ought to know. Without being her granddaughter, though, you'd be ours all the same *now*. You work in Whiskey; that makes you family."

"Does she work for you, then?"

Uncle Karl laughed. "I'm old, but I'm not a fool. Don't nobody cross your grandmama, not if they have a lick of sense." He shooed me toward the car. "Go on, then. You need to get on home, and I have paperwork to tend."

I was still relaxed when I pulled into my grandmother's

neighborhood—at least until I saw the cruiser and ambulance lighting up the street outside my grandmother's house. My panic ebbed only when I realized that it wasn't *her* house that had been burgled. One of her neighbors was sitting in a lawn chair with paramedics at her side.

Grandma Maureen stood with a group of senior citizens. Most of them looked more angry than afraid.

"What happened this time?" I wrapped an arm around my grandmother's waist.

She reached over and patted my hand. "Idiots with a brick scared Christine halfway to a heart attack."

"Is she hurt?"

Another of the women said, "No one is ever hurt. So far they just scare us, mess up our things, and vanish." She motioned toward my grandmother. "If Maureen wasn't retired, I'd be asking if she was passing out a stack of failing grades again."

My grandmother *hmph*ed. "It's not students. There's a reason for it, but it's not kids angry at us."

The senior citizens' conversation lifted and fell as they talked about possibilities. The small group was mostly women. There were a few men, but it looked like either the women here outlived their husbands or the men were elsewhere. A cursory look around located several more old men talking to police and paramedics.

"They feel as helpless as we do," my grandmother said.

"Not Beau or Elliot," another woman quipped. "Beau's feeling like he's Perry Mason, and Elliot's making time with half the girls 'so they aren't home alone.' Old codger thinks he's clever."

"Least Christine can't pretend to be in the family way this time," one of the women said.

"What do we do?" I asked.

"We catch the bastards," my grandmother said. "I'm too old to be woken up all the time like this." She sounded tough, but I knew her too well to believe it this time. There was a new and noticeable tremble of fear in her voice, and *that* frightened me more than the sirens and the crimes.

"You could make that call," one of the women suggested quietly. "He'd handle it. For you, he'd fix this."

Grandma Maureen pressed her lips together in a tight line and looked away. Her reaction further confirmed my suspicions—and created new ones. Whatever the story between my grandmother and the bikers, it was one with some serious complications. Sooner or later, someone was going to fill me in on it. I was starting to think it would need to be soon. The simple truth, for me at least, was that if her mysterious Echo was able to ease the stress on her face, I was with the neighbors on calling him in. If I met him at the bar, I might just tell him myself.

Chapter 8

THE NEXT MORNING, GRANDMA MAUREEN ACTED LIKE the trouble hadn't happened. I wondered how often I'd failed to notice her being worried or stressed because she hid it so well.

"So who do they want you to call?" I asked as I poured a cup of coffee.

"What, dear?"

I had to give it to her, my grandmother was great at feigning ignorance when it suited her. I obviously hadn't realized just *how* great she was at it. "Your neighbors. Beau mentioned Echo and—"

"There's a saying about sleeping dogs, lovie," she interrupted. "You let them stay that way. You know what I'm saying?"

I sipped my coffee, weighing just how much I wanted to push this. I didn't want to upset her, but things weren't getting any better and if Echo could fix it, I wasn't entirely opposed to waking him. In a voice only slightly tremulous, I asked, "What about sleeping Wolves?"

"They're worse than dogs, I suspect." She nudged me to the side so she could get to the coffee pot. "You're getting your sass back. It looks good on you."

I shook my head. "I don't have any sass to get back. You must be thinking of some other grandchild."

Grandma Maureen clucked her tongue at me. "You're my only one. When you were a tiny thing, you had more attitude than pounds to you. You grew into your attitude, and then . . . you locked it all up." She lifted her gaze from the sugar she was spooning into her coffee. "I thought the mess your parents were making of everything was going to bring you back around to that little girl who was all fire and defiance. You just created another of those schedules of yours." She sighed and pressed her lips together for a moment before adding, "My son and his wife are being idiots. They need to stick together and sort out the mess your dad got into, as a *team*, but . . . no one asked me for my advice . . . except you."

"I don't want to be a burden. With the job, I can pay you rent or get a car—"

"You don't need to pay me rent, lovie, and that car's yours as often as you need. We'll sort that out just fine." Grandma Maureen sipped her coffee. "It's good to see you trying to get up on your feet, though, and I'm not of a mind to object to your questioning me. These past years you haven't challenged me no matter what I said or did. It was disappointing."

"Oh."

She reached out and patted my hand. "Yes, 'oh.' A little bit of sass is a useful thing for a woman." Then she topped off her coffee and walked away, calling out, "You need to get a move on. Beau said there's construction over by the school."

For a moment, I stood and stared after her, trying to figure out what had just happened. Then it occurred to me that she'd dodged my question. "Don't think I missed that you didn't answer my questions about Echo," I yelled as I walked toward my room to get dressed.

Her only answer was a laugh.

I got ready and headed to campus—not ending up late only because of Grandma Maureen's warning about the road construction.

Ellen waved as she sailed by me in the hallway. "I expect free drinks. Finder's fee."

I laughed.

"And we seriously need to brighten up your clothes," she added as she walked backward away from me. "It's no good for my reputation as a designer if I don't update your look."

"Pushy," I said.

"Guilty as charged," she acknowledged before she ducked into a classroom.

I was still smiling when I walked into American Lit: The

Romantics. I could do without ever trying to read Thoreau again, but much like my history course, Am Lit was one that would undoubtedly either transfer for a requirement or at the very least have a match at Reed or wherever I ended up if Reed remained too expensive to swing. A matching course meant that the credits wouldn't be dismissed. That was my priority when picking the classes I'd be taking in Tennessee. I wished I could take something more unusual. There was a 300-level "Animal Fables Through the Ages" course at Reed, and the Intro to Fiction 200-level course that focused on "The American Con Artist." Those were the sort of courses that I'd been looking forward to taking. Instead, I was stuck reading Thoreau and Emerson. It made me want to cry.

Noah joined me in the classroom, sliding into the seat next to mine. It was still early enough that he had a cup of coffee that he'd obviously picked up at the little kiosk on campus. He took a sip of it, and I couldn't decide if I was envious that he had coffee. I'd had the one cup at the house, but I could've gone for at least one more. I had become fond of fussy coffee drinks when I was in Oregon, which was a veritable coffee mecca. Here, I had adjusted to only having the good stuff at home. Basic literature courses and bad coffee . . . this was so not the life meant for an English major.

"What's that smile for?"

"English major humor," I said sheepishly.

He made a "go on" gesture with his hand, as if he could

spool the words out of me, so I explained what I'd been pondering about Thoreau and the classes I missed at Reed.

"There was a con man class?" He shook his head. "I think I'd have liked your other school."

I sighed. "I did."

Noah shot me a sympathetic look. "Sorry. I'm not sure what happened, but I'm sorry you're not where you want to be."

"Can't pay the tuition right now," I said with a shrug.

"Sucks."

"It does."

He paused for a moment before his expression switched to the sort of grin that made me think he would've understood the con man course innately. "Give me a chance, though, and I can help you see the delights of wondrous Williamsville."

It was impossible not to smile back at him, but I still said, "No thanks."

There was an easy charm to Noah that made me wish he tempted me the way Zion did—just as much as I suspected I shouldn't want that. Noah felt *safe.* Nothing about Zion felt safe, even with the bar rules in place. With a shake of my head for letting my mind wander to *him* again, I forced myself to look to the front of the classroom, where the instructor was opening her bag.

She had the harried look of someone who taught too many courses in too few days. I'd guess she was as thrilled to be here as I was. Without saying a word, she began passing

[handwritten margin note: BULLSHIT YOU SAID HE WAS SCARY AND UNCOMFY.]

90

out the syllabus, and I readied myself for another rousing class of outlining rules and expectations that truly should be obvious to anyone who had taken even one course prior to this . . . which meant *everyone here,* since there were prereqs.

Noah caught my eye. "I expect tutoring. Name your price."

I remembered his earlier remarks that he wasn't as good at English as at numbers, so I figured he might be serious. I also guessed that he could be quite persuasive if I tried to say no. I whispered, "I'll think about it."

And then I forced myself to stay focused on the course review that the instructor, a Ms. Malowski, was inflicting on us.

By the time class ended, I felt a surge of guilt. English majors should like classes in their major . . . but honestly, half the syllabus was stuff I'd read before. The rest was stuff I had no desire to read.

As the class let out, Noah stayed beside me. "I wasn't joking about the tutor thing."

"I'm not sure that's a good idea." I tucked the syllabus into a folder and slid it into my bag.

"Because . . ."

I shook my head, ignoring the question and any potentially awkward answers. Maybe he didn't mean anything by it or the flirting at the bar. Maybe he was just friendly.

"Aubrey?"

"I have work and classes already."

"I'm not *that* stupid," Noah said lightly. He motioned for

me to precede him out the door. "I'm talking about a few hours here or there."

There was no way to ask if he was interested in something beyond that without . . . well, asking it outright. But that could sound like I *wanted* him to be interested. I hated this part of talking to guys. I decided to ignore the question entirely—my typical answer to the problem. "I need to head to the bar."

"Come on, then. I'll give you a lift."

"No."

"I need to go over anyhow," he continued. "We can carpool. That's an Oregon sort of thing to do, right?"

"It is, *but* I have a car with me, and I can't leave it here. Thanks anyhow."

Noah met my gaze and stared at me like he was looking for some sort of clue in my eyes. "You're not sore about something I said or did, are you?"

While we were talking we'd walked to a side door of the building, a shortcut to the parking lot from the looks of it. I said nothing as he pushed the door open and waited for me to exit. Outside, I stepped to the side so the people behind us could pass. "Why are you offering me rides and asking for tutoring?"

"Because we're going to the same place and you seem to already know the authors we're going to be reading," he said.

When I didn't reply, he added, "*And* because you're easy on the eyes, you seem pretty smart, and you're different. If you had been here (before,) either Killer or I would've already been chasing you." He held his hands out. "I like the look of you . . . and the whole virgin thing is tempting." *THE FUCK*

BEFORE WHAT?

I held up one hand and counted off facts on my fingers. "One, thank you on the compliments. Two, I'm not that different. Three, I don't date. Four, I'm not a virgin." I was down to my pinkie finger. I held it up and said, "*Five,* I'm not interested in being chased."

He was silent for so long that I thought I'd offended him. Then he looked at me. "But you'll think about tutoring me? As friends . . . or [friends who will flirt with their tutor but are willing to pay for tutoring?]"

"I'll think about it." I folded my arms. "Stop with the flirting, though. I seriously *do not date.*"

"Can't." He shook his head. "Especially now that you're a bartender. Your job is to sell us drinks and flirt. I'm just helping train you. You don't have to go out with me, but I'm duty-bound to flirt with you. All of us are. [That's why Uncle Karl only hires people who are pretty or interesting.] He paused, then became exceedingly serious and added, "Take Mike, for example. He's very pretty. Brings the whole look of the place up by two or three degrees."

I laughed. I couldn't help it. Mike was, like most of the people I'd met at Wolves so far, a bit rough around the edges. "The whole bunch of you are ridiculous."

"Yeah, but you like us. Admit it."

"Maybe. *Some* of you."

Noah walked me to my car and waited till I was situated

before he gave me a cheeky grin and said, "I didn't really need to go to the bar. That was just a ploy to get you on my bike."

I rolled my eyes, pulled the door shut, and drove off. I could get used to Noah, maybe even call him a friend in time. Sure, he was gorgeous, but he didn't make me feel like I was going to combust just from looking at him. Only Zion did that.

Walking into the bar a short while later felt a lot less comfortable. The first two hours, I'd be on my own. Mike was going to come in before it got busy, but until then, I was the bartender on duty. I could handle the register well enough. The fear of someone ordering a complicated drink was the only real issue.

I went into the ladies' room and changed into bar clothes. I felt funny changing here, but the alternative was changing at WCC. It was one thing to wear bar clothes *here,* but it was totally different to wear them on campus where classmates would see me. I generally tried to dress to downplay my body, but the T-shirt Uncle Karl gave me to wear was tight and the black skirt I had brought was above the knee. It wasn't risqué by any standard, but it felt more revealing than what I was used to wearing.

I took a deep breath and walked out of the restroom—only to find myself all but frozen in place by the biker who'd just sauntered in the back door.

"Red."

Trying to match his relaxed tone, I greeted him. "Zion."

His gaze swept me from top to bottom and back up.

"Do I pass?"

"More than. But you passed in your schoolgirl clothes too." He smiled, making my knees unsteady and my throat dry, and then asked, "Can I get a cold beer?"

"Any particular *type* of beer?" I started toward the bar, determined not to rush despite the heat of his gaze searing into my back. I knew he was right behind me, knew he was watching me, and I was not going to let him see the way it affected me.

"Longneck Bud."

My first customer as a solo bartender was the man who'd rescued me and filled my dreams. I bit my lip to keep my smile from looking deranged as I opened Zion's beer. It was a silly thing to be so pleased by.

He dropped money on the bar and took a swig of his beer before asking, "What's the smile?"

"When you took me home, I'd never been on a motorcycle, never talked to a biker, never been in a bar . . ." I shook my head. "There's a lot about leaving Oregon that sucks, but this"—I gestured around the bar—"isn't on that list, and you seem to be there for all of it." I shrugged. "I guess *you* make me smile."

"Good." Zion looked like he'd say more, but a group of bikers came in laughing and loud.

"Killer! Leave that little lady alone, boy!" one of them hollered.

Another added, "You flirt this one out the door, and I'll kick your scrawny ass."

Zion flipped the man off without looking his way. "Good to see you, Red." Then he took his beer and walked over to join the crowd that had just come into the bar. I didn't even pretend not to watch him walk away.

Chapter 9

WORK AND SCHOOL CONTINUED TO BE FAIRLY CALM. My teachers tried to be interesting. Ellen spent far too many hours trying to get me to let her treat me like a dress-up doll. Noah flirted and tried to get me to go out. Quincy went out of his way to say hello to me, and I went out of my way to ignore him.

My grandmother tried to keep calm while waiting for the next break-in and ignoring the questions I asked. Zion and I talked about everything from my classes to the people in the bar or random bits of news he brought up. He paid a lot of attention to world politics. It was a bit like talking to my friends back at Reed—except Zion made me have the sort of thoughts that were more vivid than I wanted. He was smart, funny, and gorgeous. It wasn't fair that the first guy to catch my interest so completely was off-limits for multiple reasons.

I tried not to obsess over every little word or look Zion spared for me. I mostly failed at that. He filled up a lot of my thoughts.

On the other hand, while I wouldn't say I was exceptional at bartending, I'd gotten better. Uncle Karl no longer seemed as worried—a fact I realized only when he stopped coming through the bar flap to make sure I didn't need any reminders every hour or so. I'd thought that was just how he was, until I noticed him checking in less and less often.

Today I was experiencing one of the less exciting parts of my job: a shift with too many dead hours. I'd already learned that weekends were amazing but exhausting. Wednesdays and Thursdays were pretty good, and Sundays were unpredictable. Mondays and Tuesdays were quiet. The hours of the day varied too. Daylight was only busy if it was raining—or sometimes on the weekend. The evening and the hour after midnight brought the best tips on busy days. Right-before-closing was stressful.

Early afternoon *and* a Tuesday was going down as the most inactive time I'd worked so far. I'd already stocked the coolers, and I'd even dusted the liquor bottles, turned them all face out, and mopped the floor. I was *bored.*

Zion was here. He drank very little, but he made his presence known most days. Today, though, he was with a group of bikers. Often during my shifts, he talked to me a bit before wandering over to the pool table. Even more often, he was only here for part of my shift. Either way, I usually got to have some sort of conversation with him. Not today. Today, I had barely received a wave and nod.

Much like with any group of bikers, I didn't interrupt when they had discussions in low voices. They liked their privacy, and I liked not knowing what they were discussing. If they needed drinks, they'd come to me or motion me over. It was pretty simple. Since no one was alone or in need of a drink and I'd already done all the cleaning I could stand to do, I pulled out my Am Lit syllabus and course book. Fortunately, we were starting with historical context and parallels with the British Romantics. I wasn't a fan of Wordsworth's actual poetry, but his "Preface to *Lyrical Ballads*," where he shared his theories, was actually interesting. Give me Coleridge, Byron, Shelley, really *any* of the first- or second-gen Romantics, and I was dizzy with geeky glee. Wordsworth himself was more useful on the theory than the poetry.

By the time I'd read a few pages, two men had come and sat at the end of the bar. They were bourbon drinkers. That was easy. So far, I was getting why Mike had snorted when I'd asked about complicated drinks. There was a metal recipe box on the counter for anything I didn't know, but so far, bikers seemed to be a beer, bourbon, and whiskey crowd. I could handle that.

Periodically, I glanced up to see if anyone needed a refill or my attention. One of the bikers with Zion looked my way a few too many times, but when he caught Zion glaring at him, he laughed and stopped. I'd met him a couple of times so far, but honestly, their names were so damn weird that I still had a hard time keeping them all straight.

"Barmaid!" someone called out.

I tensed as I looked away from Zion and his friends. The new man who'd walked up to the bar—like the two at the end of the bar—wasn't wearing Wolves colors. We had patrons who weren't Wolves, and up until now, they'd all been polite. The way this guy stared at me made me feel the same way cockroaches did.

"Hi," I said, forcing myself to sound pleasant. "What can I get you?"

"A Budweiser and your number." He smiled at his lame joke. That one had gotten absurd by day two at the bar. My job was to serve drinks, nothing more. Even a few of the Wolves had tested the waters with equally weak lines.

Silently, I got the newcomer a can of beer. He hadn't asked for draft or longneck, and I didn't feel like talking to him to ask if he had a preference, so a can was what he got. If I felt bitchier, I would've given him a warm one, but I wasn't quite that irritated by lame lines yet. I put a cold can of Bud in front of him on a bar napkin and told him the price.

"Can I get some of those nuts?"

After I got him a bowl of bar nuts, he still hadn't made any move to pay, so I said, "We don't run tabs."

"What if I want to add to my order?"

"We don't serve food."

His hand came down on mine. "What about you? What's your hourly rate?" *AINT no fuckin hooker*

I jerked away and glared at him, unsure whether he was serious. The Wolves and the assorted clientele at the bar might be a little crude and raucous, but they'd never once insulted me. If anything, I'd felt both more protected and more feminine than ever in my life. There was something about fierce tattooed men treating me like a delicate but respected treasure that made me feel both safe and sexy.

"Well?" the cockroach prompted.

A chair screeched as it was shoved back quickly, and in what seemed barely a fraction of a second, Zion was standing beside the cockroach. He had one hand on the bar; the other hung loosely at his side. He didn't even glance at me.

"Apologize."

"Hey, I was just—"

"Apologize," Zion interrupted.

I looked at Zion and told him, "I'm fine. Really." I reached out and covered his hand with mine. The tension under his skin made his fist feel like a rock. "It's *fine.*"

Zion's attention stayed riveted on the cockroach. My words weren't getting through. He simply repeated, "Apologize."

"You heard her, man."

Zion stepped closer to the cockroach. "Right fucking *now.*"

"Sure, whatever." The cockroach couldn't have sounded less sincere if he'd tried. He shrugged and looked at me. "Sorry I offended your boyfriend here."

The emotionless expression on Zion's face was unchanged. "Now, walk out. You're not welcome here."

I didn't know him that well, but even I could tell that Zion wasn't joking around. There was something in his tone that made me want to shiver. Admittedly, it wasn't *fear* that I was feeling because he was defending me, but I wouldn't want to be on the receiving end of that anger.

"I have a beer sitting here," the cockroach protested, reaching out for his can.

Apparently, that was the end of Zion's patience. He grabbed the man by the back of the neck and started toward the door. The jackass was struggling and cussing, but he was being towed to the door nonetheless. I wasn't sure what to do or say, and no one else was reacting. Uncle Karl popped his head out of his office when the guy started yelling.

"Trouble?"

"Touched the new barmaid and asked what her hourly rate was," one of the bikers offered.

Uncle Karl nodded and returned to his office.

Zion jerked open the door, shoved the man outside, and followed him.

"Should someone go after them?" I asked loud enough for everyone there to hear.

"Nah. Killer's not going to hurt him, just escort him to his car," one of the bikers said.

Should *I* follow? Should I insist someone else did? I wasn't sure what to do. I must've looked as frustrated as I felt because the biker who had answered me came over to the bar. He stood in front of me as I tried to decide what to do.

"Aubrey, right?" he said after a few seconds.

I nodded and looked up at him. Now that he was standing at the bar, I realized that he was one of the tallest men I'd ever met, coming in well over six feet in height.

"It's okay. We might be loud and rude, but we're not stupid."

"Speak for yourself, Alamo," another biker called. "I'm stupid right regularly."

Gratefully, I grinned at the speaker and said, "I'm sure you're perfectly lovely." Several guffaws greeted my words, but I ignored them to tell Alamo, "I just don't understand why . . . he did that."

"We protect our own," Alamo said. "The jackass made you uncomfortable. Killer decided that wasn't okay."

"Oh."

"Grab me a bowl of those peanuts," Alamo said. "And another round for the table."

"I'll bring it out." I nodded and went to scoop out a bowl of the nuts.

I was torn between worry over Zion and gratitude that he'd stepped in when the cockroach was rude. I didn't particularly like being spoken to as if I were a hooker, but having the kind of curves I had meant that guys said stupid things to me. They'd been doing it since I was fifteen.

I tossed the cockroach's Bud and took four cold beers over to the table.

"Killer doesn't get one?" asked a biker with the palest blue eyes I'd ever seen.

"Fuck off, Hershey," another biker said.

"Alamo said a round for the table," I said, feeling stupid. "There are *four* of you at the table, so . . ."

Alamo smacked Hershey on the back of the head and told me, "Thank you, darlin'. Killer won't mind his being kept cold."

After giving him a grateful smile for covering for my stupidity, I gathered the empties and returned to the bar. Although I had told the cockroach we didn't run tabs, that wasn't completely true. We *did*, but only for Wolves.

When Zion walked back in about ten minutes later, I was reading again—or at least pretending to read. He didn't stop at the table for more than a moment before coming up to the bar.

I closed my book and set it on one of the coolers as he approached.

"I hear you kept my beer on ice." DUMB THING 2 ADMIT

"Something like that," I said. [I was flustered and took] four beers to the table instead of five. Alamo covered for my mistake."

"Alamo's good people." Zion looked at the table. "Theo and Hershey are all right, too, and Big Eddie's a bit of an ass."

I looked at the group of men. I knew who Alamo and Hershey were, but there was no way to know which of the other two was Big Eddie.

Zion offered quietly, "Big Eddie's the loud one in the shirt with paint on it."

"I'm never sure whether the names are realistic or funny or what they are."

"Hershey is from Hershey, Pennsylvania. He claims he's sweet as chocolate." Zion sat down on a stool. "Dash is easy. That's his last name."

"What about Skeeter? Alamo? Big Eddie?"

"Eddie lies about his. That's all I'm saying." Zion gave me a look that made quite clear that the origin of Eddie's name was vulgar. "Later when you hear the story, you just remember that. No idea about Skeeter or Alamo . . ."

After a moment, I had to ask the obvious question. "And you? What's your name mean?"

He shrugged. "Just a name, Red. Not everything is that mysterious."

"It is when you avoid my questions."

Zion met my gaze; then he lowered his voice as he asked, "So does that mean you have a lot of other questions, then?"

"Maybe."

"Ask one," he challenged. "Anything you want."

"Favorite book?" Maybe it was silly, but I'd always thought that the best way to know a person was to know what books they liked. It could be an English major thing, but that was my "who are you" topic: what the person read.

Zion smiled before replying, "No one has ever asked me

that. It's either *Heart of Darkness*, Kerouac's *On the Road*, or maybe Kafka's *Metamorphosis*."

I gaped at him.

"What? You expected me to say *Zen and the Art of Motorcycle Maintenance*? Or maybe a Hunter S. Thompson book?" he teased.

"I don't know what I expected," I admitted.

"Not a Thompson fan, really." Zion kept his voice pitched low. "Now, you're not going to spill my dirty little secret, are you? They thought it was funny as hell that I never went anywhere without a book when I was a kid. I had favorites, though, ones I've read a few times."

"Oh."

"They knew I read, but most of them never bothered to question *what* I read, so that was handy. Racy romances or King's horror or classics. It was all the same to them."

I laughed. The image was simply too much. "Racy romances?"

"Hell, yeah! No better way to figure out what women want when you're fourteen and trying to get a little sympathy." He offered me one of his panty-dropping smiles. "Want a demonstration of what I've learned?" HOW MANY TIMES...

And just like that the conversation had gone from surprising to teasing to something dangerous. His gaze dropped to my mouth, and without meaning to, I bit my lip.

"That's not a no."

"It should be," I said, then quickly corrected myself. "It is. It *has* to be."

He picked up his beer, studied me for several moments, and pronounced, "No. It's a 'not yet.' It might even be an 'I can resist,' but it's definitely not a no."

I didn't have the words to argue with him. The best I could do was force myself not to stare at him as he walked over to Uncle Karl's office. Everything illogical in my body screamed that my answer was far from a no, but a tiny logical voice reminded me that I couldn't let it be anything *but* a no.

Chapter 10

WHEN I LEFT WORK THAT NIGHT, ZION WAS SITTING on his bike beside my grandmother's car. Uncle Karl was at my side as I stepped out of the bar, so it wasn't like I needed an escort.

"Mind the rules, Killer," he said tersely, and then spun around and left me standing there with Zion.

"You were done with your schoolwork earlier," Zion said. "Mrs. E. has her card night tonight. That leaves you alone for dinner."

I stared at him for a moment, wondering how he knew all that. I must've looked either alarmed or angry because his posture shifted and he reminded me gently, "You told me about her card night, Red."

"Right."

I walked closer to him, not so close as to touch him, but near enough that I could hear him when he spoke softly like he just had. That was how he was at the bar too. Sometimes I wasn't sure whether it was a way to lure me closer or to let him be more open without the other Wolves hearing.

"And the homework?" I prompted.

He offered me a grin, the one that made him look less dangerous and more approachable. "I watch you, Red. You closed that textbook with a thump and a smile. That meant you were done."

"Maybe I have other homework." I folded my arms.

"Do you?"

"No," I admitted. "I can't leave the car here, though. Gran needs it."

Zion shrugged. "I'll follow you home. You can drop it off *or* we can stay there. I'm a decent cook. I'll make dinner."

"I don't remember agreeing to go out with you," I said lightly.

He laughed. "Dinner. We don't even need to call it a date, and even if we did, we get three before there's an issue."

I liked talking to him, liked it in a way that was not just about how mouthwateringly *gross* gorgeous he was. He was funny and smart, and he loved books. I wanted to be able to be around him, and not just three times. *this book is the biggest cliche*

When I turned back to him, he was still sitting on his Harley watching me.

"Dates include kissing," I said bluntly.

He stared at me for a long moment before asking, "Is that an invitation?"

"No." I folded my arms and met his gaze unflinchingly. "It's a negotiation. You can meet me at the house, and we can get dinner, but it can't be a date."

"Which means no kissing?"

"It does."

Zion shrugged. "I'm not *only* interested in kissing you."

"No sex either," I added.

The smile that came over his face was the same one he'd turned on me in the bar. "Well, then, it looks like I'm not the one with the dirty mind here, Red. I meant that I liked talking to you too, not that I was thinking about more than kissing."

My face flamed, but he didn't comment, and I certainly wasn't going to do so. Instead, I stepped around him and unlocked the car door. I tossed my bag inside and only then did I meet his gaze again. "I'll meet you at my house."

Zion nodded and started his bike.

I felt almost guilty at how much I wanted to be on his motorcycle. Both the man and the machine tempted me. Steadfastly ignoring the urge to look at him, I slid into the driver's seat and started the car. It gave a pitiful little rumble, as most cars do, and I sighed.

Finally I glanced back at Zion, who gestured for me to pull out.

The drive to the house was a tense one. I had to resist staring in my rearview mirror, and I worried about stopping too suddenly or doing something stupid that endangered him—which was ridiculous. He'd been riding for at least a decade, and most drivers didn't do everything cautiously to keep bikers safer. It was a cliché, but that was where the "loud pipes save lives" expression came from: most people didn't pay attention to bikers, not like I had always done. Now I realized why my grandmother had pressed that issue when I was a teenager. A lot of things made more sense now that I saw how integrated the Wolves were into her town.

I pulled into the drive at the house, but when I got out of the car, Zion was still on the bike.

"Come on, Red," he called. "I need to pick up a few things for dinner."

"You could've gone without me," I said as I accepted the helmet he held out to me.

"You looked like you wanted a ride," Zion said.

"Thank you."

He watched me while I put on the helmet, fumbling a little with the chinstrap but doing it myself this time. "Climb on."

I climbed on the bike behind him. Gingerly, I put my hands on his sides and my feet on the pegs. "You need to carry a second one of these."

"Haven't needed a spare helmet until this month."

While I was still trying to figure out what that meant, he grabbed my hands and pulled them forward so I was hugging him from behind like I had the night he carried me home on the bike. I sighed. He glanced back briefly and grinned. Then the Harley roared to life, and Zion eased us into the street.

Riding this time was even more exciting than the first night I'd been on the bike. That night, I was tired and drunk. Now, I was wide-awake. Every nerve in my body was almost painfully alert. Both the thrill of the machine and the man in front of me were overwhelming. Maybe it wasn't a date, but it was already more fun than any actual dates I'd had.

We picked up a few things at the store and went back to the house. It was an odd realization that all we had for carrying supplies were two small saddlebags, which weren't usually on his bike. When I pointed that out, Zion shrugged.

"You planned this," I accused.

"Maybe it was a coincidence that I put the bags on the bike today and they came in handy tonight," he said.

"Uh-huh." I opened the door so he could carry the groceries inside.

"Or maybe I was being an optimist," he added as he stepped into the kitchen and looked around. "It's been a while since I was in here."

He looked a little uncomfortable, but it wasn't something I wanted to ask about just then, and even if I had, he put the bags on the counter and said, "Skillet?"

And somehow in the next twenty minutes, I had become his sous chef. After I'd washed up, we worked in companionable quiet. I'd never made jambalaya or cornbread, and Zion was aghast at the "shortcomings in my education."

By the time he was putting the cornbread in the oven, it was hard to believe we didn't know each other well.

"So tell me about Aubrey Evans," Zion prompted as he set the timer. "You know my reading taste. What about you?"

"I like Chaucer, Flaubert, a little bit of Eliot." I went over to the fridge and got the sweet tea. "Tea?"

He nodded. "What about your family? I know Mrs. E., obviously, but what about your parents? Are they still in Oregon?"

"More or less," I hedged. My father was a criminal. I didn't think his crimes were any less awful because they were "white collar."

"Tell me what I'm missing," he prompted after a few more moments of silence.

I didn't know what I was doing here with him, but I did know that I wanted him to stay. So I answered him. I told him about my parents, about my father embezzling and my parents turning on each other, about the divorce and the fact that I had no money for tuition. I explained how college loans were based on the taxes of the person who claimed you as a dependent, so I was basically unable to get any money for tuition for a full year—and then only if my parents cooperated on the tax thing. I told him that my home was gone and my parents were so caught up in their drama that I wasn't sure if I could handle Reed right now even if I did have tuition money. It was the first time I'd admitted that to anyone—including myself—and I felt somewhere between embarrassed and weak. I'd spent so much effort trying to pretend I had it all together that being honest was terrifying. *This begs the definition of a copout.*

"So, 'stronger than she looks' and 'has trust issues' go on my list of reasons to like you," Zion said gently.

I felt tears gather in my eyes, but I didn't deny the trust issues. I wasn't sure about the strength part, but I hoped he was right. He *saw* me. I didn't know why, but he did. *He's known you for a week* I hoped he saw the real me, not the scared version or the confused version that I felt like most days.

"I'm sorry," I said.

"For what?"

"Unloading all that." I sipped my tea and tried to pretend I wasn't shaking. I hadn't talked about most of what I'd just told him with anyone. It left me feeling vulnerable, but the way Zion looked at me went a long way toward making me okay with that too. "I don't usually do that."

"Admit to being badass?" he teased. Once I smiled, he added in a more serious tone, "You can trust me, Red. Whether we end up just friends or something else, I can promise you that."

I nodded.

"I can also promise you that this is some of the best corn-bread you'll ever have," he said lightly as the timer went off. "Meals like this aren't what you'll find just anywhere."

"So you're going to get me hooked on Southern food?"

He grinned at me before picking up the oven mitts. "I didn't say I would play fair in my pursuit of you."

I paused and met his eyes. "Are you pursuing me, then?"
He didn't answer as he pulled out the cornbread. Once
it was out to cool, he met my gaze, leaned in so his lips
almost touched my ear, and told me, "The better question
is, what are *you* going to do if I am?"

EW.
So disgustingly
cheesy.

Chapter 11

OVER THE NEXT TWO DAYS, I ONLY HAD TWO CLASS SESsions and one short shift at the bar.

Oddly, Quincy stopped by the house before I left for class the second day. I wasn't even sure how he knew where I lived, but it was a small town, so I couldn't be *too* surprised.

"I thought you might want to carpool," he said when I stepped outside and found him approaching the porch. He motioned to a glossy red pickup truck with oversize tires. If I were the sort of girl to care about vehicles, I might've been impressed, but all I could think was that it wasn't a Harley.

"I have work after class," I said.

Quincy shook his head. "Out there at the bar, right? I

could help you get a safer job. Between living here where you've got all these troubles lately and working out there, you're not safe."

My temper spiked. Sure, bartending wasn't exactly the long-term career I aimed to have, but I certainly didn't feel unsafe there. "I like Wolves," I said.

"The bar or the bikers?"

For a moment, I almost answered that I'd meant the bar, but I wasn't going to deny liking the people. I hadn't intended a double meaning, but it was true all the same. I folded my arms over my chest and asked, "How is that any of your business? I don't know you, and you don't know me. You couldn't even get my name right the night we met."

"And I'd like to make that up to you," he said, his voice slightly less friendly but not angry. "You seem like a nice girl, *Aubrey,* and we had fun, so—"

"We didn't. *I* didn't." I felt guilty about being blunt, but he seemed to think we had a connection that didn't exist. "We drank, and we kissed, and it was a mistake . . . and not fun."

"So that's it? If I'd been sober, Killer wouldn't have had—"

"Stop, please," I interrupted. "It's not because of him or anything else. I'm just not interested."

Quincy shook his head. "Your loss, then, if you'd rather spend your time with bikers than someone with a *real* future."

He turned and left, and I pushed down the urge to call him back and try to rephrase what I'd said in some way he didn't take as an insult. I'd never had to refuse a guy before. Men didn't ask me out much, and the ones who did were so sweet that it wasn't a big deal if I misunderstood—on purpose or accidentally. They usually gave up before it got to overt questions like this. Until I'd moved to Tennessee, I'd never had to flat-out reject someone.

I watched Quincy tear off down the road, driving like he thought he was being chased, and sighed. It hadn't gone gracefully, but at least it was done. I got into the car and headed off to class.

Two days later, the surprise outside my door was a lot worse. I had neither class nor work, so I was planning on a leisurely day of doing nothing—until I went outside and saw the vandalism and graffiti on my grandmother's house. Her porch swing was dangling from only one chain, and two of the hanging planters were ripped down.

Grandma Maureen had gone with her friends on some sort of bus trip early that morning, so I hoped that it had been dark enough when she left that she hadn't seen the spray-painted words on the house. I couldn't imagine she missed the swing, but I hoped so . . . or maybe it had been done after she left.

I didn't think it was Quincy. We'd had enough trouble around the neighborhood that I was all but positive that this was more of the same. I'd mentioned my argument with him to Grandma Maureen, and she'd told me he was harmless. Since she'd taught almost everyone in town, I trusted her judgment.

That left me dealing with another case in the growing list of neighborhood dramas. I wasn't sure what to do about it, though. What was the right step when people vandalize a house? Did I call the sheriff or not?

I sipped a cup of coffee while I thought about it and settled on taking pictures. I didn't call the sheriff. Grandma Maureen had nothing nice to say about Sheriff Patterson, and goodness knew that his son was a jerk.

After I changed into a pair of cutoff jeans and a paint-stained tank top, I went out to the shed. Inside was a massive extending ladder, but I couldn't even move it. There was no way I could carry it to the porch.

Plan B, then. I went back to the house and grabbed a chair from the kitchen. That, I could move. I brought the chair out onto the porch, careful not to step on anything sharp. Shards of flower pots littered the edge of the porch and the yard. The soil and red blooms looked wrong on the white boards. I shoved some of the mess aside with the side of my foot and focused on the swing for now.

With my improvised ladder, I climbed up and looked at where the hook had been ripped out. The chain was intact, so the fix was a simple one. I just had to drill a hole and put in a new screw eye. I could do that—assuming I could stretch that far. The downside of my height was that simple tasks grew complicated sometimes. Putting away dishes often required a step stool. Drilling a hole in the ceiling boards of the porch might be a bit of a challenge.

A few minutes later, I'd found the cordless drill and a

screw eye and was on tiptoe on the chair drilling into the porch beam when I heard a Harley roar by. I resisted the urge to look. I needed to stop craning my neck every time I heard the growl of pipes. In a town with a sizable biker population, I'd spend half my time staring at the street.

I concentrated on trying to reach the ceiling without tumbling from my makeshift ladder. It wasn't happening. Being short sucked sometimes.

"The ladder's too heavy, and the chair's too low," I muttered.

I pondered other possibilities. There was an actual phone book in the house, which had seemed odd to me when I'd seen it. I was so used to everything being digital. Right now, though, that phone book sounded downright useful.

"What are you doing?" a voice asked.

The drill slipped out of my hand as I startled. I glanced over my shoulder to find Zion at the edge of the porch.

"Yoga," I said with an eye roll. I looked down, hoping I hadn't broken the drill. It had landed on the chair and looked fine. I bent over to grab it.

Zion groaned.

I straightened and looked at him questioningly.

"A sight like that's better than coffee at waking a person." He gestured to my cutoff jean shorts.

Hearing him flirt was growing easier every shift at the bar. I didn't feel like the same quiet girl who had lived in Oregon only a couple of months ago. The new me, the bolder me, looked at Zion and grinned. "Thanks."

He did another of those toes-to-top stares and made an appreciative noise. "Anytime, Red. Anytime."

Before I could reply, he'd put both hands on my waist and lowered me to the ground. He held out a hand. "Drill."

As much as I wanted to claim that I didn't need help, I wasn't going to deny the obvious. It wasn't because I was a *girl;* it was because I was *short.* If he'd been a taller woman, I'd have had no hesitation. That was one of the lessons I'd been trying to sit with since moving to Tennessee and starting at the bar: I had my own gender biases. I wouldn't say they weren't legitimately caused, but I also couldn't say they were fair.

I handed him the drill and said, "Thank you."

In a few short minutes, he'd repaired the porch swing. Once he was satisfied that it was straight and steady, he motioned to the house. "Where's Mrs. E.?"

"Out with her friends on a seniors' bus trip," I said as I sat on the newly repaired swing and pushed with my feet. "Nashville, I think."

Zion didn't pretend not to look at my legs before he pointed at the rude words on the house. "Do you have anything to remove that?"

"I wasn't sure what to use. Would turpentine or something work?"

"Maybe. There's a couple things that work: Goof Off and Lift Off. We can run over to the hardware store to get them."

I paused, hating that I felt like I had to ask, but not wanting to break any of the rules that would result in problems at the bar. "Will you get in trouble with Uncle Karl?"

"No."

"Will *I*? This would be the second time we were somewhere alone. Well, third if you count the fair, but . . ." My words faded as he shook his head.

Zion held a hand out to me. "If the hardware store is your idea of a date, Red, we need to talk."

After a brief pause, I took his hand and let him pull me to my feet. I didn't want to comment on the fact that our dinner *had* been a date. My attraction to Zion made me break rules, mine as well as the bar's.

"As much as it pains me to say this, you need to put on some jeans." He opened the door to the house and ushered me inside. He stayed on the porch as he said, "You can't get on the bike dressed like that. If we laid the bike down, you'd have a nasty road rash."

I paused. "You're awfully sweet for someone who goes by a name like Killer."

He smiled but didn't say anything.

"There's coffee if you want a cup," I offered.

"I'm good." He stepped back farther from the house, refusing to cross the threshold. "Go get dressed, Red."

I turned to go, then glanced back at him as I heard the clomp of his boots crossing the porch. He was confusing. He flirted, but it was casual. I wondered if that was because of the rules at the bar, or because he was just being polite and I'd misread the signs I thought showed a real interest in me, or because of something else entirely. It didn't really matter, I supposed. Even if the bar rules were changed, I still intended to get out of Williamsville as soon as I could.

I quickly shucked my shorts and changed into something more appropriate for being on a bike. It amused me a little that I now knew what that meant. The things I'd learned at work weren't limited to what it meant when a patron asked for a "generous pour" or the signs that someone needed to be cut off.

When I came back outside, my legs covered by jeans and short ankle boots, Zion had gathered up the broken flower pots and hanging baskets. He was sitting on the porch, surrounded by shards and flowers. His legs were stretched out, boots resting on the steps in front of him, and a cigarette burned in his hand. His ever-present gun was visible. In Tennessee, gun laws allowed him to carry it openly. None of the other bikers seemed to do so, though.

I tried not to wrinkle my nose at the cigarette smoke. Being around the Wolves, I was getting used to the nasty things, but I still thought the smell was gross. It clung to everything too.

Zion pinched it off and stood. "What happened anyhow?"

I shrugged. "Same thing that's been happening the past month or so, I guess."

He frowned. "Anyone hurt this time?"

"No."

"Mrs. E. have any weapons in there?"

I almost laughed out loud, but then I realized that the

image of my grandmother armed and chasing off the vandals wasn't truly *that* out of character. "No weapons that I'm aware of," I said finally.

Zion frowned again. "I don't like the idea of anyone messing with you *or* her. She told me it was under control when we came around a while back, and you didn't mention it."

"We're fine," I said. "It's a hassle, but that's all it is." When he didn't respond, I motioned to the Harley parked in front of the house. "Are you sure you don't mind? I can take Grandma Maureen's car."

He gave me a disbelieving look, and then he walked to the bike. "Come on, Red."

I followed him to the street and paused to examine his bike up close. The tank wasn't simply black. It was a flat black paint that made the red and glossy black of the wolf stand out even more. I reached out to touch the painting before I could stop myself. I traced down the wolf's throat with one finger. "This is gorgeous."

"Thanks," he said quietly.

Something in the tone of his voice made me look away from the painting and study him. He didn't look embarrassed, but he seemed uncomfortable.

"You painted this," I half asked, half declared.

He stared at me for several heartbeats before he nodded once.

I thought back to the wolves painted on other bikes in the parking lot of the bar; there were wolves prowling, resting, or howling. They were all stylistically similar in some way. "Do you do *all* of them?"

"Yeah . . . but no one outside the club knows that, so . . ." He shrugged. "It's just a thing I do when I'm thinking or whatever."

"You're good." I looked back at the painting. "*Really* good."

He cleared his throat, obviously not at ease with the direction of the conversation. He handed me a helmet, new from the look of it. "Here."

I held it, trying to decide if I should comment. He slung a leg over the bike and looked back at me. "It's yours. Won't no one else be wearing it either."

"Oh." I touched my hand to the helmet, smiling broadly. It wasn't a romantic gift in the traditional sense of the word, but I'd learned enough to realize that it was a statement— one that was dangerous to my resolve.

"Don't overthink it," he told me.

I nodded and climbed onto the back of the bike.

Zion drove slower than I would've liked, but he looped far out of the way, crossing streets a few times, before eventually pulling into the lot of the hardware store. I knew he had been extending the ride, and it made me smile.

He slowly rolled into a parking spot, putting his feet down to steady the bike. He idled for a moment until I reluctantly loosened my hold on him. Once I released him, he cut off the engine.

I slid off the bike. "I'm not so new to town that I don't realize that the drive took twice as long as it would've if I drove on my own."

Zion didn't bother seeming abashed at being caught. "I could've been lost."

"Uh-huh."

"Distracted by the woman pressed up against me, then."

I glanced his way, admittedly pleased at the idea. "Were you?"

"Every day since I met you."

I bit my lip to stop myself from saying something foolish. I had a feeling that getting involved with him was a bad idea for more reasons than my new job and intention to leave Tennessee. The looming question I hadn't even begun to consider was what Zion did to pay his bills.

"Where do you work?" I asked as I pulled a shopping cart free of the stack.

Zion hesitated a beat before saying, "I work for the Wolves, Red."

"That pays enough that you don't need another job?"

"The club owns my apartment, and my bike's paid for. Some food and gas." Zion shrugged. "Not a lot of need for money."

When he said nothing else, I prompted, "So you work for the club president, then?"

My excessive hours of googling motorcycle clubs the day I accepted the job at Wolves & Whiskey had taught me a little bit about them—enough that I stopped reading.

Zion nodded.

"Why?"

"Habit? Loyalty? My mother was one of their women, but she bailed when I was still in diapers." Zion shrugged. "One of them is my father."

We were silent for a few minutes while we walked across the lot.

He opened the door to the hardware store. "It doesn't matter. They're my family. They all raised me. Uncle Karl did the most of it, but they all took their turns minding me and Dash both."

The image of a bunch of bikers raising two little boys struck me as odd, but just because the Wolves made their money in ways I didn't want to know about, it didn't make them heartless. I'd only worked at the bar a few weeks, but I could already see how the Wolves were like a family of sorts. Even as a barmaid, I already felt welcomed and respected.

Zion and I were silent as we walked through the store, but I didn't miss the curious looks we got from a few people. I had no doubt that Uncle Karl and my grandmother would both hear about my impromptu shopping trip with Zion. I was glad I'd changed out of my shorts. Even dressed properly and not touching Zion at all, I was being judged. Zion received several friendly greetings, and I suspected that whatever business he handled, it wasn't something that caused problems around Williamsville.

"You have more questions," Zion said quietly while we walked.

My hands tightened on the handle of the cart. "What do you *do*?"

He met my gaze unflinchingly. "I work for the club."

"Right. I got that, but—"

"That's all there is," Zion said. "I do what needs done."

I opened my mouth, but there wasn't a reply to that. I thought of my question about his name—a question he wouldn't answer. My imagination filled in things like shooting or drug deals or any number of crimes I couldn't even think about when I looked at Zion. "You can't give me examples?"

"I run errands. I make sure our president is safe," Zion said carefully.

The meticulous way he answered made clear that there was a lot that was illegal about his job, things he wasn't going to tell me and I probably didn't want to know. I didn't want to leave it at that, though. I already had feelings for him that were a bad idea. Even if I broke my no-dating rule, it couldn't be with Zion. I'd lose my job—and in the couple of weeks I'd been there, it had become very clear that bartending paid better than anything else I could do.

"Do you carry the gun because of your job?" I asked very quietly.

"Yes."

In an even lower voice, I asked, "Have you used it?"

He nodded slightly, just one brief dip of his head.

"I've never been around them. Until the bar, I mean. It scares me to have to handle them there, but next to you . . ."

"It isn't going to go off on its own," Zion said, not mockingly but in a tone I knew was intended to reassure me. "And everyone at the bar knows not to—"

"You said something," I interrupted, thinking back to how there had only been a couple of times that I'd actually had to touch a gun at the "weapons check-in" at work. That was Zion's doing.

He shrugged. "Saw that it made you nervous. Handled it."

My hands felt sweaty on the handle of the shopping cart. I tightened my grip as if it would keep the shiver of fear at bay. I didn't want to ask how he'd handled it or why they listened or why he'd used his pistol. I wasn't afraid of him hurting me; he'd done nothing but be kind and protective of me. That didn't change my reaction to the things he could've done for his job with the Wolves.

We continued in uneasy silence as he pointed me toward the aisle with the supplies he'd said I needed to remove the paint. I didn't know what to say, and he didn't push me. There were more questions that I didn't want to ask than I knew how to admit.

He put the paint-removing supplies in my cart, and then instead of stepping away, he caught my chin in his hand. Gently, he made me look at him. "I would never hurt you, Red. Ever." His thumb slid along my jaw. "You're safe with me. I told you that the night we met, and I meant it."

I swallowed hard.

"None of us would hurt you," he continued.

Words still wouldn't come. I nodded.

"You work for Uncle Karl, and you're . . . my friend." He moved closer to me. "Aren't you?"

What I felt when I saw him, when I rode with him, wasn't simple friendship. But it had to be. He was called Killer for a reason. He was the enforcer for the club president. That part was clear now. I'd certainly suspected that he was more dangerous than most of them. Very few Wolves moved through the crowd with the kind of respect Zion received.

"Are you still my friend, Red?" he asked again.

I nodded. I couldn't even pretend that I was no longer feeling the exact same things I had before he answered my questions. I *liked* him. In a very soft voice, I said, "I am. I *still* am."

Zion rewarded me with a smile, but then he took his hand away from my face and stepped back. It took more effort than I could explain not to follow him, to remove the distance between us. I wanted the comfort of his touch, even as he was the reason I needed comfort. I felt safer when he was near me.

I had to remind myself of the things he'd told me about his job. He was a criminal. He wasn't someone I could fall for, even if I *did* break my no-dating rule. "We should head back," I said, not meeting his eyes this time. "I appreciate the ride, but I have work to do."

He stared at me but didn't argue. In fact, he said nothing as we checked out and walked back to the bike. *Friends.* I had never met anyone like him in Oregon. I certainly hadn't ever expected to be interested in a motorcycle-riding criminal. *I'm friends with a killer.* The thought tripped through my mind like the refrain to a bad song. Unfortunately, it did nothing to erase the way I felt when I pressed up against him as we rode back to the house. He took a direct route this time, and I wanted to whimper when we arrived home too soon. In a tiny, well-hidden corner of my mind, I admitted that what I still wanted when I was near Zion was not just friendship.

Chapter 12

WHEN WE REACHED THE HOUSE, I SLID OFF THE BIKE, wondering if that had been my last ride. If I were smart, it would be. If I were smart, I'd tell him to leave now. Instead, I handed him the helmet and asked, "Can I get you anything before you go?"

He looked at me silently.

"A drink?" I added.

"Are you asking me to leave, Red?"

I wanted to run, but I wasn't sure whether I wanted to run toward him or away. Okay, I *was* sure what I wanted to do right then, but *want* and *should* were pretty far apart where he was concerned. I took two steps away from him. "I figured you had better things to do and you already took the time to help and—"

He got off the Harley in a fluid move and walked toward me. "There is nothing I could do that would be better than being here."

"Oh."

He advanced on me like he expected me to bolt and invited, "So tell me more about the life of Aubrey before Williamsville."

"It's not very exciting," I said.

"Is that a no?"

It should be. It really should be, and I was sure he knew that too. "Let me grab sandwiches and drinks."

I walked to the house, aware of the heat of Zion's gaze as he followed me.

I stopped on the porch, looked back, and added, "I don't have any beer."

"Whatever you've got is perfect." He sat on the swing he'd fixed, and I couldn't help but smile at the sight of him on my grandmother's white porch. The geranium and daisy planters were destroyed, but even without the flowers there, Zion looked out of place.

"Right. Let me change and grab a snack for us, then." I went inside and changed back into my work-in-the-yard clothes while Zion waited on the porch. I had a moment where I considered putting on something other than the shorts I'd been wearing, but that led to worrying that it would look like I was dressing for him. I put on the same shredded jean shorts, gathered up bread, cheese, and lunchmeat, and went back outside.

"Here," he said, holding out a hand.

I left him with the basics while I grabbed drinks and condiments. Stepping back outside to see him putting together sandwiches made me grin.

"First porch picnic?" he asked.

I nodded and sat next to him. "Maybe."

"So, Red's parents weren't country. That's another fact for my list."

"There's a list?"

"Oh, yeah." He took the tomato slices and added one to each sandwich. "From Oregon, not happy being in Tennessee, never been on a Harley until coming here but already likes it, doesn't date, college girl, hard worker, not a drinker." He paused, glanced at me, and added, "Looks damn good in whatever she wears."

I blushed. "Thank you."

"No criminal record," he said.

I thought about my father, about the things he'd done. Was that worse or better than the things Zion had done? It wasn't about the individual crime. It was about the kind of life I wanted for myself, and that life didn't include criminal parents *or* a criminal . . . whatever Zion was.

"Red?" His voice interrupted my growing panic.

When I looked up, he said, "I've never been arrested."

I nodded. I didn't add "yet," but I thought it. What was I doing with a guy like him? What was *he* doing here with me?

"Me either," I managed to say.

"Not used to men finding her irresistible," he said, returning my attention to him.

"I'm not."

"Liar," he said softly. When I looked up, he continued in a more serious voice, "I like you, Red. Most everything about you. It's nice being with you outside the bar."

"I like it too," I admitted. Then, before things veered into forbidden territory, I prompted, "Best song ever?"

"Ever?" He shook his head. "That's a hard one. Maybe a few of the best blues songs or something. I could answer that. But one song? Not possible."

I laughed at his expression of absolute certainty and steadfastly refused to admit that he was lulling me back into calmness. He was good at that, like trying to lure a wild thing to trust him, but the truth was that I wanted him to succeed. I *wanted* to trust him.

"I don't know," I said. "What about something like 'Nobody Knows You When You're Down and Out' or 'Boom Boom' or . . ." My words dried up at the way he was looking at me. "What?"

"Little Miss Oregon's a closet blues lover," he said with a note of awe.

"No closets," I stressed, thinking back to discussing the blues with Ellen a few times. "It's no secret. It just hasn't come up when we talked."

"Well, all right then," Zion murmured.

We ate in a comfortable silence that was punctuated by

little notes on bands we liked or movies we'd enjoyed. We continued that way as we cleaned up and then started to work on removing the graffiti from the house. Every so often, his hand brushed against me, and it didn't take long for me to realize that it was intentional.

I'd never wanted to throw caution away as much as I did in that moment.

When he took off his vest, his gun holster, and then his shirt too, I couldn't find the strength to pretend I was immune. I stared at him.

"Not quite running yet," he murmured.

"Friends," I reminded him. "We're friends."

"For now." He turned back to his task, and I bit my lip to keep a sudden whimper from escaping. Whatever he did in his free time, more than a little of it was obviously devoted to fitness. Muscles rippled as he scrubbed the side of my grandmother's house.

Criminal. No dating anyhow. Would lose my job.

The words played like a self-hypnosis recording in my head for the next hour as we worked. It didn't cure me. I couldn't stop myself from looking at him. It was one thing to see such defined muscles in pictures of models; it was another to see them on a person beside me.

By the time we finished, I was ready to forget every last reason I knew for staying clear of him. He was sweet and funny, and he listened when I talked, and to top it all off his body looked like statues I'd seen in museums.

"That's all of it," I said. "Thank you."

I stepped back.

"You keep looking at me like that and I'm going to need a cold shower soon, Red." He didn't glance my way when he spoke. "Do you remember what I said when we met?"

"I do." I bit my lip again, keeping any other words from escaping. I couldn't believe I'd been drunk enough to proposition him, but when he looked at me like . . . like he was right now, the words slipped out. My voice was a whisper when I told him, "I shouldn't have said—"

"It's fine." Zion paused, giving me an opportunity to say something that I couldn't, and then he motioned to the house and said, "You'll call me if you need anything."

It sounded more like an order than a request, but I answered it like it was a question all the same. "I will, and about the other thing . . . I *do* think about it, you know?"

"Oh?" Zion's fingers curled into a loose fist, like he was resisting reaching out.

Somewhere in a hazy part of my mind, I realized that he wasn't used to having to exercise self-control. I liked that he seemed to feel as drawn to me as I did to him. Softly, I said, "I think about it, and you, a lot."

"Good."

"You never said why you were here this morning," I pointed out, giving us both an excuse to stay together a few moments longer.

He shrugged. "Riding by and saw you. It looked like you could use a hand, so I stopped."

"Really?"

"Maybe."

"Are you planning on showing up every time I need rescuing or help with something?" I stepped closer to him as I spoke. I knew it was a bad idea, but I couldn't seem to stop myself.

His eyes darkened. "Do you have something else I can help you with, Red?"

A droplet of sweat rolled down his chest and over his stomach. I watched it like I was transfixed. I reached out and traced its trail with one fingertip. Standing this close, I could smell a mix of bergamot, musk, and the lingering scent of leather. I flattened my hand on his stomach, relishing the feel of taut muscles.

Zion caught my wrist, holding my hand in place against his skin.

I looked up and met his gaze. "I'm . . . sorry." My uncertainty caused my voice to lift, making my words sound like a question.

"Don't be," he said in a voice that made me want to lick my lips.

His grip on my wrist loosened, and I gave in to the urge to slide my fingers over his chest and stomach again. I didn't break our gaze as I admitted, "I wish you could help me."

"Say the word."

"I can't," I whispered. Then I steeled myself to be bolder than I usually was and told him, "But I'll think of you when I handle it myself."

He sucked in a breath at that. "Yeah?"

My cheeks burned, but I didn't look away. "It wouldn't be the first time."

"Jesus, Red, you're testing any control I have saying things like that," he rasped.

"I'm sorry." I started to step back but his hand tightened on my wrist again and slid my hand back up his chest.

"No apologies," he ordered.

He pulled me in close for a hug. This time I was the one drawing in the unsteady breath. He leaned close enough that I thought he was going to kiss me, but he shifted and his lips grazed my jaw instead. I tried not to be disappointed. I failed.

"I'll think of you too," he whispered as his lips barely touched my throat. Again, it wasn't a kiss. He moved close enough that it was only a moment from a kiss.

His breath was warm on my throat, and then on my cheek.

I stepped back. I felt like he was both respecting my rules and proving to me that I wanted to break them as much as he did. I shook my head. Spending these hours with him had made me forget reality. He was a *criminal,* and I had already decided that I wasn't going to get caught up in anything here.

"I . . . I'm sorry. I shouldn't . . ." I swallowed hard, but my words were still rough whispers. "I wish I could do one-night stands. You make me wish that."

Zion stared at me for a moment, and then turned and walked away without speaking.

Chapter 13

ZION HADN'T GONE LOOKING FOR A FIGHT IN YEARS. HE had enough with his job that he didn't need to find some idiot to let off steam. Since he'd left Red, he'd spent several hours simply riding. After he'd crossed Williamsville several times and followed a few dirt roads that weren't meant for Harleys, he headed to his apartment. If not for his responsibilities, he would've gone for a long ride like he had in his teenage years, but he was never too far for Echo to reach now.

Red might not see it, but Zion *was* responsible—and that was the problem. Leaving the club, even briefly, would feel like ripping his lungs out, but if that was what it took to have her, he'd talk to Echo. If it came down to it, he couldn't swear that he *could* give up the Wolves for her. They'd raised him. That wasn't something to walk away from. On the other hand, it was reason enough that they might let him walk without pain. Membership was for life, but maybe Echo would be understanding.

Or maybe Zion should just let her go.

The very idea of walking away without seeing what could come of their connection renewed his need to break something. Aubrey was special. He *knew* it, and he wasn't sure he could walk away.

"Should've known better." He tossed the keys on the table as soon as he was inside. "Idiot."

He let out a growl and hit the wall of his apartment before he realized Echo was sitting in a chair in the living room. The older biker announced his presence by asking, "What's got into you, boy?"

If he had been anyone else, Zion would've punched him for asking—and for being in the apartment. Eddie Echo wasn't anyone else, though. He was the man Zion had most wanted to impress growing up, the man he'd wanted to become, and the man he'd sworn to serve.

"Nothing." Zion jerked the fridge open, willing his temper to cool.

"Grab me one."

Mutely, Zion pulled out two longneck bottles, opened them, and walked over to Echo.

"It's not about work," Zion told him as he flopped onto the worn sofa.

Echo's voice was deceptively soft when he asked, "Are you telling me to mind my own business, Killer?"

"No."

"So talk."

"I was stupid. That's all." Zion took a pull of his beer. "No consequences. No trouble. Nothing that reflects poorly on the club."

Echo watched him for almost a full minute. That tactic worked on most people. Silent stares tended to invite confessions, but Zion had been on the receiving end of those stares since he was a kid.

"When are you going to stop trying that on me?"

"When it stops working," Echo said.

"Like hell it works."

Echo raised one brow. It was another familiar look—one that was all the more common because Zion had seen it in his own mirror. No one called Echo his father aloud—or if they did, they certainly hadn't done it in front of Zion. Still, he suspected they all knew the same fact he'd figured out on his own: Eddie Echo was very obviously his father.

"So, girl troubles," Echo announced. "The new girl at the bar or someone else?"

Zion sighed. "Do I do *anything* you don't know about?"

"Do you see a need to keep things from me?" Echo's voice grew gentle, at least as gentle as Echo could be, and he said, "You're my right hand, Killer. It's never been a secret that I have plans for you. That means I pay attention."

Zion felt like a jerk. He was grateful that he had Echo's

respect and trust. Being valuable to the club president—to his *father*—was what had given Zion focus for years. Until Aubrey, he hadn't wanted anything more in his life.

"Yes, it's her. Aubrey." He looked at Echo. "You already know about what happened at the fair?"

"My most trusted punching Sheriff Patterson's kid over a girl?" Echo drawled. "Yeah, that tidbit made its way to me."

"Right." Zion took another swallow of his drink. "I didn't figure on seeing her again, stayed clear of her when I realized who her gran was . . . Then she took a job at the bar."

"That was the plan."

Zion blinked at him. "The . . . what?"

"Bitty's girl is in one of her classes. I asked her to reach out to Aubrey." Echo shrugged. "I wanted information. It turned out she needed a job, so Bitty's daughter took the initiative and sent her out to Wolves."

Zion couldn't say he was truly surprised. If there was anything that Echo needed to know, there were any number of people he could call upon. The town of Williamsville was well looked after by the Wolves. They kept order far better than the sheriff did—which meant that folks trusted Echo enough to do what he asked when he called in a favor. A lot of people thought ill of bikers, but even those who did couldn't deny that Wolves took care of their own. Echo kept the town safe, and he looked over it as if he were a warlord yanked out of history. His territory was important, and his subjects mattered. Perhaps his methods were crude sometimes, and admittedly the club had less-than-legal income streams, but no one could accuse the Wolves of being bad for the citizens of Williamsville.

Zion was usually proud of their role in town, but this time, he felt betrayed. "So you had Uncle Karl hire her to keep her out of my reach? That's a new level of cockblocking."

Any remaining gentleness in Echo fled at that remark. "Watch your mouth, boy. You might've gotten a lot better with those little fists of yours, but I can remind you of your manners if you need a lesson."

Zion ducked his head. If they'd been in public when he'd mouthed off, he'd be bleeding now, but even though Echo had never openly claimed him as a son, he was often kind to Zion in private. Both Zion and Dash had a lot more leeway than the older bikers. It didn't mean they'd escaped bloodied mouths and black eyes all the time, but Echo was more patient with them than he was with anyone else.

"I sent Bitty's girl to check her out—both because of Maureen *and* because of you." Echo met and held Zion's gaze. "You have far too many secrets in that thick head of yours to have them spilled because you were caught up by a piece of ass—"

"She's not—"

"You know better than to interrupt me," Echo spoke over him.

Zion nodded.

"As I said, I needed to get your piece of tail checked out because I've never seen you act like this." He shook his head. "Do you think I didn't know you drove past her house more than a few times? That you risked trouble with the sheriff over her? Think, boy. What if she was undercover?"

"She's not," Zion said. "She's Mrs. E.'s granddaughter."

Echo sighed. "Which you didn't know when you got into it with Sheriff Patterson's boy, but it *is* precisely why you have my blessing. Karl's rules at the bar make good sense, but I can overrule them for you." Before Zion could thank him, Echo snatched up his beer again and drained it. "Now, if you're done whining over a girl, I need you to arrange security on the run down south to pick up supplies. Drop them. Bring the payroll up. Skeeter, Big Eddie, and Theo will go with you."

For a moment, Zion considered explaining that the fact that he was about to go along for security on a drug run was precisely why Red was out of his reach. Then he realized that their personal talk wasn't *really* personal. It was about Echo reminding him of his responsibilities if he was going to get involved with someone—and letting him know that Aubrey was cleared.

"When do we leave?"

"Morning."

Zion nodded. "I've got it."

"See that you do." Echo stood and leveled a hard stare at him. "Nothing wrong with having a woman, but don't forget where your loyalty belongs. Make sure she understands what it means to be your old lady if you decide to keep her."

Zion nodded. Echo wasn't saying anything new, but that

sort of mind-set wasn't one that would work for a woman like Red. He was loyal to his family, proud to be a Wolf, but he'd never wanted the responsibility of an old lady. He'd seen too many fights and too much nonsense to think relationships were worth the hassle. Maybe the problem was that the sort of woman who'd be okay with being second place to his family wasn't the right sort. He didn't want to put Aubrey *above* the Wolves, but he wanted her as an equal to them. Unfortunately, he didn't see either her or them being okay with that plan.

Chapter 14

THINKING ABOUT ZION WAS A BAD IDEA. I'D KNOWN IT before he'd spent the day with me, and I knew it now. After he'd left earlier, I busied myself planning—and baking. I needed to focus on things I could manage, and with classes and work under control, that meant figuring out who was targeting the neighborhood and why.

The sheriff hadn't done anything, and I kept thinking back to his son saying my grandmother's neighborhood wasn't safe. Maybe Quincy knew more, or maybe he was just in a temper. Maybe I was just desperate for a clue. Either way, I needed help from someone who knew the locals. It wasn't a great plan, but it was the best I had. The sheriff had been useless. The only other people I knew were Zion, Ellen, and Noah—and I didn't think any more entanglement with Zion was wise. That left me with seeking out Ellen or Noah, and I had to do that somewhere other than the bar.

I called Ellen, and after chatting for a few moments, I asked, "Where would I find Noah?"

On the other end of the line, Ellen grew silent.

"I have questions," I clarified.

"So ask *me*." There was something off in her voice, or maybe I didn't know her that well yet.

"Please? Where can I find him? I can wait till class, but—"

"He hangs out over at the garage sometimes. It's where his non-Wolves friends meet up." She gave me the address, paused again, and then softly said, "Be careful with him, okay?"

"It's not like that."

"I'm here if you need to talk," Ellen said before we disconnected.

I did want to talk, but *not* about Noah.

I had developed a completely inappropriate interest in a man who as much as admitted to having committed at least one felony. There was no way that Zion had meant that he'd fired his gun at a range when he'd acknowledged having used it. He'd understood what I'd been asking, and that was what he'd answered. I needed to keep my distance from him unless he was willing to accept being only friends.

And that was assuming *I* could handle that too.

Noah, on the other hand, seemed somehow safer. He teased and flirted, but not in the way Zion did. With Zion,

I felt like it was a crime to resist him. Noah also wasn't one of the Wolves. Both he and Zion had pointed that out. I could ask him to help me figure things out or at least point me in the right direction without involving the Wolves—which Grandma Maureen still seemed opposed to, and now that I'd gotten closer to Zion, I understood a lot more.

Resolved, I drove to the address Ellen had given me.

I parked the car and walked across the patchy grass until I was at the table where Noah sat with several strangers.

"Looking for Killer?"

"No. I was looking for this guy I met at school. Offered to be my friend. Asked me to tutor him . . ."

Noah nodded and motioned for me to walk with him. "Come on, then."

A whistle followed his terse statement, but neither of us acknowledged it. I didn't much care what his friends thought I was doing there. I needed help, and there weren't a lot of people I thought I could talk to. Noah seemed more likely to have answers than Ellen, but less likely than Zion to make me feel indebted.

Mutely but with my head held high, I followed him.

As Noah led me away from the garage, I tried to remind myself that Uncle Karl and Ellen both swore he was a good guy. He'd offered to be my friend. He had seemed nice. I was *safe*.

"I need your help," I said as we walked. "It's about the break-ins."

When he stopped, I took a few steps away from him and leaned against an old car that was up on blocks. For a moment he simply stared at me, and then he started pacing. I waited. If he said no, I wasn't sure what else to do. Grandma Maureen wasn't going to get any legal relief if I was right about the sheriff.

"The sheriff knows something, but he does nothing. I need help," I started.

"Do you want me to talk to Echo for you?"

"Echo?"

"The president," Noah said.

I felt stupid. Of *course* Echo was the club president. The remarks Beau had made replayed in my head, as did Zion's explanation that he worked for the president. My grandmother . . . my sweet schoolteacher grandmother had a relationship of some sort with the president of the Wolves. My grandmother had dated Zion's boss.

"Echo's the president of the Wolves," I repeated, trying to remember if anyone had pointed him out to me.

"Tall. Zion is always there when he is," Noah said. "Goatee. Dark hair. Usually keeps his riding gloves on."

"Right. Echo. He's the president. Zion's boss." I had a vague image of a very fit older man who spoke quietly and had never stood to retrieve his own drink. I had realized by the way people acted that the older biker was influential. I hadn't known his name, though.

Noah frowned. "Yes . . . everyone's boss. He likes your

gran a lot. We all do. When Killer and I were in school, Echo always went to the parent meetings if he could."

I smothered a laugh. I was pretty sure by now that the way Echo "liked" my grandmother was a bit different from the way Noah did. This whole thing was surreal. "Okay, but I just wanted *your* help. No Echo. No Wolves."

"Then there's nothing more to say," Noah said.

"My grandmother doesn't want to call Echo," I blurted out.

Noah's voice was kind as he said, "Sorry about the trouble. If you want help, though, you need to go through Echo."

"I'm not asking the *Wolves*—" I started.

"Then you need to talk to the sheriff," Noah said firmly. "Those are the two choices."

He walked away without a pause, and my eyes threatened to fill with tears. It wasn't that I was unused to things going poorly, or that I expected everyone to fall in line with my wishes. Noah was the second person to walk away from me today, and I felt like I was going to scream.

"Wait!"

He paused and looked back at me.

"I don't know what else to do," I confessed. "The sheriff isn't doing anything, and my grandmother *really* doesn't want to call Echo. The neighbors suggested it. I brought it up . . . before I knew who . . . or *what* he was."

Noah stared at me for a long moment, and then he looked skyward like he was seeking some divine answer. When he lowered his gaze and met my eyes, he asked, "Why aren't you talking to Killer?"

I shook my head.

"He put you under his protection at the bar," Noah said, his voice falsely casual. "He's never done that. He looks out for his club brothers, and for me, but he's not the sort to take on responsibility for other people."

"I didn't ask him to," I said, as if that was any sort of answer.

Noah shook his head.

"I *can't* date a Wolf," I said, knowing as I said it that it wasn't an excuse that held up very well.

Noah snorted. "So says the girl who was on Killer's bike all over town today. I heard already, so Uncle Karl will know by now too . . . Three dates, Aubrey, that's all you get, or you lose your job."

"He was driving by, and he stopped to help me out." I stared at my hands as I spoke.

"Aubrey?" When I looked at him, he said, "Neither of us believes that."

There wasn't anything I could say that was true *and* didn't involve confessions, so I shifted the topic back to what I wanted to discuss. "Look. I just need help figuring out how to keep my grandmother and her friends safe. I thought you might be willing to help me. I don't know anyone other than people at the bar and—"

"Why aren't you asking Killer to help you with this, Aubrey?" Noah cut me off, repeating his earlier question.

"Because I thought maybe you could deal with it less violently? Because I don't want him to do something stupid? Seriously, you *had* to have heard how he got with Quincy and with the cockroach at the bar." I flung up my hands. "I don't know what else to do."

Noah reached out like he was going to touch my face, but then lowered his hand. He took a steadying breath and then said, "I don't keep secrets from the Wolves. I can't."

I stared at him, not sure what that meant.

"I'll ask around, but I need to tell Uncle Karl and Echo first. I'll leave Killer out of it, and I can tell them *you* didn't want him or them involved. If they overrule me, that's the way it is. That's the best I can do," Noah said quietly.

I looked past him to his friends, who weren't even pretending not to watch us. The curious looks of a few people weren't my biggest concern. My grandmother being angry, Zion being livid, and having to deal with the fallout from all of it—those were all more pressing. I didn't know what else to do, though.

"Okay." I nodded at Noah. "Thank you."

"And Aubrey?" he said gently. "My cousin's not a bad person, but whatever you two are doing needs to get sorted out. He's never acted like this, and I'm not sure if that's a good or a bad thing for you . . . or him."

"There's nothing to sort out," I stressed. "I told him that earlier. I didn't break Uncle Karl's rules. Zion helped me clean up after someone trashed my grandmother's porch. That's all."

Noah sighed. "Don't lie to yourself, Aubrey. It would take a blind, deaf dead man not to see the way he watches you *or* the way you soak it up."

The thought that I was being unfair to Zion washed over me again. "I'm sorry. That will all stop."

I straightened my shoulders and walked past Noah, past his friends, and to the car before tears started sliding down my cheeks. Willing this thing with Zion away wasn't working at all. Maybe it would be better now that we'd talked . . . or rather, now that I'd talked and turned away.

Chapter 15

AFTER THREE SHIFTS AT THE BAR WHERE ZION HADN'T even stopped by, it was pretty clear to me that he'd taken my inability to have a one-night stand as a total rejection of everything. Maybe it was for the best. I tried telling myself that repeatedly, even though I was fairly sure I was lying to myself the whole time. I wanted him. I *liked* him—too much to consider a one-night stand and *far* too much to consider more. I wasn't going to get involved with a criminal. I couldn't.

Noah had stopped me on campus once to tell me that Echo had agreed to allow Noah to ask around for information, but he hadn't heard anything. There weren't any break-ins or vandalism that week either. Everything seemed strangely calm. I, however, felt like I was half-asleep. I looked up at the sound of every Harley on the street and greeted every door opening at the bar with hope. It was absurd that I missed the brief exchanges with Zion; it was foolish that I missed the smiles he sent my way when he walked into the bar. I told myself repeatedly that I'd blown the whole thing out of proportion. He was an interesting guy who paid attention to me. It was rare, and I had made it into something bigger. Obviously, if we'd been becoming real friends he wouldn't have vanished just because I pulled away.

None of that changed how I felt. For the first time in my life, I couldn't rationalize away my feelings for a guy. It sucked.

Despite the way I felt about missing Zion, juggling work and classes was going well. I was as settled as I'd been in Portland. I had a job, a home, and school. I was even feeling less lonely. Ellen and I had lunch together several times, and she was fast becoming a good friend. Her need to sort through my closet and try to lend me clothes was a little weird, but as far as quirks went, it was more endearing than off-putting. So far, she'd been gentle in her suggestions for me, although her own style went from neo-hippie to old-fashioned country to grunge to black-and-white film goddess. Fashion was her future career. She'd told me so several times. She never wore anything awful, though, and maybe dressing up like I was a different person would make me *feel* different too.

After my Friday class had ended—and a whole week had passed without a single sighting of Zion—I decided to treat myself to some comfort food. It was stereotypical, but curling up with ice cream and a sappy movie seemed more tempting than it ever had in my life.

I headed to the grocery store, deciding to pick up proper groceries to assuage my guilt at my upcoming ice cream binge. As I was walking in, I saw Quincy walking out. He didn't even acknowledge me, but I still said, "Hello."

Being disliked was never something that felt good, and it added to my already surly feelings.

I was piling my cart with produce—mostly berries and fruit that would go nicely with ice cream—when a familiar voice whispered, "Don't look, but Mrs. Connors is giving you her death glare. Put the tomato in the cart and keep walking."

I glanced over my shoulder to find Noah standing right behind me with an onion in one hand and a bright red Ryerson's shopping basket in the other. The woman in question was watching him.

"Actually, I think it might be you she's watching."

"I never attract the right sort of women. Always the ones old enough to be my mother."

A laugh escaped me before I could help it. The way she was glaring wasn't anywhere near a come-on. Mostly, she looked like she thought he was going to snatch purses or cuss in front of young ears or any number of things that Nice Young Men shouldn't do.

Noah and I walked farther away from her before I asked, "Did you hear anything new?"

Noah shook his head. "I'll tell you if I do. I was actually just out shopping and thought I'd say hello."

I glanced at his basket: steak, several potatoes, and some sort of hot sauce with flames on the side. My cart was a bit more varied, and I'd only made my way through part of the produce aisle. We walked in relative silence as I selected fruits and vegetables.

"You should come to the races tonight," Noah said suddenly.

"The what?"

"Races."

"You mean cars driving in circles?" I frowned at him. "Why would I do that? Why would *anyone,* actually?"

"It's fun." He shrugged. "I'll even let you sit with me, but you need to bring your own cooler. I don't want to be seen toting a bunch of girly drinks."

"I can't." That was the best I could say, and it sounded lame even to me.

Noah put a hand on my arm. "I'm not asking you to go on a date, Aubrey. You said we could be friends, though, right? I'm just introducing my new friend to the wonders of Williamsville. I need to go either way because Killer's like a kid who got the lead in the Christmas pageant. He *needs* applause. Just come with me to watch my cousin drive in circles."

The thought of seeing Zion, even though it would just be

from a distance, changed my mind. I felt instantly guilty that hanging out with Noah—who was being a good friend— was more appealing to me because I would be watching Zion. I couldn't admit that, although I was fairly sure Noah suspected as much. I didn't want to mislead him, though, so I asked, "Would it be okay if I brought someone? Since you are just asking as a friend, I mean."

"Hell, bring your grandmother if you want. Mrs. Evans has probably never been to the track."

"So we're agreed that this is *not* a date?" I prompted.

"Exactly."

"You've hardly said a word to me the past week at the bar *or* on campus. What changed?"

Noah's light tone vanished. "I wanted to see what you decided about Killer. I might not approve, but I don't poach from family, especially him."

"Nothing to decide." My voice started to waver, so I took a breath before continuing, "Zion has apparently decided my friendship isn't good enough. I haven't seen him all week."

"I know." Noah sounded almost sorry. "That's why I'm asking you *now*. I waited and . . . Just come out with me, Aubrey. No strings. You look like you could use a night out, and it's fun. Killer will be on the track, so it's not like you're going to need to talk to him."

In the month I'd lived here, my only social events had been the fair, which was a disaster of drunken stupidity, and a day of cleaning graffiti with Zion, which was best not pondered at all.

"Fine," I told Noah. "I'll meet you there."

"Great. Text me when you're at the track." He held out his hand. "Phone."

Mutely, I handed it over. After a few moments, he passed it back to me. His name and number were still on the screen.

"And Aubrey?"

I looked at him.

"It's not a date, but so we're clear, since you seemed confused when I offered you a ride before"—he put his finger under my chin and tipped my head up so I was looking into his eyes—"if I thought you'd say yes to a real date, I'd ask. Zion had his shot. I'd like a chance to take you out, but I'll settle for your friendship until you're ready for something else."

I was still trying to find words to reply when he said, "See you tonight," and left.

I watched him walk away, not knowing if there was any sort of normal response in these sorts of circumstances.

My phone was still in my hand, so I did the logical thing: I called Ellen.

"Miss me already?" she answered, instead of saying hello. "Class *just* ended."

"Are you busy tonight?"

Something in my voice must have given me away because her teasing tone vanished as she said, "What happened?"

Even after glancing around to make sure no one was near enough to hear, I still lowered my voice to say, "I think Noah sort of hit on me . . . or something."

"And you're offering him to me instead? I'm not sure he's going to go for that idea."

I quickly summarized as best I could without being overheard and ended with, "So I need you to come to the races with me."

"Go to the races with you and Noah to watch Killer drive like he has a death wish? What the hell, it's better than my big plans for the night."

"If you have plans—"

"My plan," she interrupted, "was to see if you wanted to watch a movie, since you seemed like someone kicked your puppy all week, *but* since you're already busy, I'm guessing that wouldn't work out for me anyhow."

Cautiously, I asked, "So did you want to watch a movie instead?"

"No, sweetie, I want to go with you to the races. I'll be over at half six to get you dressed up, okay?"

I exhaled in relief, and then paused when I realized what she'd said. "Wait. Dressed up?"

"That's my fee. I get to use you as my model three times."

"Model *how*?"

"Just wearing the clothes I pick during your normal day," Ellen clarified. "I've been moderate, but . . . this one will cost you."

I couldn't say I was genuinely surprised. Ellen was pushy, but somehow she made it seem charming. Truth be told, I got more compliments when she made clothing suggestions than I ever had in my life.

"Deal," I agreed.

When I got home and told Grandma Maureen my plans, she nodded and said, "Good. You've been about as chipper as a wet cat all week."

"Sorry."

She waved my words away. "I'm here if you need to talk."

"I know."

We fixed a light meal, and by the time I was putting the last of the dishes in the drainer, Ellen was ringing the bell.

Grandma Maureen let her in with a welcoming smile. "Are you planning on cheering sourpuss up?"

"That's my mission. Cheer her up, dress her up, and take her out . . . not necessarily in that order," Ellen announced.

I waited as they exchanged a few words. Then Ellen turned to me and eyed me as if she was mentally cataloging potential outfits and rejecting them. "Country casual tonight," she finally said.

"Do your worst."

Ellen gave me a faux stern look. "As if my taste is ever anything but *fabulous*."

My grandmother laughed, and I couldn't help but join in. Ellen sounded like she'd just pronounced an edict. I had no idea what exactly country casual was, but I was game to find out.

A couple of hours later, Ellen stood at my side, pointing out the landmarks and layout of the track. Despite never having been to a racetrack, I wasn't feeling out of place. I *did* feel a little silly in what I was wearing, but I didn't look silly. The jeans I had on were my own, but the almost too tight green tank and the cute aqua cowboy boots were hers, as were the bracelets and necklace. The makeup was all Ellen's doing too, and the way my hair was pinned up and curled was her work. The good news was that we were the same size in general; the bad news was that my chest was a little bigger, so her tops seemed more risqué than my normal style.

"Aubrey?"

I turned to find Noah staring at me. "Hi." When he said nothing further, I motioned to Ellen. "Do you know Ellen?"

"Ellie," he said to her, politely nodding. "It's been . . . a while."

The look she gave him was mocking. "Has it? I hadn't noticed."

Noah tensed, and I was fairly certain I was missing something. Again. He stared at her for a moment before looking back at me. "Is that Ellie's shirt?"

"She needed a dress-up doll," I told him. "Apparently, I'm going shopping with her too."

He nodded. "She has a great eye for that sort of thing."

Rather than seeming pleased by his compliment, Ellen bristled. I'd need to ask her what the history was there. I was starting to think the whole evening was going to be a fiasco, but then she folded her arms and, in a far lighter voice, asked, "So where are we sitting?"

Noah didn't quite shake his head, but for a moment he simply stared at her. Then he was fine, smiling and seeming as comfortable as he usually was with me. "Right. I'll walk you over, and then I'm going to go check on Killer."

We had only gone about three steps before someone called Ellen's name. She looked at me. "I'm *not* bailing on you. Just tell me where you are, and I'll meet you there."

Noah gestured toward the bleachers and told Ellen, "We're over in the usual Wolves section."

"Got it." She leaned in close to my ear and said, "Not a date, my ass. He's certainly hoping. You could do a lot worse than Dash." Then she squeezed my hand and left me there with Noah.

Chapter 16

BEING AT THE RACES FELT A BIT LIKE ATTENDING A HIGH school football game in a small town: it was half about watching some of your friends kick the ass of some rival team and half about seeing the rest of your friends in the stands. Williamsville had a hometown feel to it that I'd only ever read about. It didn't make me want to give up all my plans and stay here forever, but I was really starting to understand why people did.

"Do you mind if I don't go with you to talk to Zion?" I asked Noah. I felt exceedingly weird at the idea of Zion seeing me here with him.

"I figured on it." Noah raised his arm and motioned someone over.

Billy, a sometime bouncer at the bar, came to join us.

"I need to check on Killer. Show Aubrey where we are?"

Billy flashed a wide grin at us, looking like he'd just won a prize. "Oh, the things I have to do. Keep an eye on the pretty girl, Billy. Escort the pretty girl, Billy. Run away and marry the—"

"Pretty sure I didn't ask you to do that," Noah interrupted with a laugh.

Billy winked at me. "My Aunt Ettie worked as a carnie. Saw the future, she did." He linked an arm through my elbow and started walking away. " 'Billy,' she said, 'one day you'll meet a gorgeous girl not even a third of your age, and you'll have to marry her.' It's a long time I've waited for you."

"She better not be engaged when I get there," Noah called out.

Billy just rolled his eyes. "Poor young men, always trying to steal the girls away before I can find out if they're the heartbreaker my Aunt Ettie warned me about."

"So this young girl is a heartbreaker," I prompted.

"It's a curse. Ettie's fault, of course." He sighed mournfully. "Ettie made a move on the Strong Man. She liked a big man, you know. Unfortunately, one of the trapeze girls was descended from a *bruja*."

"A what?"

"Witch, girl. She had witch blood in her. Spanish temper, magic skills, and . . . well, you can guess what happened. Ettie got us all cursed." Billy nodded at a few bikers I hadn't met as we climbed to our seats in the bleachers, and when they looked at him in question, he switched from storyteller to protector. "This is Aubrey. Karl's new bar girl. Sweet as molasses with a wit like cayenne-coated jalapeños."

Obviously, they were well used to Billy's tendency toward story. Most of the men simply smiled or said hello. A few of the women did too, but others looked at me like I was there to steal their men. I was starting to get used to that attitude, but I'd also found a few standard replies that helped.

"I'm just out here for a few months saving up money to go back to school full-time. I live with my grandmother, Maureen Evans."

"The schoolteacher?" one of the women asked.

"That's her," I said. "I'm staying with her while I save up to move."

As they had before, those facts seemed to calm any thoughts that I was here on the prowl. I debated going over to Ellen when she appeared, but she stopped to talk to several of the Wolves I'd seen at the bar with Killer, and I felt self-conscious about going to talk to them when I was here with Noah. Instead, I stayed where I was and used the tactic Noah had suggested I use if all else failed—point out that I was his friend. I understood that they read it as "girl who sleeps with him," but since I wasn't interested in landing one of the Wolves, I was okay with them thinking the wrong thing.

"I'm a friend of Noah's," I said. "He invited me and Ellen to see the race because I'd never been to one."

That had the benefit of turning the remaining looks of

doubt into dismissal or friendliness. A few of them started pointing out the cars and explaining different races and rules. Honestly, most of it was perplexing to me. All I knew was that I was here with people who were laughing and friendly, and I felt safe and embraced. It was a little like being a part of one of those big families I'd always envied.

By the time Noah arrived, I was giggling and sipping on a wine cooler that one of the girls had handed me. It wasn't as ghastly as beer, but it had relaxed me a little too much already.

"Let me take you for a ride after the races," Noah whispered.

I licked the drops of wine cooler from my lips. "Maybe."

Noah stared at me until I thought I was going to get up and flee. I don't know what came over me to make me say that. I didn't like him that way, but he knew that. He opened his mouth to say something, but before he could, I looked away.

I motioned Ellen toward me, feeling like I was flailing and needing a friend without ulterior motives at my side. She came and slid into the seat on the opposite side of me.

"Can I have a sip?" Ellen asked.

"Here." Another woman passed a bottle down from a cooler behind us.

I turned to get it, and Noah whispered in my ear, "Just so you know, we could turn this into a date if you wanted."

Instead of replying, I started chatting with Ellen, who

seemed to be alternating between glaring at Noah and smiling at me.

"Is everything okay?" I whispered.

"Dash and I grew up together," she said. "Sometimes he irritates me."

"Do you want to go? We can—"

"No," she interrupted. "I want you to have fun. Enjoy the races. Enjoy *Dash*. He really is a great guy. We just had words last time we talked, and seeing him . . . I forgot how angry I was until I saw him."

I wanted to ask more, but she'd looked away to stare at the track. I felt like a fool, trying to figure out this whole dating thing. I wasn't sure if I wanted to date Noah or not. I liked it well enough when he flirted with me, but I couldn't help looking toward the track in search of another biker— one who was off-limits.

The races started, and everyone seemed to want to make sure I was having fun. I tried to follow their explanations, but honestly, a lot of it just looked like people driving in circles really fast. I knew there was more to it than that because they would point out when a driver was going to do something before it happened sometimes. It was fun cheering and yelling.

Ellen was at ease here in the way that comes of knowing people one's whole life—as long as she didn't talk to Noah. Whatever their drama was, it meant that her expression grew icy when she so much as glanced at him. Aside from him, she was completely at ease. Apparently, most of the Wolves knew her and her mom, Bitty, who was the widow of one of the Wolves.

Then the motorcycle race started, and my attention was on the track again.

Ellen had moved a few steps up the bleachers and was talking to an older biker with a snow-white beard and a shaved head, and Noah moved closer to me. We were almost knee to knee, not quite touching.

"This isn't a date," I told him quietly. "Friends I can do, but no dating."

"Because of him?"

Noah didn't say Zion's name, but he didn't have to. We both knew whom he meant. After a longer pause than I should've needed, I said, "No. I just don't date. I told you that already."

"Me either." Noah turned his attention back to the race.

We watched the bikes zip around the track, and I tried not to gasp as several of the riders leaned almost horizontal.

"They know what they're doing," Noah said.

On the track in front of us, the motorcycles whined as they zipped around. Zion was easy to spot. He was the only one on the track wearing the Wolves' insignia. We both watched him.

"He's good, right?"

"Yeah." Noah reached out and twined his fingers with mine. "He's also a lifer with the club, Aubrey. If you want to take a turn playing with danger, I'll volunteer. I have a job, and I'm working on a degree. Killer is . . . not housebroken. You need to let it go."

I glanced at our hands. "Is that why you asked me out? To distract me from him?"

"No. I like you, and you looked like you could use a night out." He looked down at the track for a moment before adding, "If I *didn't* like you, I'd tell you to give him a shot."

I thought about it. There was a strange truthfulness to his words, but it wasn't enough of an answer. "So . . . what do you want? You say you like me. What's the goal here?"

"Straight up?"

I nodded.

Noah lifted my hand, turned it over, and kissed my palm. "Since you don't date either, I'm hoping we can be friends with more. That wouldn't technically be breaking your no-dating rule."

I froze. *Friends with benefits.* That's what Noah was offering. I'd known people who had that sort of arrangement. It was more or less how I explained my one experience with sex. Could I do that? Did I want to do that with *him*?

Since being in Williamsville, I'd been having the kind of thoughts and urges that I hadn't had in years. I caught myself imagining kissing and touching Zion. I'd dreamed about him. *He* was forbidden, but Noah wasn't off-limits for a fling. He was gorgeous too, and he was okay with my refusal to date. Maybe being with Noah would help me get my focus back, work through the lust I had, but *safely.*

I kept my voice low as I asked, "And there'd be no strings? Just friends?"

"Exactly."

"And *no one* would know"—my gaze darted to the track, to Zion, and then back to Noah—"what we did?"

"If that's the way you want it," Noah said. "I've had a friend with no strings before. I can keep a secret, Aubrey."

"I just can't . . . I don't want to hurt him or . . ." I didn't even have words for what I meant.

Noah squeezed my hand. "Understood."

I nodded, and we watched the race in silence. I didn't object to Noah's hand in mine, but I didn't move closer either. Was I really considering this? I felt guilty even thinking it. I stared at the motorcycles zipping around the track.

When the race ended, Zion had come in second. Now that he was done, I didn't feel like staying around in the bleachers waiting for him to come over and see me with Noah. I stood and motioned to Ellen.

"I'll let you know what I decide," I told Noah mildly, and then I called to Ellen, "Let's walk a bit."

Noah stood too. "I'll head down to see Killer while you're with Ellie."

"Thank you," I whispered.

Noah squeezed my hand again and then he let me go.

Chapter 17

BEFORE WE GOT VERY FAR FROM THE STANDS WHERE WE'D been sitting, Zion was in front of me. I wasn't sure how he'd managed to get there so fast, but he was headed my way. I was torn between excitement and fear as he walked toward me. He'd already yanked his helmet off. It dangled from his hand, looking foreign in comparison to the small helmets I'd started to think of as "normal." This was a full-face helmet. With it on, I couldn't have identified him . . . well, aside from the club insignia on his leathers.

"Regulation at the track," he said, answering the question before I even asked about the markedly different helmet. "They worry about us spilling our brains and ruining the race."

Suddenly, Noah's voice interrupted all the words I wanted to say. "Great race," he started. He'd obviously seen Zion and come to intercept him.

Standing there beside Noah while Zion watched me like I was a gazelle he'd like to stalk and carry off was enough to make me want to whimper. I wanted to ask where he'd been, to tell him I was sorry for upsetting him, to beg him to at least be my friend since we couldn't be anything else. I wanted to ask him to take me home. I wanted to explain again that it wasn't that I didn't feel all the things he seemed to feel. I wanted to make him understand. It felt like a million things clashed in my mind, but all I could say was "Hi."

Ellen saved me from madness then. In a deft move, she stepped in front of me, blocking me from Zion's gaze. "Come on," she urged. "I want you to meet some people."

"Red and I have some things to discuss," Zion said in a tone that left no room for argument.

But Ellen was a force to reckon with too. She acted as if the tension weren't there and said, "Sorry, Killer. Aubrey is with *me* tonight." She flashed a bright smile at both men and led me away.

We weren't but yards away when she looked at me and said, "Dash looked ready to throw down with Killer."

"He just doesn't want me to get mixed up with Zion," I told Ellen. I left off the fact that I already had, and I was trying to stop it from going any further. I debated telling her what Noah had suggested, but I wasn't sure what she'd think—and I wasn't sure I could do it.

"Because they both want you for themselves."

"Maybe," I started.

Ellen gave me an incredulous look, but said nothing.

"Okay, *yes*, I know Noah wants me. That doesn't mean he wants to date me—or that I want to date him. And it doesn't matter if Zion does. He's . . ." My words faded. I didn't want to talk about what he did. "Zion's a Wolf. I need the job at the bar, and I don't need a criminal."

"And Dash?"

"I don't know, Ellen. It doesn't matter, though. Like I keep telling everyone: I'm not staying here, not forever."

"Since when did *dating* mean forever?" Ellen nudged me with her elbow. "This is not the 1940s or '50s, despite your current gorgeous hairstyle."

I laughed. It was either that or cry. She was right. I'd as much as said to Noah that what I was considering was a far more . . . modern relationship. No strings. No romance. Friends who might get naked. It was practical. I could do practical, right?

Despite myself, I glanced back at the boys. Some of the other Wolves had joined them. Noah was talking with one of them, but Zion was watching me. I wished I could do casual with him, but I couldn't. Whatever it was I felt when he looked at me, it wasn't casual.

I snapped my head back around and asked Ellen, "So, who are we meeting?"

"Stick with Dash," Ellen said quietly. "I see the sparks between you and Killer, but he's not the sort to be okay with someone else calling the shots. If you gave him a chance and then told him you were leaving in a few months, he'd find a way to make you stay. He doesn't do relationships any more than Dash does, but when either of them fall for real, they'll be harder to dislodge than ticks on a black dog."

"Maybe I don't want a relationship either," I said.

"You do, but not with someone who will break your heart. Trust me on this."

"You and . . . Zion?"

"No!" Ellen shuddered. "We went out once, but he's not the guy for me. There was someone else I . . . cared about, but it was a mistake. I thought we wanted the same thing, but I realized I wanted more so I broke it off."

"Who?"

"Never mind," she said firmly. "The point, my dear, is that Dash could be what you need. Casual. You're not going to fall for him like you are for Killer. Anyone can see that you only have eyes for Killer. Take it from me. The best way to get him out of your mind is to find someone else."

I opened my mouth to protest, but no words came. Her theory seemed wrong to me, but I couldn't argue from any personal experience. The best I had was "Did it work for you?"

Ellen flashed me a smile that was more wicked than usual. "I haven't fallen back into his arms since then. Trust Dr. Ellen. What you need is a distraction from Killer."

Noah did seem willing to settle for no strings. Maybe that was all the answer I needed: I could enjoy being Noah's friend with a side benefit of finding out if my initial impression of sex was mistaken. But I felt like I was being disloyal to Zion to even consider kissing anyone but him.

Ellen stopped beside a group of people, and I tried to push all my thoughts away. Being here was supposed to relax me. That was the point of coming out tonight.

"Aubrey," Ellen said, and then started nodding at people and saying names.

I caught Toby, Cheyenne, and possibly a LeeAnn. They all seemed friendly enough, and I happily let Ellen steer the conversation. There was something comfortable about being on the periphery of a group. It was where I'd always lived, not the social butterfly or the one leading the group in plans, just a girl quietly at the edge of the conversation. Ellen, obviously, was exceedingly assertive. She was the type of girl I always ended up friends with: someone who led, decided, acted.

We weren't with Toby and the rest of Ellen's friends for more than ten minutes before the surprisingly easy conversation stalled. Toby was talking about going mud bogging and asked, "Do you want to come?"

"Me?" I clarified.

"Yeah, you."

Mud bogging, which as far as I could tell was driving a truck into swampy areas and over bumps, wasn't my thing. I was about to politely decline. Thoughts of the awkwardness of my night out with Quincy put me even more off of things that might be dates. Before I could answer, Toby and the other guys with him tensed. The two guys with girl-friends both reached for their partners.

"Or not," Ellen said quietly.

"Aubrey? Ellen? Are you ready to head out?" Noah was at my side then.

I glanced at him, and saw Zion there too. He smiled at me before saying, "Tony. Ken. Ladies."

"Toby," the one girl corrected.

"Right, *Toby*." Zion smiled in that mocking way of his. "I'm not as good with guys' names as with women's."

One of the girls looked down, and I knew she was on the long list of panty-droppers. Obviously, so did everyone else. They all excused themselves and in a matter of minutes, I was once again standing with the two guys and Ellen.

I couldn't exactly chastise them for being intimidating. Considering how angry Zion seemed tonight, his behavior was downright proper. Neither of the boys had been *rude* per se. Okay, maybe Zion had been a little derisive, but he hadn't done more than pretend to not know one of their names and imply that he slept with a lot of girls. That wasn't reason for them all to leave. They had, though.

"Nice of you to bring a date for my cousin, Red," Zion murmured, pulling me to him in a hug. "We need to talk."

The feel of his arms around me made me want to forget every warning. For a moment, I leaned into his embrace, but then reluctantly I stepped back. "I can't."

Noah looked between us. "Don't do this, man. Aubrey and I are here as friends. I told you that."

"Friends?" Zion scoffed. "Don't lie to me, cuz. I've seen how you look at her."

The boys exchanged some sort of silent conversation that I didn't understand, and the moment passed.

"Red?"

I shook my head again. "I'm . . ."

"I can take you home," Noah offered.

Zion's hands fisted. "You *rode* here with him?"

"No," I said. "I came here with Ellen."

Zion's darkened expression faded as quickly as it had come. "You need a ride home?"

"Not from you," I said

Zion met my gaze and, in a terse voice, said, "I see."

He grabbed for my hand, but I jerked out of reach. "Don't. Please, don't do this."

"Fine." He drained his beer. "Go with Ellen then."

"No," I said softly. "Noah is my friend, just like you are."

"Is that what we are?" he challenged. "Friends don't back away all skittish like you are, Red."

"Fine." I stepped closer and hugged him briefly.

When I tried to pull away, he said, "Not so fast. Don't give up on me yet. Please?"

"I can't—"

"Just tell me you missed me," Zion insisted, holding on to my hips. "I missed you. I was away until last night. I know what it looked like, but I had work. It was shit timing, but I had to go."

"To work for Echo?" I prompted, pulling away finally. "I

can't . . . We . . . It's not going to happen, not with what
you do. I just *can't*."

"So that's it?"

"Friends," I said in a shaking voice. "That's all I can do."

Zion turned to Ellen. "I'll walk you to your car, Ellie."

"I *can* take you home, Aubrey," Ellen offered.

"No." Maybe it was foolish, but I needed to prove to
myself that I didn't need Zion's permission to talk to another guy. I needed to prove to myself that I could let him
go despite how miserable I'd been all week. It didn't matter
that he'd been out of town. What mattered was that there
was a better than good chance that whatever he'd been
doing was illegal.

I felt Noah's arm come around me after Zion and Ellen
turned and walked away.

Noah didn't say anything, though, until they were well
gone. Then he said, "I've never seen him like this. He's not
sure how to cope with whatever you two had going on
and—"

"Wait," I interrupted. "Did you proposition me to protect
him? I understand if you did. It's not nice, but . . ."

A flash of anger filled Noah's eyes, but his voice was level
when he pointed out, "In case you weren't listening earlier,
I already told you: I like you. It has nothing to do with protecting Killer *or* competing with him."

"Okay. I just . . ." I sighed. "Never mind. I don't even
know anymore. This is why I don't date, you know? I'm no
good at any of this stuff."

"You're fine," Noah said. "I'm not sure anyone would deal well with my cousin."

The urge to defend Zion warred with my common sense. I bit my tongue, and we walked in silence toward the lot where I assumed we'd find Noah's bike. Before we reached it, though, he motioned to a trail that twisted into the darkness. "I can take you home, we could ride, or we could take a walk. Lady's choice."

"I feel like I'd be using you," I admitted.

"It was my idea," he reminded me. "So . . . go directly home, ride, or walk?"

"Walk," I said quietly. "I want us to take a walk."

He followed me into the shadows, catching my hand in his as we walked deeper into the copse of trees.

"This"—I gestured between us—"isn't dating. It's friends deciding if there will be benefits."

"Right."

I put my free hand flat on his chest. I pushed him toward a wide tree, as if I could actually move him. He didn't resist, stopping only when his back was to the tree.

"No strings," I said. "No relationships. No dating. And no one knows."

"Promise," Noah said.

I faltered a little then. My experience at the start of high school and with a few scattered dates hadn't prepared me for whatever we were doing here. "Okay then . . . so now what?"

Instead of answering, he smiled, and I remembered why

I'd thought he and Zion both looked like angels that first night. The thought of Zion made me falter, but then I looked at Noah and decided to stop thinking. I didn't want to be pursued. If I was doing this, I needed to *choose* it. I reached out and tugged him toward me for a kiss.

He let me have control at first, and then he spun us around and hoisted me into the air. My legs wrapped around him, seemingly of their own accord, and suddenly I was the one who was leaning on the tree. As he pressed closer, I gasped at the pain of the rough bark against my back where my shirt had been pulled up.

Kissing Noah made every other experience seem nonexistent. This was why I didn't get involved. In that moment, I didn't care that we were in public. I didn't think about anything. It was just *want*, and the last threads of logic were slipping away. Somehow, though, it still felt . . . lacking.

A giggle interrupted my kiss-fogged mind.

When Noah pulled back, I looked up to see a group of teenagers.

"Show's over," I announced, a bit breathless.

Noah looked over his shoulder. "Get lost. Now."

The last giggles died, and the kids left.

Once it was just us, I said, "You should take me home."

"Are you okay?"

I gave him a small smile. "Not really. I need a little time to think."

Noah stared at me in silence for a moment before saying,

"I suddenly feel like I should apologize. Did I . . . do something wrong here?"

"No. No apology needed either." I reached out and took his hand. "I'm just not sure I could handle the benefits part of this friendship." I forced myself to look up at him. "When I was fourteen, I discovered kissing and boys, and I was hooked. People got weird, talked, were rude, and I realized that I'd lost track of everything else *but* boys. I stopped. I decided to be . . . someone else, someone different, someone who had a plan that led to a career of some sort."

He squeezed my hand.

"I guess I'd told myself that kissing wasn't as much fun as I remembered. I've only kissed a few guys since then, and I even had sex with one. It didn't leave me . . . like this."

"Like what?"

"Wishing I could justify kissing and more," I admitted. "I like you, and I think we could be great friends, but to get more of *that*, I might lie to myself and call it something else, something it's not."

"Maybe it could be something else in time," Noah suggested. "Maybe you could be the girl who—"

"No," I interrupted. I swallowed, feeling ten kinds of awful for what I was about to say, but needing to admit to it just once. "If I couldn't deal with the whole biker thing for Zion, I can't do it at all. I won't say I love him. I don't, but . . . I *could*. I know it, and unfortunately, so does he." I folded my arms over my chest. "What I wanted, what you *offered* was a distraction, but I don't think I can do this with you."

"How do you know?"

That was the answer, the admission I didn't want to keep making, but I was already in this conversation so I kept going. "Because I don't dream of you. Because I don't watch the door for you. Because I don't think of you when I wake or want to hear what you did all day." I looked at him. "I want us to be friends, but I don't think benefits can work for us."

"I'm a big boy, Aubrey. You're not going to hurt me," Noah said, unfolding my arms and taking my hand.

"I want to feel like that . . . physically, I mean." I made myself look into his eyes. "I want the emotions too, though. I can't do just physical, not with the feelings I have for Zion. It just feels . . . empty somehow."

Noah gave me a smile that didn't look entirely sincere, but he said, "If you want to be just friends, that's fine too. Okay?"

I nodded, and we walked back to the parking lot without speaking. Surprisingly, it felt comfortable instead of awkward. I climbed on the bike behind him, and I let myself enjoy the sheer pleasure of riding—even though Noah wasn't the biker whose Harley I wanted to ride.

I liked him, and he was certainly a good kisser. But I couldn't get past the suspicion that what he was proposing wasn't good for *any* of us. He might say he wanted to wait before he dated someone, but I didn't completely believe him after tonight. I thought back to Ellen's earlier warning that both boys would fall hard when they fell. I was pretty sure that whatever girl either of them fell for would be exceptionally lucky—but I couldn't be that girl.

After Noah pulled his Harley up to my grandmother's house, I slid off the bike and removed the helmet he'd brought for me.

Noah stayed seated for a moment. He put one hand on my hip. "Maybe—"

"Don't." I leaned in and brushed a kiss on his cheek. "Be my friend. That's what we are."

"We could be friends who enjoy each other. Nothing's changed because we kissed."

"Liar," I said. "Maybe that's normal for you, but—"

"It's not," he interrupted. "But good chemistry isn't a reason to say no."

I met Noah's gaze and said, "We're friends, but the sort who won't . . . have benefits."

I turned away and walked inside the house. Noah was a great guy, and after tonight, I was sure that we could have a fabulous time in bed—or against a tree. He wasn't the one I dreamed of, though. He wasn't Zion, and my being with Noah would be unfair to all of us.

My grandmother looked up from the news when I came into the room. "That sounded like a motorcycle."

I nodded. "Noah brought me home."

"Noah Dash?"

I nodded again.

The television clicked off, and my grandmother looked at me for a moment. "I thought you liked your job at Karl's place."

"Noah isn't . . . he doesn't . . ." I started. Finally, I managed to say, "He's not a Wolf."

"Just because there are no patches on his jacket doesn't mean he's any less a Wolf than the rest of them," she said gently. "Eli Dash was their president. The club raised Noah his whole life."

My grandmother motioned to the sofa, and I sat down. "I'm not in any danger of falling for Noah," I promised.

She continued, "Keep it that way. The Wolves keep trouble out of Williamsville, donate to charities, and insist their kids graduate high school. The Southern Wolves—this chapter at least—aren't as bad as some bikers, but make no mistake, Aubrey, they're still a criminal organization. I don't have any problems with you working for Karl or being friends with Noah, but don't get mixed up in their business."

I nodded.

"And Noah might be a good-looking young man, but he and his cousin Zion have both had a lot of passengers on their motorcycles—and not the same girls very often." She met my eyes and added, "If being here means you're going to get involved with either of them, you need to get a plane ticket back to your mother or father right now."

"I don't date," I reminded both of us, thinking not about Noah but about Zion.

My grandmother didn't let it go that easily. "I'm not so old that I can't tell when someone's been doing more than riding on a bike. Your lips are swollen, and there's bark clinging to your shirt."

I took a deep breath. "Noah and I are friends. Even if we did . . . kiss, he knows I don't want a relationship. He doesn't either." I felt increasingly guilty as I continued, "You know I'm not staying here forever. I love you, and I love being here with you, but I'm going to leave. I'll get things sorted out, and then I'm moving back to Oregon. I can't risk everything for a few kisses . . . and I already told Noah that we wouldn't ever be doing that again. It was a mistake."

My grandmother didn't reply for several long moments, and then she said, "Just be sure you're being careful if those kisses turn into something more. There are other ways to throw your plans off than falling in love."

Cheeks flaming, I told her, "I didn't have sex with Noah."

She nodded. "If you do, be careful." Then she stood and bent down to kiss my forehead. Once she straightened, she added, "And don't think I missed that you aren't mentioning Zion in your protestations. I heard you were out in town with him, and I know he carried you home a few weeks back too. People talk."

"Zion's a Wolf," I said weakly.

She gave me the same look she'd used on hundreds of students, but all she said was "You're an amazing young woman, and neither of those boys are stupid. They're a lot of things, ones that are easy to like, but trust me when I say that falling for a Wolf is a path I wouldn't wish on you."

Willing myself not to blush, I said, "I know better."

My grandmother patted my shoulder and headed to her room, and I sat in the living room thinking about Zion's words and Noah's kisses. The one I couldn't have at all was the one I dreamed of, and the one who was offering me all the fun and none of the strings was someone I could only like as a friend. I couldn't be fair to either of them, not unless I kept to a strictly platonic friendship. I muffled a grumble over the fact that I'd finally figured out what true desire felt like—only to be unable to do anything about it. Life had been simpler before I'd met Zion and Noah.

Chapter 18

I HADN'T EVEN FINISHED MY FIRST CUP OF COFFEE THE NEXT morning when I glanced out the window and discovered that someone had messed up my grandmother's car pretty severely. Both driver's side tires were flat, and the hood had been forced open. I had no idea what other damage the vandal had done, so even if I had a way to change the two flats, I'd still be trapped.

I went outside, pulled the spare from the trunk, and was midway through changing the first tire when my grandmother came outside. I looked up to find her on the porch in her housecoat and slippers, two cups of coffee in her hands.

"I have another one under a tarp in the shed," she told me. "Possibly two more."

"You have *several* spare tires?"

"When I got the new ones, I kept the ones that were salvageable." She lifted the cup of coffee that I assumed was for me. "Do you have work?"

"I can take a taxi." I walked up to her and gratefully accepted the coffee. "I left a message at the bar telling Uncle Karl I might be a little late, but that I'm hoping not to be." It was a Saturday, one of the busiest nights at the bar, so I needed to find a way to get to work.

Grandma Maureen sipped her coffee, and after a quiet moment, she returned to the kitchen to fix brunch for us. I thought about the flats. I wasn't sure if changing them was the right move or not. Even if I did, I had no way of knowing what had been done to the engine.

Doing nothing wasn't an option, though, so I set my coffee on the porch step and went to get the second spare from the shed.

By the time I was done, my grandmother had finished fixing omelets. She also told me that Uncle Karl had called to say he was sending a ride over for me that afternoon.

A few hours later, I got ready for work and waited for my ride. I expected that ride to be Noah, so finding Zion on my grandmother's porch when I opened the door was unexpected. He smiled at me in that dangerous way of his and said, "Uncle Karl said you didn't have a ride to work. I volunteered to come fetch you."

"I thought Noah—"

"He was busy," Zion interrupted. "I'm not sure what Dash said about m—"

"Nothing bad."

Zion frowned. "So this is still about when I was at the house with you? Or because I was away this week?"

"I was wrong," I said quietly. "I'm sorry I . . . touched you."

"Don't be," he said.

After a long pause, I said, "I *did* miss you this week."

"Enough that you went out with Dash."

"I was there to see *you* race." I stared at him. "Even if Noah and I were to end up more than friends, that doesn't change anything with us."

"And did you?"

"Did I what?"

"End up 'more than friends' with Dash?"

"Noah's my friend," I said, not quite answering the question and looking at Zion's feet, but then I looked up and met his eyes as I admitted, "I don't want to know about the things you do for Echo, but even without the details, I *know* they aren't legal. You carry a gun. You run 'errands' for him."

For a moment, neither of us spoke. Then Zion motioned toward the house. "Go get your things."

When he stepped back from me, I realized we were still standing in the doorway. I stepped back. "Come in."

Somehow he looked bigger once he was standing inside

the house, surrounded by Grandma Maureen's innumerable Willow Tree figurines, vases, and assorted knickknacks. Zion didn't blend in here at all.

Then my grandmother came around the corner and saw him. "Zion! I didn't know that you were coming to pick up Aubrey."

"Uncle Karl sent me."

"Are you still living with him?"

"No. I got a place of my own a few years back," Zion said.

She nodded and then looked at me, as if willing me to remember what she'd said the night before. Then my grandmother pressed her lips together and gave him a look that would make most men quake. "I best not hear that you're leading my girl astray, Zion. It's bad enough that Noah brought her home last night."

"Mrs. E., I . . . I wouldn't endanger your granddaughter, ma'am."

"Don't ma'am me, Zion." She *tsk*ed at him. "And don't think I missed that you skipped replying to what I actually said."

"Killer is here to give me a ride to work," I interjected, using the name everyone else did as if it would provide distance.

"Killer?" Grandma Maureen sighed. "I think I liked it better when they were calling you Ladykiller." She looked at me and reminded me of our talk last night when she said, "This one's lucky he doesn't have a passel of kids running around by now. I swear a few of those young teachers were a smile away from ruining their careers over him."

"Now, Mrs. E.—" he started.

"Don't think I'm going to forget a thing about you just because I'm retired now," she said with a wag of her finger. She gave me a stern look. "I thought he was going to run out of girls to bed. If he hadn't gotten a license for that motorcycle of his, he might have. I swear he's the first boy I met who needed a license so he could get to a new pool of bedmates."

"Right," I muttered.

Before she could launch into the importance of birth control in casual sex like she had last night, I not-so-subtly steered the conversation into safer areas, reminding her, "Uncle Karl sent him to give me a ride to work."

"And Billy and Noah are going to come by to see what's wrong with your car, Mrs. E." Zion flashed her a sweet smile. "If it's all the same to you, we were wondering if you could tell your neighbors that the boys will be walking around the neighborhood the next few nights."

At that, my grandmother sighed again. "They don't need to do that, Zion. It's generous, but we're fine."

"Echo ordered it." Zion shrugged. "You know how it goes. We look after our own."

She stared at him until he looked like he was going to squirm. Then, softly, she said, "I don't want trouble, but if there *is*, I certainly don't approve of you doing anything illegal about it, Zion. You could do so much more with your life than be here."

Zion's expression was unreadable. "All I'm doing is taking your granddaughter to her job. Noah's better with cars, so he'll be looking at your engine. It won't do to have the two of you out here without wheels." He shrugged again. "Then a few folks are going to look into your trouble."

A long, tense moment passed, and then my grandmother met Zion's eyes again. "I won't accept anything if it means either of us is indebted to the Wolves. I know the ride to work isn't a debt, but the rest . . . I'm not that old, Zion. What are the terms?"

Zion laughed, breaking the tension. "Echo said you'd ask. He told me to tell you, 'You taught most of the Wolves, so we're already in debt to you. This is just us paying respects to you.'"

Grandma Maureen nodded once. "You tell him that I appreciate the help, then. We've had a lot of problems out here, and most of us aren't spry enough to be walking around looking for the ones that are breaking into folks' homes."

"Yes, ma'am."

"And, Zion, I'll expect you to bring my girl home safe and sound after work," she told him. "No detours."

I was mortified. For all of my grandmother's liberalism, she sounded like she thought I couldn't say no on my own. I could. I *had*.

"Yes, ma'am," he repeated.

Then she glanced at me. "I'll see you in the morning.

Remember what I said last night? I'm underlining it today."

After a quick kiss on my cheek and a pat to his, she was gone.

I grabbed my keys and phone and followed Zion to his motorcycle. He handed me my helmet, and I put it on as he swung a leg over the bike.

He was silent while I got on the bike, and he stayed that way as I wrapped my arms around him. I could feel the steady rhythm of his breath as I held on to him. Still he was silent.

"Zion?"

He didn't answer, but he started the bike and in the next moment we were moving. After only a few rides, I was already hooked on the joy of being on the back of a motorcycle. I had no desire to ride on my own, but there was something gloriously primal about being wrapped around a man on an immense, growling machine.

If nothing else, I wished I could keep riding as a regular experience. It was more than the power of the Harley, though. There was something perfect about the way my body connected to the rider. I leaned when he leaned, and straightened when he straightened. We were moving together, in tune with the other's actions without words or complication.

I admitted to myself that it felt even more natural with Zion than with Noah. Everything felt natural with Zion . . . well, everything but pulling away like I had to keep doing. That felt wrong, but feelings didn't overcome logic.

A few minutes into the ride, Zion pulled off the road. He guided the bike over toward a picnic table that was all but hidden by the long, draping branches of a weeping willow. The sudden silence when he cut off the engine seemed dangerous.

"Hop off."

I did, and then I turned to face him as he stood.

"Just hear me out, Red."

"About?" I took off my helmet as he did the same. I walked the few steps over to the picnic table, but I didn't sit. The branches of the weeping willow provided almost as much privacy as a curtain, giving us a sense of intimacy that made me simultaneously excited and afraid.

Zion stayed leaning on the bike in front of me. He met my eyes, as if he was daring me to find a lie in them. "I like you, and . . . I *care* about you."

I didn't flinch away, but I didn't say anything either.

"I know you have doubts," he continued, setting his helmet on the ground beside the bike.

"Zion . . ."

"No, just listen for now." He took the three steps that brought him up beside me. Then he reached out and took the helmet from my hand. "I'm not asking you to be mine, not *yet*. I talked to Echo about you already. I just want you to know that I'm serious. Don't listen to them talk shit about what I *used* to do. Listen to what I do now. Look at how I am with you. Give me a chance to find a way."

"Even if you do change, that doesn't change *my* plans," I

admitted quietly. "Williamsville is a pit stop. This isn't my forever. I want to get my degree, to have a career . . . maybe teaching, maybe something else. I can't be involved with a criminal, and I can't stay here."

"So if things with us work out, I get a different job and move wherever you go after here," he said.

"Leave your family, the Wolves, everything? I wouldn't ask that of you even if we *were* dating." I thought back to what Noah had said, how troubled he sounded at even talking about it, and *he* wasn't wearing the Wolves' colors already. It was even worse for Zion to suggest it. I didn't want him to hate me or even just resent me for making him give up his whole family.

"You didn't ask me," Zion reminded me. "That doesn't mean I wouldn't do it if it meant we had a shot."

I shook my head. "How is it that I can go my whole life without meeting one guy who's interested in me until I come here?"

Zion studied me for a moment before he said, "How many guys are *you* interested in, Aubrey?"

"I shouldn't be interested in anyone," I said.

"But you are," Zion said.

I was too chicken to say there was only one. Noah and Zion were like two sides of a coin: Noah was measured where Zion was impulsive, calm where Zion was vibrating with energy. Then, in other ways, they were similar. They were both gorgeous and passionate. If I hadn't met Zion first, or if I could get him out of my mind, maybe I could be interested in Noah. I wasn't, though. The truth was that there was only one man who had my attention, and I didn't want him to realize just how much of it he had. It was hard enough admitting my feelings about Zion to myself.

"Has Dash kissed you?"

"Please," I asked, not wanting him to do this. I had talked myself out of kissing Noah again, but I wasn't sure I could convince myself to do the same with Zion if he finally kissed me.

"That's a yes." Zion pulled me closer, and in the next moment, his hands landed on my hips. It felt like his skin was burning through my jeans and searing me everywhere we touched.

"Please," I repeated. This time, though, I wasn't sure what I was asking.

"It's not fair if you're kissing only him when there are *two* of us you're interested in," Zion said.

Only one, I admitted silently. *Only you.*

The mere idea of kissing Zion was enough to make me lose all common sense—even worse than last night with Noah.

"Don't think he's innocent, Aubrey. He might not wear the same patches I do, but he's the son of a former Southern Wolves president. His dad died for the club. Noah's had more pu—"

"Stop." I shook my head. "Don't talk about him like that. He's your family."

"Okay." Zion slid his hands from my hips to my ass and pulled me closer. "No talking is fine."

I didn't try to resist, not anymore. I wanted this more than I'd ever wanted anything.

"Just one kiss," I lied to us both. I already wanted the *next* kiss when the first one hadn't happened yet. "Only one."

"One for every time you kissed Dash," he countered.

I was hip to hip with Zion. I wanted to be sensible, argue all the reasons this was a very bad idea, but the words weren't coming. They'd be lies anyhow. I wanted this. I wanted *him*.

"And if you let him touch you"—Zion leaned down and breathed his words against my throat—"or hold you"—he slid one hand up my spine—"I get to do the same."

Since I had convinced myself that there wouldn't be anything more happening with Noah, it wasn't as risky to let Zion set terms like that. Zion didn't need to know that there was no competition, and to be honest, a not insignificant part of me reveled in the possessiveness in his voice. I liked the way it made me feel. I liked how *he* made me feel—like he needed me, like I was special to him, like I was worth his time and temper and kindness. From the night he'd rescued me, I'd wanted this feeling, and every moment I'd had it, at the bar or at my house, I'd treasured it.

"What if I let *you* do something first? Do I owe him?"

Zion laughed against my throat. "I'm not negotiating for him, Red. Just me. Just *my* rights." His mouth trailed down to drop kisses on my collarbone. "I don't want to help anyone else have even a second of your attention."

"Oh."

And he kissed me.

God help me, the man could kiss. My lips parted under his assault, and I was grateful for his arms around me. I wasn't sure I'd have had the strength to stand otherwise. I pressed myself closer to him and felt the hard length of him against me. For a desperate moment, all I could think was that I wished we weren't divided by his jeans and mine.

That thought, however fleeting, was reason enough to jerk away. "Stop . . . please?"

He didn't even hesitate. He stepped back immediately. "Whatever you want, Red."

"Not what I *want* at all," I admitted quietly.

"Good." He reached up and cupped my face in his hand. "Remember that. You like me, and you want me. We can go from there."

Calmly, I listed off reasons why this wouldn't work: "I don't date. I won't be staying here. I can't date a Wolf . . . that means you *or* Noah. He and I are just friends, by the way. I told him that, and he agreed. That's all I can give *anyone*."

Seemingly ignoring everything I said, Zion stepped back, adjusted himself, and swung a leg over his bike. "Come on. We'll get you to work, then."

Mutely, I picked up my helmet.

Before I could climb onto the bike, Zion pulled me into his arms. "I want you, Red. Not just because of this"—he leaned in and kissed me until I was all but boneless in his embrace—"but because I like talking to you. I like the way you try so hard, the way you don't give up on your plans, the way you treat everyone like they deserve respect, the way you tilt your head when you study . . . I like *you*."

"Oh."

"I'm going to find a way to make you give me a real chance," he vowed.

"I want that," I admitted quietly. "I shouldn't, but I do. I want to throw all the worries away and give in to this, but . . . there are things I can't be okay with. The things you do for Echo . . . they aren't things I can accept."

"So I'll change that," he said, as if it were that easy, as if there weren't insurmountable obstacles in our way. No one had ever made me feel like I was worth battling impossible odds. No one had ever made me feel like I was that precious.

We stood there with his hands holding me to him and kissed, not like we had been, but like people who were a little afraid of the fragile thing that was growing between them.

"It feels impossible, but I want to be wrong," I said after several minutes of soft touches and tender kisses. "I want there to be a way that we *can* date."

He smiled. "I'm working on that, Red. I talked to Echo some already. Just give me a little time and trust."

I swallowed nervously and gave him one last kiss. Then I slid onto the back of the bike, already very comfortable there. Between Noah and Zion, I was very at ease as a passenger on a Harley.

Or maybe I was just relaxed as *their* passenger.

Either way, I put my feet on the pegs, scooted closer to Zion, and wrapped my arms around him. I knew that whoever had messed up my grandmother's car wasn't a friend, but the benefit of having Zion chauffeur me was almost reason to thank the mystery vandal.

Chapter 19

SATURDAY AT WOLVES & WHISKEY WAS AN EXPERIENCE I'd had only once so far, and that had been as a backup bartender. It hadn't prepared me for walking in to discover that Mike had been called away.

"It's all you, Aubrey," Uncle Karl said.

Zion was silent at my side. I could feel the tension all but radiating from him, but I didn't know why.

"So what does that mean?" I asked Uncle Karl.

"Trial by fire, li'l bit. Trial by fire." He patted my hand. "Noah stocked the coolers, and we have a few cases on ice, but you're going to work those muscles tonight. Hillbilly Bob is playing."

"Who?"

"Country and blues band," Zion said quietly. "Who's on the door?"

"Billy." Uncle Karl motioned to the front door. "I'll be inside the bar in case of the usual 'Bob trouble.' Echo sent a few boys to handle the back door and be on hand if I need them inside."

"Billy was supposed to be at Grandma Maureen's, though," I said, confused.

Uncle Karl looked at Zion and said, "Echo wants Billy here."

"We can take the car to a garage," I started. "That way you're not short staffed, and—"

"We aren't short staffed," Uncle Karl cut me off. He turned his attention to Zion. "He tells me you get special rules from on high."

Zion tensed, but he said nothing.

"I don't appreciate you going around me," Uncle Karl said.

The way Uncle Karl was watching Zion made me realize that about half the conversation was in subtext I was starting to fill in for myself. I had a growing suspicion that whatever Zion had done, it had to do with me. "I don't understand."

"Killer here will be hanging around tonight looking after you. The boss gave him the night off from any other responsibilities."

"So Echo sent Noah away, and he's sending others here to help mind the door?" I asked.

"Correct." Uncle Karl bit off the word.

"And he's ordering Zion"—I caught myself and corrected quickly—"*Killer* to be here at the bar. What's the special rules part?" I suspected I knew, but I wanted to be sure. I did want to be with Zion, but I didn't want trouble.

Uncle Karl looked from me to Zion. "Why not come to me?"

"I answer to one man these days, Uncle Karl. I work for Echo," Zion said levelly.

"And Aubrey works for me. I don't like being told how to run things in *my* bar." Uncle Karl crossed his arms and glared at Zion. "You need to think about someone other than yourself, boy."

Zion said nothing, and I didn't know *what* to say. I couldn't say for sure whether or not I'd broken the rules. We hadn't really even gone on a proper date.

Uncle Karl was still staring at Zion. "Think about what you're gambling with here. She's not cut out for this life."

"I'll be at the front door until Billy gets here. Then I'll be at the bar *with* Aubrey." Zion glanced at me briefly before turning and walking away.

"He was raised by the club." Uncle Karl put a hand on my shoulder. "He's never asked for anything but to work for Echo, and Eddie Echo . . ." Uncle Karl cleared his throat. "Take a good look at him, at both of them, before you make any decisions about what you're getting yourself into here."

I thought about the club president, trying to remember what he looked like. I hadn't spent a lot of time studying him. Staring at the biker who ruled the roost wasn't something that had seemed like a particularly bright idea, but when I thought back on the things I knew about Zion, I had a good suspicion as to what Uncle Karl expected me to see.

"Killer has more ties to the club than anyone says outright," Uncle Karl remarked, just in case I was slow to catch the clues he'd already put in front of me. "He just used those ties to get permission to date you without you getting fired."

I nodded, but it wasn't the job that was suddenly pressing. Zion's offers to leave the Wolves were a lot more serious than he had admitted.

"And he knows?"

Uncle Karl shrugged. "Echo's been harder on him than on most when it comes to training, but he also indulges Killer. Dash too. He treats the boys well. Always has. Killer's all but marked to fill Echo's shoes someday."

I glanced toward the door to the bar. Zion must be standing outside, since I couldn't see him. The hope I'd started to let myself feel when we'd kissed felt like a weight in my chest now. I walked over to the bar and started double-checking that everything was ready to go. So far, there were only a few people scattered around, but the band would start in a couple hours and I'd be too swamped to think.

WHEN HILLBILLY BOB came through the back door an hour later, I was as ready as I could be. The band wasn't what I'd expected from the name. For starters, Hillbilly Bob appeared to be five people, and one of them was a woman in the tightest pair of jeans I'd seen at the bar, which was saying something. She had a leather jacket without any patches, fire engine–red boots, and straight blond hair that brushed her red belt.

"New barmaid?" she said as she approached me.

"Aubrey." I held my hand out. "Can I get you a drink?"

She took my hand and squeezed it. "Just water right now. I'm Bobbie." She motioned to the band. "They need three longneck Buds and a Miller Lite."

Silently, I pulled her beers out of the coolers. Bobbie ignored me, looking around as she perched on a stool. Up close, I could see that she was in her late twenties or maybe early thirties.

"Who's on shift with you?" she asked.

"Billy, a few guys I don't know, and Z— *Killer*." I lined up the bottles on the bar. "Dash is off, and Mike's away."

"So you're manning the bar *alone*?" She gave me a surprised look and *tsk*ed. "You poor girl."

I straightened my shoulders. "I'll manage."

She laughed, not in a friendly way. "Sure thing, babe."

Then she lifted her water in one hand and gathered the four beers in the other with the sort of careless grip that only someone used to carrying a lot of drinks can make look easy. I made a mental note that it was wrong to hate her for her attitude, but I still frowned at her as she strolled across the bar with a sway in her hips that made every man in the room watch her.

I was grateful that Zion was still outside. At least I was

until she dropped off the beers and went out the door where I knew he stood.

Apparently, Bobbie didn't need to help with setting up. The rest of the band was at work, but she was off chatting up my . . . I didn't know *what* Zion was. He wanted more, and he'd managed to get Uncle Karl to suspend the rule about dating. I felt like that meant we were moving in the right direction—or at the least, moving in the direction I wanted us to go. None of that entitled me to be quite as possessive as I suddenly felt.

I shook my head and turned my attention to the bikers and locals who were starting to come into the bar. I hadn't understood what Uncle Karl had meant when he said that Wolves & Whiskey wasn't a private club, but now that I'd been here a couple of weeks I understood. The bar served more than the Wolves. It was obviously their hangout, but it wasn't closed to others. It was a place where the Williamsville residents could socialize with Wolves, and I could see that it resulted in a lot more comfort than I suspected there would be without a chance for people to mingle.

It was already clear too that the Wolves went out of their way to do just that. Sometimes in the afternoons when it was mostly bikers, they seemed more serious, and I'd learned that there were business meetings that happened in the bar, but in the evenings it was different. The Wolves greeted townspeople and made them feel at ease. It was obviously a sort of PR move, but it quite evidently worked.

Only a few minutes passed before Zion was back inside.

Bobbie followed him. They were just inside the door when she reached out to him. He looked at her hand on his wrist and then at her.

"Hello?" someone said.

As I looked away from Zion, I could tell that he'd just said something Bobbie didn't like. She looked irritated as she walked past him and joined the band.

I couldn't help the bright smile I gave my customer before I asked, "What can I get you?"

That smile was a bit less bright an hour later when the crowd had started to grow to the point that I wasn't sure why there was only one bartender.

The customers weren't disagreeing with my silent thoughts.

"What in the hell is Karl thinking?"

"When does the second bartender get here?"

"Darlin', you are doing jus' fine. Steady and focused. Get the order, move on, work your way from end to end," one older biker drawled.

"And don't make eye contact," the woman next to him added. "They'll take it to mean they're next and get pissed when you don't agree."

"Thank you," I said, handing them their drinks.

"It gets easier," she said as he tucked more money in the tip jar. "And if they disrespect you, shut 'em off. You have the power."

"Don't teach her your bad habits, Shelly," another man teased.

Another added, "Go back there and give her a hand if you want to be useful."

"Mind yourself," the previously sweet biker with Shelly growled, pulling her closer to him.

The man who'd suggested Shelly help me held his hands up.

"And that, Red, is why there's usually a rule about not working here if you date one of us," said Zion from my side, where he'd apparently crept up without my noticing.

Then he went to the other end of the bar and started taking orders.

Together, we managed to get everyone served before the first set. When the music started, the crush at the bar let up, but I had no illusions that it would stay that way.

Zion came over to stand behind me. "It looked like you needed a hand."

"Or three." I leaned back against him briefly before I caught myself and pulled away. "Sorry." I looked over my shoulder at him. "Something you meant to tell me earlier about the rules for barmaids?"

"I talked to Echo. He talked to Uncle Karl. It was *his* call, though. I didn't ask him to talk to Karl." Zion spun me to face him. "I can't fix everything right now so you'll give us a chance, but I'm not objecting to one less obstacle. Is that okay?"

I nodded. It *was*, but at the same time I didn't want to cause trouble—and I certainly didn't want to come between Zion and his father. I was grateful when a girl came up to get drinks, and even more so when Zion motioned for me to get her order when she was ogling him so blatantly.

"Echo told Uncle Karl not to fire you," Zion continued when the girl walked away. "He's likely the one who called Mike away so there was no chance of you being sent home tonight because Uncle Karl was pissed off at me."

He pulled out a few more beers, obviously knowing people well enough to guess their orders before they spoke.

Finally, Zion grabbed my hand and tugged me into his arms. "Talk to me."

"*Your* job is the problem, not mine, not anything else. Uncle Karl is letting me stay at the bar and be with you. I can work around the whole 'what if we don't split up and I'm ready to move thing.' The thing I can't do . . . that I *won't* do . . . is be with a criminal."

For a moment, he stared at me, studying my expression as if there were words he could find there. Then he asked, "And if I wasn't? If I didn't do the things I've done before? What then?"

"Zion, we hardly know each other," I started. "It's a huge thing to change what you do, who you are . . ."

He caught my chin and tilted my head back so I was looking at him as he asked, "Will you give us a chance to correct that if I'm not doing what I do now?"

I couldn't speak at first, but that was it, the last objection, the one obstacle that made me cling to the others. "Yes."

Then, right there in front of anyone who cared to look, he leaned in and kissed me. Not the way he had before, but possessively enough to make me sigh when he pulled away.

"Let me talk to Echo," Zion said. "I'll find a way to make it work. You're worth it. Just give me a little time to sort it out, okay?"

I was grinning so wide that I knew I looked ridiculous, but I couldn't help it. "Okay."

"So we're good, then? We're really going to do this?"

I grabbed him and kissed him until someone started whistling and someone else called out, "So, I guess that answers the questions, doesn't it?"

Zion kept an arm around me when he pulled away. "Mine," he whispered against my lips.

"I guess so."

"And I'm yours," he added.

"Good." I stepped back and smiled. "Now, go . . . do whatever bouncers do." I shooed him away. "I'm working here."

"Yes, ma'am." He brushed his lips over mine one more time and then went back to the other side of the bar, leaving me to deal with the townsfolk and bikers in need of cold drinks.

Chapter 20

Zion was grinning like an idiot when he saw Echo sitting with Skeeter and a man in jeans who obviously had brought concerns of some sort to Echo. A brief flash of amusement crossed Echo's face, but all he did was raise a brow.

But when Zion started to walk away, Echo stopped him with a word. "Killer."

Sometimes Zion felt like a two-legged guard dog when he did this, but if Echo was going to tell Zion to heel and stay, so be it. At least now Zion was a hell of a lot better at it than he'd been as a kid. When he'd realized that Echo was his dad, he'd felt like he finally had a real place in the world.

"Let me protect you," thirteen-year-old Zion told Echo.

"You're not even wide enough to stop a bullet," Echo teased. "Skinny little thing with your head in a book half the time. What are you going to do?"

Zion heard the question that Echo was really asking, so that's what he answered. "Learn."

"Karl!"

The old man poked his head out of his office.

"The boy wants to learn how to protect me." Echo stared at Uncle Karl. "See that he does."

Back then, Zion had worked out until he ached and signed up for every martial art or self-defense option at the community center. He'd learned how to fight, how to fire a gun, how to handle the fear of guns and knives in someone else's hand. For well over a decade, Zion had lived for his father and, by extension, the club.

Maybe, though, he could learn to do something else. For Aubrey, he wanted to. She made him want to be whatever he needed to be in order to find out if the spark they had was the start of something he'd never thought possible. He'd become what he'd thought he had to in order to earn Echo's love and trust; now, he wanted to learn to be something more in order to earn Red's. It wasn't that he had no interests of his own, but none of them drove him the way his desire for acceptance had. He just hoped he wasn't about to lose Echo's affection in order to gain Aubrey's. Echo had never seemed to want anything more than the Wolves. It made him a little less likely to accept Zion's request.

Zion stood at his boss's side and waited for the others to

finish their business and leave. Once it was just the two of them, Echo gestured at the chair across from him.

"Bobbie doesn't seem to age," Echo said. They watched the band for a few moments. For the first time in years, Zion wasn't feeling the usual pull to the bluesy singer. She'd found him outside and asked for a ride after the show like usual. It was more of a routine than a question, typically. She asked; he said yes or that he had work to do first. He'd never turned her down before—and she wasn't particularly pleased that he had tonight.

"Maybe *I* got older," Zion said. "I turned Bobbie down. Not even tempted."

Echo quirked his brow again.

"Aubrey's willing to give us a shot," Zion explained.

"I already told Karl that he wasn't going to fire the girl." Echo paused when Skeeter's old lady stopped by with a drink. She didn't approach, simply stood there waiting to be acknowledged. Zion couldn't picture Aubrey ever doing that. She didn't seem offended by the way the bikers' old ladies acted, but she didn't try to emulate it either. He couldn't see her ever wearing a "property of" patch—and that didn't bother him. This world wasn't for her.

As Echo motioned the woman in, she smiled, dropped off a drink for each of them, and disappeared. She was happy. Most of the wives or serious girlfriends seemed to be, but that didn't mean that every woman would want to be a biker's old lady. Hell, a lot of women didn't even like the *term* "old lady"—although those rare women who wore a "property of" patch owned it like it was a crown. He could respect both attitudes, but Aubrey was somewhere between the two types. He'd seen her treat the old ladies with respect, but she was pretty clear that it wasn't for her.

"What would it take for me to walk away?" he asked Echo.

Echo didn't stop raising his drink to his lips, but Zion saw the brief shake in his hand. He had held control over the club too long to be truly rattled, but there were moments when Eddie Echo was more human than others. Zion felt guilty for provoking one of them. For the first time in his life, he wanted something—*someone*—more than he wanted his father's approval.

They watched the band in silence. The song ended. A second song passed. Finally, Echo said, "How far away?"

"All the way."

"For her?"

Zion nodded. "I think she might be the one for me, and this life—"

"*Our* life," Echo interjected.

Zion nodded. "Our life isn't for her."

"She's asking you to choose?"

There wasn't a good way to answer that. She wasn't, not really. She would walk away from him, and she'd been trying to do just that. "No," he explained. "She's not comfortable, though. With my job. I said I'd give it up for her."

"I mean for you to be president," Echo said. "We haven't talked about it, but I thought that was clear."

"I know."

"And you'd give it all up for a girl?"

Zion glanced over at her. Aubrey was laughing and talking to one of the customers. The crowd had thinned enough that she seemed to be enjoying her job again. That was what he wanted, to see her happy like that. He looked back at Echo. "No, not for *a* girl. For *this* girl. She's different. I'm different with her."

As was typical when he was thinking something over, Echo resumed his silence. He finished his drink before he spoke again. "We'll work something out if you're sure. Take the month to think before you do anything rash."

"I don't need—"

"Take the month," Echo repeated, louder this time. "I still need you, Killer. If you're going, it's not today or even next week, but we can work it out if you're sure."

Zion reached out and clasped his father's arm. "Thank you."

But all Echo did was nod. It was obvious he didn't approve, but he wasn't a monster. Later, when the idea settled in on him, Zion could encourage Echo to talk to Dash. He'd been raised in the club too. No one would object to Echo grooming Eli Dash's son for the role.

Echo and Zion sat in silence for a few moments, a tentative peace between them.

"Skeeter's old lady found out that there's a development company quietly buying up property in town," Echo said. "Mostly old businesses or vacant properties, buying them up cheap."

Zion shook his head. "And how close are these businesses to Mrs. E.'s house?"

"Close enough that our good sheriff should've been asking some questions by now." Echo's tone made his disdain for the sheriff clear enough that Zion could almost pity the man. "I need you to go talk to his boy."

There was a wealth of words never uttered aloud in their world, but sometimes things needed to be clarified. Messing with Quincy Patterson was such a situation, especially on the heels of Zion letting his boss know he wanted out. Ending up in jail was exactly what he didn't need right now. He'd known it was likely sooner or later, and he'd once accepted that as the price he might have to pay. Right now, though, there was a much higher cost on the line.

"How much talking?"

"You want Maureen—and Aubrey—safe?" Echo pushed to his feet and looked down at Zion. "Find out what Patterson's involvement is. His kid will know something. I want to know what it is. Do what you think necessary."

Zion nodded once. Echo didn't care about the cost, about the risk; all he wanted was the result. That was typical. Echo looked after the big picture, made the decisions. He had people who turned those decisions into reality. Zion had fought and bled for the privilege of being one of them, and until he was no longer a Wolf, he would have to continue doing so.

Once Echo was gone, there was no need for Zion to be anywhere but at the edge of the bar, keeping an eye on Red and helping her out if she ended up in the weeds again. The side benefit of not being at Echo's beck and call for the night was that Zion could run interference if Bobbie decided to cause trouble. It wasn't that he doubted Aubrey's ability to look after herself, but dealing with the temperamental singer when she was unhappy wasn't anybody's idea of a good time.

Once he reached the bar, he lifted the flap and went back. Aubrey finished ringing up an order and glanced at him.

"After one month," he told her.

"Really?"

"He needs me to take a month to consider it." Zion pulled out a stool at the far end of the bar, back to the wall so he could keep an eye on everyone, and settled in for what he hoped would be a calm night. The worst, at least, was behind him.

Chapter 21

A FEW HOURS LATER, I WAS NEAR WHIMPERING FROM THE ache in my legs, but I was holding up better than I'd expected—and the tip jars were stuffed. Aside from that first rush when Zion had helped and a fifteen-minute quiet spell where he'd taken over so I could grab a break, I'd managed to serve drinks to the hordes on my own. He'd stayed in reach all night so far, making a point to come back to my side of the bar as the band took a break.

I saw why as soon as I noticed Bobbie swinging her hips like an invitation he very clearly was pretending not to notice.

"I've got this," Zion offered.

I stepped in front of him. "Not your job. Go on."

He paused, and when I saw the worry in his eyes, I relented a little. In a low voice, I asked, "Do you think I'm going to run because you're not a blushing virgin?"

He quirked a brow.

"Every day, *someone's* told me you can't seem to figure out how to keep your pants from falling off." I paused and kissed his cheek. "Relax. Unless you're planning on having that problem now—"

"Never."

I nodded. "Well, then, why don't you pull out another case of Corona and three more of Bud to restock after the band break ends. Unless they swarm, I've got this."

About as subtly as she seemed to do anything, Bobbie watched him walk away. I wanted to be catty. It was a new feeling for me. Possessiveness had never been something that made sense to me, but right now it made more sense than anything else I could think of.

"Jack and Coke," she said.

Mutely, I poured her drink, generous on the whiskey so she couldn't complain. I set it in front of her and turned away.

"Barmaid," she called.

I pasted a friendly smile on my face as I glanced her way and said, "The band's drinks are comped." Then I moved on to the next customer. I wasn't going to stand and engage in conversation with her if I could avoid it—and *because* of her, the bar was crowded enough that I could.

"Good on you," Shelly, the woman who had offered

advice earlier, said quietly. "If that boy's yours . . ." She paused and looked at me. Once I nodded, she continued, "You make clear that you aren't going to put up with shit from any of the ones who were around when he didn't have an old lady to answer to."

"I don't share," I said.

Shelly laughed, a husky rasp that made me wonder if she had a bluesy singing voice to go with that depth. "None of us do, sweetie. That don't make bitches like her stop sniffing around."

I nodded. I didn't know what else to say. Part of me wanted to point out that I wasn't *really* his old lady because he was going to leave the club, but at the same time, I knew that it wasn't my place to quibble over details or talk about his business. I might not intend to wear a patch literally proclaiming me as "property of," like Shelly and a lot of the others did, but I'd picked up enough of the rules. I respected her. I respected anyone who chose their path. It wasn't a fit for me, but the Wolves' partners had a power that I hadn't understood before starting here—a power my own grandmother had, whether she wore Echo's claim on her body or not. I understood that now.

Once the crowd thinned again and Bobbie took the stage, I walked over to the corner of the bar where Zion sat.

The rest of the set was easier—or maybe I was just used to the chaos after a few hours. Either way, the next few hours went well, and then it was last call.

The remaining patrons were starting to drift out while the

band tore down. I might not have been very impressed with Bobbie as a person, but I couldn't deny that the woman had a hell of a voice. Now that they were tearing down, someone had already cued up a bunch of songs on the jukebox. The sounds of the eternally amazing Etta James were filling the bar, adding to my good mood. I'd made more tonight than any other night, and I'd held my own. Even better than that, I was going to actually try *dating* the man I had all these feelings for. Things were looking up.

At least, they were until I turned around to grab empties from the bar only to find Bobbie standing there. I'd been sending her drinks over with Uncle Karl or one of the bikers since the break. Now she was in front of me, and Zion was not here to dissuade her from being rude.

"Jack and Coke."

Silently, I turned to grab a new bottle of Jack Daniel's, hoping to avoid actual conversation again, but fate must not have been feeling generous.

When I turned back around to grab a clean glass, she added, "So I guess you're Killer's newest flavor of the month."

With a comfort that came from a good many hours mixing drinks the past few weeks, I poured hers without hesitation and set it in front of her with a tight smile in place. "Your drink."

Bobbie swirled the icy mix in her glass and took a sip before asking, "You mind if I ask him for a ride home tonight?"

I shrugged. I knew she already had, and I knew what his answer had been. "Ask away."

"Killer isn't going to make some wide-eyed child his old lady, you know?" she said conversationally.

"I don't see how what Zion does is any of your concern," I said as politely as I was able.

"I've been on that ride more times than any other woman," Bobbie added.

And my temper slipped a little more than I meant for it to. "I'd expect that, at your age, you've certainly had plenty of experience. If that's what he wants, that's his business."

The music cut out midway through my reply as the jukebox switched to the next song.

Slowly, Bobbie took another swallow of her drink and then tossed the rest in my face.

I gasped as the liquor and ice trickled down my neck and soaked my shirt. As calmly as I could, I snatched up a bar towel and wiped my face. "Billy? Zion? I need her removed."

"You okay, shug?" Billy asked me as he approached the bar. He already had Bobbie's hand caught in a firm grip.

"I'm sure Zion can kiss it away if I'm not," I said sweetly.

"Fuck you," Bobbie spat.

"He can manage that too, I suspect." I smiled at her.

Billy snorted in laughter and scooped her up like she weighed no more than a grocery sack.

Zion was partway across the bar, headed toward me,

when Billy added, "Killer, get the door. Miss Bobbie needs some fresh air."

He looked at me, and I nodded. "Thank you *both* for removing her."

Then I turned my back on all of them and resumed putting away the garnishes and returning the bottles to the racks. Closing down the bar was something I'd done solo already, but usually it was already fairly dead by then. Doing it while there were still so many people around was different. Doing it when I was fuming mad and soggy was even worse. No one had ever thrown so much as a cup of juice at me in my whole life. I wanted to do a lot worse than make a catty comment.

I was running over the reorders when I heard, "You've put me in a spot, Aubrey."

I looked up to find Eddie Echo sitting at the bar. It was the first time I'd been quite this close to the Wolves' president. Maybe if I had before, I would've noticed that it seemed like Zion's eyes were looking out at me from the older biker's face, or maybe that was just the result of Uncle Karl planting the idea. Either way, I looked into those eyes and admitted, "I didn't mean to do anything. She was—"

"I don't care about Bobbie," he cut me off. "If you're Killer's lady, I'll tell Karl she's done playing here." Echo shrugged.

"Oh."

For a moment, neither of us spoke. He studied me like

I was a problem he needed to resolve. Maybe I was. The thought wasn't very comforting. I had the distinct impression that Eddie Echo wasn't casual about resolving problems. Then he sighed. "You look like Maureen."

"I've heard," I said quietly.

"I have people looking into the situation over there," he announced. "If there are other troubles, I expect you to call Killer . . . not Dash. There's an order to things."

As much as I didn't love being issued edicts, this was the man who Beau said would pluck the stars from the sky for my grandmother. Plus, Echo was Zion's father, his boss. It wasn't ever explained outright, but I knew he was ultimately *my* boss too. Uncle Karl might own and run the bar, but that didn't mean he was free of Echo's orders. There were a lot of reasons to listen to Echo, but the most significant of them was that Echo's orders could solve the problems that my grandmother and her friends were having. I didn't know how, but I did understand that people didn't disobey him.

"Understood," I said. I wasn't sure what else to say, though. I couldn't ask him if he needed anything else, and not a single person in the room had approached since Echo had stepped up to the bar. I lifted my gaze briefly to scan the crowd. There were Wolves scattered around the bar like normal, but it was telling that one of them was stationed at the door where Zion had exited when he escorted Bobbie out.

"You know, there are a lot of young women who wouldn't ask Killer to change," Echo continued in that same level tone.

I resisted the impulse to shiver. "I didn't ask him to change."

"You also rejected him unless he *does* change." Echo's gaze was unwavering, and for a moment, I was afraid. So far, I'd seen the protective side of bikers because they were embracing me like I was part of their family. The censorious expression on Echo's face reminded me that in this case, I was on the wrong side of that equation.

Ignoring every instinct telling me not to argue, I said, "There's no law saying I have to accept someone's interest. If I did, I'd have had to accept Quincy or Noah just as much as I'd have to accept Zion."

"The sheriff's boy?"

I nodded. "Zion, um, rescued me. I have no interest in Quincy."

"And Dash?"

I crossed my arms to keep from either trembling or being lippy, but I still shook my head. "No."

Echo's stony expression cracked a little, and an unexpected softness came into his voice. "I don't want to lose Killer."

I looked over to the doorway, where Zion was now returning. "I'm twenty. I don't have a clue where I'm going half the time. I try. I had . . . *have* a plan." I waved my hand around the bar. "None of this is part of it."

"Your gran had plans too," he said. "She never asked a man to change for her, though."

Maybe it was supremely stupid, but I'd seen the mix of happiness and longing on my grandmother's face when

Echo's name came up. I didn't like it either, so I said, "And my grandmother is alone. I'm not going to do something halfway."

The only reaction Echo had was a slight lift of a brow. He didn't reply to my intimation that my grandmother had only been halfway committed. We both knew it was true, and I suspected they were neither one over it. I glanced away, unable to hold his gaze.

After a moment, Echo pointed out, "Killer's never known another life. Tonight he told me he'll give it all up for you. His family. His position."

When Echo paused, I looked back at him, which was obviously his intent because once I did, he added, "There are *consequences* of walking away once someone's been patched in. He's offering to face that for you."

I looked past Echo to where I could see two bikers step in front of Zion. One of them was Alamo, and I didn't know the other. Zion obviously wasn't used to being stopped, and he looked furious about it. Neither man budged, though.

I didn't ask Echo what the consequences were. The tone of his voice already told me more than I wanted to know.

"You could tell him not to do it. Forbid him . . ." I shook my head. "I don't want him to get hurt. I *do* care. I could care a lot more if I let myself, but you can make him stop, walk away from *me* instead."

Echo's smile was grim, and his words weren't much better. "If he's going to hate one of us over this choice, it's not going to be me."

He pushed to his feet and was already away from the bar when I found my voice. "I didn't mean to get involved. I keep trying to walk away."

"What you *meant* to do doesn't matter, Aubrey. What matters are the choices you make now, and if you can't figure it out, maybe you ought to move back to Oregon." Echo said it mildly. It felt like a threat, but I wasn't sure if it actually was.

I nodded.

And Echo walked away. He paused at Zion's side, grasped his arm, and pulled him close, and from the looks of it, said something in his ear. After a moment, Zion nodded, and Echo and the rest of the bikers left.

Zion followed them over to the door and locked it behind them, sealing the two of us in Wolves & Whiskey. I wasn't afraid of Zion—but I was afraid of the emotions threatening to consume me.

He killed most of the lights before he walked over to me, and all I could do was watch as he came toward me. I wanted to run to him, to apologize, to offer an answer that wouldn't cause him to choose between me and his family. Instead, I stood there and shivered.

"I'm sorry," he said. "Whatever he said, I'm sorry."

"Zion—"

"Whatever Bobbie said earlier, I'm sorry about that too. And the drink." He took a deep breath. "And the things Uncle Karl said . . . and for whatever Dash *will* say . . . I'm sorry about all of it."

"I don't know how this happened," I told him. "All I wanted was a job and a couple of classes. Things . . . us . . ."

He reached over the bar to catch my hand.

I jerked back. "Don't." I forced myself to meet his eyes. "I don't want you to have to leave the Wolves. I don't want to be . . . but I don't want *you* to do the things you do for them, for Echo, either."

Zion stared at me for a minute. "What do you want, then?"

"A night to think," I asked.

Instead of answering me, he pulled out his phone and made a call. "Aubrey needs a ride home. How soon can you be here?"

I felt tears start to slide down my face as I watched him.

"Dash will be here in ten." Zion motioned toward the back, where the ladies' room was. "Go wash up. I'll deal with the rest of the cleanup and restock."

"I don't need you to do my job," I said quietly.

"I'm still on the clock, Aubrey."

When he said my name instead of calling me Red, I wanted to stop him, to correct him, but I didn't. He had every right to be angry. I kept running from him, and if things had been reversed, I'd probably have been furious too. Whatever this was between us seemed impossible to ignore. When I'd told Echo that I'd tried to walk away, I wasn't lying. I didn't want to feel this confused or emotional. I wanted Zion more than I'd ever wanted anything or anyone in my entire life, and it wasn't simple lust. I wanted him, his smiles and words, his strength and kindness. The

230

package was beautiful, but it was what was inside him that made him so irresistible. Asking him to change his entire life for me wasn't fair, but I couldn't change mine either. What I wanted was a compromise, a way for both of us not to have to surrender something essential. I didn't see one.

But I didn't want to lose him.

We stood, neither of us speaking, until I looked down. Zion lifted a glass and tossed it at the wall. A bottle followed it. Another glass, another bottle. I stood there, flinching every time. I didn't know how to fix it, even though I wanted to. I couldn't change who he was—or who I was. I couldn't make being the Wolves' enforcer a tame job, and I couldn't even think about a future that would include my boyfriend in jail.

Zion paused and looked at me. "Go."

I fled to the bathroom and took as long as I could washing my face, stalling until I heard Noah outside the bathroom door calling, "Aubrey?"

"Be right out." I dried the tears that had continued to spill down my cheeks before I stepped into the dimly lit hallway. I couldn't look at him, didn't want to say anything, wouldn't pour my confused feelings out on him. All I said was "Thanks."

"No problem," he said in a soft voice. "Come on. Killer's in Uncle Karl's office putting the take into the safe."

I nodded, grateful to Zion for being out of sight and Noah for telling me, and followed Noah outside. He paused to lock the bar behind him before pulling me in for a hug.

I felt like a horrible person. Last night Noah was trying to kiss me, and now he was consoling me while I sobbed about walking away from Zion. "I'm sorry." I sniffled. "I don't know what I was thinking, especially after we . . . after last night. You probably hate me."

"I don't. No strings last night, remember? You don't owe me an explanation," Noah said, pulling back and forcing me to look up at him. "Friends, Aubrey. We're friends, and no matter what did or didn't happen beyond that last night, I'm still your friend."

I nodded.

"And no judgment today either," he added.

"I don't want to hurt him," I whispered. "Or anyone."

Noah sighed. "How about we get you home? You're dead on your feet, smell like you took a whiskey shower, add that to whatever happened with Killer . . . let's just get you home."

Meekly, I followed him to his Harley. He had to help me put my helmet on because my hands were shaking too badly.

Then I let the roar of the engine hide my sobs and the wind whip my tears away.

Chapter 22

P RYING MY EYES OPEN A FEW HOURS LATER TO THE SOUND
of a window shattering in the house was the perfect
ending to a lousy night. I wasn't even sure what the
sound was before I was running to check on Grandma Maureen.

"Bree!" she yelled as I slammed open her door and sped
into her room.

"It's me," I said as I grabbed her in a hug. "Are you okay?"

My grandmother's upset expression faded into one of
fury, and she snatched a baseball bat off the floor beside the
bed and shoved her cell phone at me. "Call 911. Someone
broke the window."

I did as she ordered, listening for the sounds of anyone

else in the house. I didn't hear anything, but that didn't mean we were alone.

The emergency operator was insisting I stay on the line, but Grandma shook her head and told me, "Tell them you're hanging up so you can call a friend to stay with us."

I did, and the operator objected. She explained that we were to stay on the line, and I repeated myself.

"Recent calls," my grandmother said quietly. Her voice shook a little, but not so much that I was more worried because of it.

"Recent . . . ?"

My grandmother gave me a look, and I disconnected.

"Recent calls," she repeated. "Eddie Echo."

"Echo?" I asked, knowing that I'd have had to call him anyhow but a little surprised that my grandmother apparently had been talking to him earlier.

"*Echo,*" she agreed.

I had questions, a lot of them, about why they were talking, what it meant, what he'd told her. For now, I simply did as I was told. Why my grandmother had a recent call with the president of the Southern Wolves was something to ponder later. I found the number and pressed it, keeping an ear out for any noises in the house while calling him.

"Hello?" It wasn't Echo who answered, though. It was Zion.

"Hello," I said. "Um . . . I was calling for Echo."

My throat froze as Zion said, "Red, is that you?"

"Tell him there's been a break-in," my grandmother said, refocusing my attention.

I repeated her words.

"Jesus! Are you hurt?" Zion was moving. I could hear the sound of him grabbing something and then the slam of a door. "Is someone in the house with you?"

"Grandma Maureen and me. That's it." I looked at my grandmother. "We don't hear anyone else, but . . ." My words faded. "I called the police, and they're sending someone, and . . . she said to call Echo. This was the number."

"Yeah, it's the right number. I was on duty. Don't hang up, just hold on a sec." He slammed something. Then I heard him on another phone, making a call, "It's me. Evans place. Yes. Now."

My grandmother was watching the closed door, and I started shoving the edge of her dresser in front of it while I held the phone against my shoulder.

When Zion came back on the line, he said, "Someone else will be there in about twenty minutes. I'm on my way now." He paused and growled, "Goddamn it! I can either stay on the line while you wait for one of the Wolves to get there or hang up and come myself. I can't ride and hold the fucking phone."

"Hang up," I whispered. "There's no one here, I think, but . . . come."

"Stay where you are till I'm there," he ordered. "Can you do that?"

I nodded as if he could see me, but realized that was foolish and said, "We're in Grandma Maureen's room. Last door on the left. Just come in."

ZION HADN'T BEEN known to be slow as a rule, but he wasn't careless. The ride to Aubrey's house was in his top three for least safe riding. The only other times were when Echo had been shot and when he'd had word of a planned police checkpoint he needed to get clear of before it was set up.

The sheriff was pulling in as Zion roared into the yard. The man was taking his time getting out of the car, and by the time he had, Zion was already busting through the door with gun in hand.

"You there!" Sheriff Patterson called.

Zion didn't stop. He called out, "It's me, Red! Mrs. E.!"

"Back here," Aubrey called. "Hold on. The dresser's blocking the door."

He could hear a *thunk* as she cleared the way.

"It's just me," he called out. He was glad too, because when the door swung open he saw Aubrey just inside the room with a baseball bat in hand.

"Well?" Mrs. Evans asked. She was sitting at the edge of the bed with her phone in hand. "Is there anyone in the house?"

"No one that I saw."

"Good." Mrs. Evans nodded and stood. The older woman had an ankle-length nightdress on and looked far frailer than he liked. When he glanced at Aubrey, he drew in a sharp breath. She had an oversize T-shirt on. That was all.

He jerked his gaze from Aubrey and glanced at Mrs. Evans. "You're okay?"

"We're fine, Zion," Mrs. Evans said, her voice shaking. "Thank you for coming over. If you don't mind waiting, I'd appreciate it."

"I'm here until Echo says otherwise," he clarified.

Mrs. Evans nodded.

Against his will, Zion's gaze drifted back to Aubrey. She was staring at the gun in his hand. She swallowed visibly. "The police are c—"

"Miz Evans?" The sheriff's voice came from inside the house.

"Do you need to hide that?" Aubrey asked in a hurried whisper.

"It's legal," Zion assured her and Mrs. Evans both.

"A young man just crashed in your door, ma'am. I'm armed and in pursuit," the sheriff called out in a drawl.

"If he's in pursuit, it's not very fast," Mrs. Evans muttered. Louder, she said, "Zion is here at my request. He's not an intruder."

The sheriff stood in the hallway. Zion tensed at the unease of having an armed man at his back. It wasn't that he didn't trust *anyone* behind him, but it was a short list that he did trust. Sheriff Patterson wasn't on it.

"Well," the sheriff announced, as if he had actually done something. "The house is clear aside from him." There was a brief pause before he added, "Hand over the gun, boy."

"I'm turning around now," Zion said in a steady voice. When he faced the sheriff, he added, "This is a legal, registered weapon, Sheriff."

"Be that as it may . . ." He nodded at it. "Slowly bend down and place your weapon on the ground."

A noise behind the sheriff startled them both. Midway to the ground, Zion straightened. The sheriff spun. Both men raised their weapons.

"Christ, Patterson! Put that away." Echo strolled toward them without a care in the world. He glanced at Zion, at the gun, and then back at Zion. He shook his head slightly and made clear that Zion should not release his weapon. "Son."

Then he met Mrs. Evans' eyes and said, "Ma'am." Finally, he looked at Aubrey and nodded. He didn't greet the sheriff in any remotely friendly way.

"The boy's gun is licensed and legal, Sheriff, and I believe he's a guest here." Echo paused and looked back at Mrs. Evans, who helpfully added, "He is."

"So why don't we take this conversation to the porch, Sheriff Patterson?" Echo gestured in the direction he'd come from. "Give the ladies a moment to collect their wraps, and we'll all have a chat. There's no need for the women to be uncomfortable."

The sheriff made no more mention of Zion's gun or anything else. He simply walked past Echo and toward the front door.

Echo glanced at Mrs. Evans. "Some of the boys are out

patrolling the neighborhood, Maureen. I'll be staying here while the sheriff talks to you."

"Thank you," she said.

He nodded and motioned to Zion. "Wait here until Maureen says otherwise. I'll keep the sheriff company."

Barely a minute later, Aubrey and Mrs. Evans came out of the room. Mrs. Evans was now wrapped in a quilted red-and-gold housecoat with a thick satin sash cinched around her middle. Her feet were tucked into matching slippers, and her red-framed glasses perched on the edge of her nose. She looked like the English teacher he remembered and respected, but fierce in a new way since Echo had arrived.

"Give us a few moments before you two join us," she ordered. "I need to look outside. Our *sheriff* might miss any evidence if I don't."

Then she walked past Zion, leaving him alone with Aubrey.

"Thank you," Aubrey whispered, leading him to another open door.

He followed her into what was obviously her bedroom and stopped just inside the doorway.

Now that they were alone, Aubrey stepped up to him and wrapped her arms around his waist. Since he hadn't stopped to grab his jacket, he was wearing only jeans and a T-shirt—which was twice as much as she had on. Aubrey's hand was under the edge of his shirt—not intentionally, he suspected, but it was there all the same.

"You're okay," he whispered, as much to assure her as to remind himself.

"All I could think about was getting to Grandma Maureen," she said, her voice muffled against his chest. "This is ridiculous. The sheriff's done nothing and—"

"Echo will." Zion didn't loosen his hold yet. "I know you didn't want the Wolves involved, but—"

"I do now." She pulled back and looked up at him. "He and I talked about it earlier." She broke off with a strained laugh. "Mostly he talked and I nodded, but you know what I mean."

"I do."

"Maybe I'm a horrible hypocrite, but I'm grateful that he made the decision—and that my grandmother insisted I call him. I don't want you, any of you, to do anything illegal or get hurt or anything, but I want to know why this keeps happening."

"You're not a hypocrite."

Her eyes filled with tears. "I am. I felt safer knowing you were coming, knowing about your gun, and—"

He kissed her. He didn't want to argue or hear why she had concerns about the Wolves, and he certainly didn't want to see her tears. What he wanted was to remind them both that she was safe and here in his arms.

But kissing her when she was barely dressed was dangerous. He wanted to prove that this wasn't just lust, that the girl he held was special, that he thought she could be the one who *got* him.

He also still wanted her.

His hand slid from her back to her ass. As she pressed tighter against him, her shirt worked up farther and his fingertips were brushing her bare hip. He needed to stop. The door was open. Anyone could see them. Her grandmother. His father. The sheriff. This was a bad idea.

But then Aubrey moaned, and his good intentions fled. He slid his hand down her bare skin, fingertips grazing the edge of her underwear. She shifted to give him better access, and what had started as a kiss escalated into more.

Aubrey whimpered, but she didn't say anything, and he needed to hear her say she was sure.

"Tell me to stop or tell me to keep going, Red." His hand stilled. He wanted this, wanted to touch her, wanted to feel her trembling in his arms, but he needed permission.

She stretched up so she could capture his lower lip between hers, sucking it and inviting him closer. Then she destroyed him by saying, "I can't."

He stepped back, wanting to get the hell out of there. She was the queen of mixed signals. "Right."

Aubrey caught his wrist. "My grandmother is in the house with your . . . boss *and* the sheriff."

For a moment, Zion didn't know what to do. She was right, and he'd had the exact same thoughts. That didn't change how tired he was of the back-and-forth.

"But I want a date," she said. "I told you I needed the night to think. I'm done thinking."

In a fluid move he pulled her to him with one hand and

then shoved the door closed. Once they had that measure of privacy, he gently pushed her back until she was pinned between him and the door.

"You're sure?"

"Promise."

He put one hand on the door on either side of her, pressed his hips tightly to her, and angled so he could whisper in her ear. "You *promised* me, Red. Don't forget that."

She swallowed and leaned against his body. Her laugh was low and unsteady before she said, "I don't think I could ever forget a second with you."

For a moment, he let himself enjoy her closeness, but reality was waiting outside the door. He stepped back again. "Get dressed."

He watched as she pulled a baggy sweatshirt over her T-shirt and shimmied into a pair of yoga pants, marveling that seeing her get dressed was somehow tempting too. Zion shook his head.

"I want to take you home with me, Red, and never let you leave."

She met his eyes and said, "You're not the only one who wants that."

Although she wasn't blushing, he could tell that this wasn't the sort of thing she admitted easily. He'd been sure that there was more here, but every time she'd started to admit it, she'd backed away. It made it hard to believe that she wouldn't keep doing so.

"Tell me you're not going to run again," he asked.

Aubrey swallowed nervously. "I'm going to try very hard not to run. I don't *want* to run. I want to try this, to try being together."

It wasn't as reassuring as he'd hoped for, but it was better than the nervousness and backpedaling she'd excelled in so far. "We'll make it work. I'll make it work," he promised.

Chapter 23

AUBREY?"

"Be right there, Mrs. E.," Zion said as he took my hand in his and walked toward the kitchen.

I pulled my hand away from his before we walked into the room and busied myself setting out glasses and a pitcher of sun tea. The whole break-in was surreal, but sitting there with the police, Zion's father, and my grandmother after what just almost happened in my room was too much. I shoved those thoughts aside and tried to focus on pouring the tea without shaking. I needed to listen to what they were saying, not think about Zion.

He stood silently behind Echo, who sat next to my grandmother. The sheriff and a deputy sat at the table looking tense. The whole situation was tense.

Then the door flew open. Echo had grabbed my grand-mother and pulled her to her feet. In a split second, he'd put himself between her and whatever threat might be at the door.

Zion had stepped in front of all of us, gun drawn.

Beau stood there with a shotgun in his hands. Behind him, the senior brigade stood in a small clutch.

The sheriff had done nothing but lumber to his feet. "For the last time, y'all need to stop brandishing weapons."

Beau ignored him. Zion and Echo simply exchanged looks.

"I'm not armed," Echo said, as if that was all that mat-tered. He leaned closer to my grandmother and whispered something to her.

She nodded and squeezed his hand. Then she walked over to the door. It was obvious to me, and to anyone with basic observation skills, that my grandmother and the presi-dent of the Wolves could work like a team. That was more telling about their history than anything else had been.

"Everyone's fine," she said to her assembled neighbors. "Eddie and Zion are here to talk to the sheriff with us."

Beau stood there grinning the whole time, shotgun held crosswise in front of him. "It's about damn time," he said. "Good to see you, Mr. Echo."

Echo nodded. "You'll be seeing a lot more of me and the boys." He looked past Beau. "I'm sorry you all have been troubled over here. We'll get it sorted out, though."

The sheriff started, "Now, wait a second—"

"Oh, bless your heart," Christine said in that sugar-sweet voice of hers. "We all know you gave it a good try, Sheriff. Sometimes a man just needs a little help getting the job done."

Beau snorted, and several titters slipped out from the others. My grandmother sighed. "Go on, everyone. I'll talk to you later. We don't want to waste Eddie's time because we're all standing around."

Zion crossed his arms and leaned back against the wall while my grandmother sent Beau and the others on their way. Once she'd shut the door, Echo pulled out her chair for her. She shot him a chastising look, but smiled at him a second later and took her seat.

"Where were we?" Echo prompted.

"Discussing how the sheriff isn't getting any results," Grandma Maureen said.

"Now, Miz Evans, we've gone over this—"

"Rubbish," she snapped. My grandmother was a few shades past angry this time. I couldn't blame her for it, and I was betting no one else could either.

Echo, however, was once more clinging to silence as she laid into the sheriff and his late-arriving deputy.

Before tonight, if anyone would have told me that the sheriff and the president of the local chapter of the Southern Wolves would be sitting in my grandmother's kitchen while both of their "deputies" took notes, I'd have laughed at them. I wasn't laughing tonight. I was trying to figure out which of the supposed resources my grandmother had called was actually more of an upright citizen right now.

The sheriff wasn't winning.

I had some issues with Echo's business, but my only *personal* one was the way he'd confronted me about Zion. Regardless of that, I had to admit that I felt a lot safer under his watchful gaze than with the sheriff. For whatever reason, Sheriff Patterson hadn't been active in stopping the crime wave here. I had no doubts that Echo would solve it.

"So you're saying these problems are related?" the sheriff said yet again when my grandmother pointed out that he'd been called out to the neighborhood more times in the past thirteen months than in the last five years.

"Don't be an imbecile. Of course they are!" My grandmother hadn't been particularly polite the last time she'd called him out to the house, or when he'd been at the neighbors' houses. She wasn't usually this blunt, though.

"Do you have any proof?"

"Isn't that your job?" Zion interjected.

Sheriff Patterson shot him a glare. "You're only here because I allow it."

"Zion and Eddie are here as my guests, Sheriff," Grandma Maureen snapped. "I called them because my hearing isn't what it used to be. I want to be sure I don't miss anything."

My eyes widened at her lie.

"And your granddaughter?" the sheriff prompted. "Is her hearing impaired too?"

Grandma Maureen gave a long-suffering sigh. "No, Sheriff, but she was shaken up. Shock doesn't make for the best focus. Eddie and I have been good friends since before you took office. In times of stress, a woman needs her friends."

The sheriff looked from her to Echo. "I see."

Echo remained silent. He'd said next to nothing the entire time the sheriff was taking our statement. He watched. He listened. Aside from his words in the hall and when Beau arrived, he might as well have not been there.

At least that was what I thought until I returned from showing the sheriff and his deputy to the door.

Once they were gone, Echo looked at my grandmother. "He's either involved or covering for someone."

"That's what I thought." She tightened the sash on her housecoat and glared in the direction of the front door, where the sheriff and his slightly more astute deputy had left. "So where does that leave me?"

"Practical matters first . . . I'll have someone fix the window first thing tomorrow." He nodded toward the broken living room window. "Tonight, we'll cover it, and I'll leave Killer here to keep an eye on you." Echo's gaze slid to mine as he added that last detail, as if daring me to object.

"Thank you," I said, answering for both my grandmother and myself. "There's some plywood in the shed. That's probably the quickest solution." I looked at Grandma Maureen. "Are you okay while I go out and get it?"

"I'll stay until you're back inside," Echo said before she

could reply. Then he looked at my grandmother. "Do you have any of that tea you kept at the school to calm upset parents?"

She smiled. "Just like old times, then? Zion's not in trouble for a change, at least."

"Oh, I'm sure he's done something we can discuss."

"Thanks, Echo," Zion said wryly. He walked to the back door, grabbed the flashlight off the counter, and opened the door for me. "Come on, Red."

I didn't mention that he'd reverted to calling me Red again, but it felt good to hear. I walked to the door. "Be right back."

"Take your time," Echo said in a lighter tone than I'd heard him use before. "I'm in no rush."

My grandmother shot a glare at him and added, "No need to dawdle either."

Echo laughed. "Afraid to be alone with me, Maureen?"

"As if. I've got no more use for a man half my age than I did the last time you came sniffing around." She bustled over to the cupboard.

Zion and I both froze. It was one thing to know in vague terms that they had history, but it was a bit different to hear it spelled out quite so clearly. I didn't know whether to tiptoe out the door or run. There were conversations best not overheard, and this was fast becoming one of them.

"Thirteen years, Maureen. I know you weren't a math teacher, but even you can figure out that thirteen years is not half your age." Echo sounded weary as he followed her to the cupboard. Then, in a louder voice, he ordered, "Close the door behind you, Killer."

Outside in the dark, the yard looked ominous. It never had before, but I guess a break-in does that. The porch light wasn't bright enough suddenly.

Zion turned on the flashlight.

"I always thought he was a little too willing to go to parent-teacher conferences," Zion said lightly.

"So you didn't know?" I asked.

"Echo doesn't have an old lady, never has, and I doubt that Mrs. E. would've been willing to be . . . that she'd . . ." His words faded away.

I laughed at his unexpected awkwardness.

Zion looked at me, frowned, and said, "Just so you know, I'm planning to forget that whole sentence that I started *and* what I heard in there. You don't seem surprised."

I shrugged. "Grandma Maureen isn't exactly a stereotypical schoolteacher, in case you don't already know that," I said mildly. I didn't particularly like the idea of her sleeping with Echo, but from the way they were relaxed around each other, I wasn't foolish enough to think it hadn't happened. "Just be glad it didn't get too serious. You'd have been my step-uncle or something."

Zion stopped midstep and looked at me. "Who told you? Or did you figure it out on your own?"

I realized what I'd said then, that I'd admitted to knowing that Echo was more than a boss to him, that I'd pointed out that the club president was his father. I'd known for less than a night and already said something stupid. Carefully, I asked, "Does it matter?"

"That you know that Echo's probably my father?" He watched me. "I don't know, does it?"

I tried to keep my expression bland. Obviously I failed, because Zion muttered, "Damn him. That's what happened earlier tonight."

"Zi—"

"He's why you . . . earlier at the bar. That's what that whole mess was, wasn't it? *He* said something about being my father?" Zion's fists clenched, and he turned back toward the house.

I stepped in front of him. "No."

"Why not? If he's going to admit it to someone, why not me? He thinks he can meddle in my life like he's a father after all this time—"

"He simply pointed out that there were consequences to your leaving the Wolves and that I wasn't being fair."

"I'm a little old for him to start talking about fair." Zion stepped to the side like he was going around me.

I grabbed his arm. "Stay here. Please?"

"Why?"

"Because seeing them doing whatever they are isn't what you want," I said lightly, hoping to defuse the mood that Zion's realization had sparked. When that didn't get a reaction, I sighed and continued more seriously, "And because Echo was right to talk to me. I shouldn't ask you to change and give up your family just for a *chance* at us."

"I don't remember *you* asking me to," Zion said mildly. His fists were still balled at his sides.

"Maybe I didn't say the words," I started. I slid my hand up to his biceps. "I'm sorry I put you in this situation."

"Jesus, Red. You're missing the point. He *knew*. He knew how I felt, and he should've stayed out of it, and you should've said something to me. We're never going to get anywhere if you can't talk to me instead of jumping to conclusions and running. Just so we're clear"—he held up a hand and ticked off statements—"I like you; I am willing to try us; I've already got permission for you to keep your job *and* for me to take a month to consider if I truly want to walk away from the club; I haven't even touched another woman since the night we met at the fair—"

I withdrew my hand and stepped backward. "I'm sorry I didn—"

He continued as if I hadn't spoken. "I might not be a college student, but I can do something else to take care of us if this works. Something legal." He caught me with both hands on my shoulders and held me steady as he added, "And aside from liking talking to you and liking the look of you, we don't lack for chemistry."

"I'm *sorry*," I repeated.

"I'm getting tired of sorry, Red. Maybe you could try a

new tune." Zion turned back to the shed then and walked away from me. Bitterly, he said, "Come on. I have orders to follow."

ONCE THE WINDOW was covered and Echo had left, Grandma Maureen kissed both Zion and me on the cheek and said, "You'll fix the sofa up for him?"

I nodded.

"Echo will have the boys patrol, and I'll be right here all night, Mrs. E. You're safe."

"I know." Grandma Maureen patted his cheek fondly. She met my gaze and said, "I expect everyone to be safe." She looked back at Zion. "Are we clear?"

I blushed, but Zion didn't so much as look away from her. "No worries, Mrs. E. I'll be out here *on my own*."

She looked at me once more and then left us standing in the middle of the living room.

"I don't need a cover or anything. You can go on," he said, and then he walked over to the front door.

I stood there silently, staring after him and not knowing what to do. Since we'd come back from the shed, Zion wasn't speaking to me any more than was absolutely necessary. All the comfort we'd had just a couple of hours ago had faded.

Mutely, I went to the linen closet and pulled out sheets, a blanket, and a pillow to fix up the sofa for him. When

I came back, Zion was outside sitting on the front porch, not quite ignoring me but certainly not being very open. I busied myself making up his bed.

He still hadn't come inside by the time I was done, so I walked over to the door.

"Zion?"

"Go to bed," he said, not even looking my way.

My heart broke a little more at that, but I didn't know what I'd say if I stayed. I watched the street, trying to think what to say. For a moment I thought I saw Quincy's truck drive by, but there were more than a few red pickups in Williamsville.

Zion remained silent, so I went to my room, trying not to obsess over what we'd shared there earlier. When I fell asleep, there were tears on my pillow.

Chapter 24

WHEN MORNING CAME, ZION WAS ON THE FRONT porch again. I could see that he'd been inside at some point: all the bed linens were neatly folded and stacked on the end of the sofa.

I went into the kitchen and found Grandma Maureen at the table with a cup of coffee in her hands.

"Sit with me," she said.

I poured coffee for myself and grabbed a banana before going to the table. When I sat next to her, we said nothing at first. I'd always loved mornings with her. There was a quiet comfort in simply being near my grandmother—but we also had the ability to talk about anything and everything.

"Did you love him?" I asked. "Eddie Echo?"

"I don't know anymore." Grandma Maureen smiled at me, looking a lot younger in that moment. "I loved the way he could make me feel, the way we laughed, the way he thought no one would ever compare to me." She shook her head. "I think I could've loved him if he wasn't who he is, but at the same time, I *wouldn't* have loved him if he wasn't who he is."

"He wasn't the club president then," I half said, half asked.

"No, he wasn't." She met my eyes sadly. "He was what Zion is, too young to have been committing the crimes he already had. He was one of the smartest young men I'd met, and back then, that thirteen-year age gap was a lot wider than now. I had a son to raise, and having a criminal around your father wasn't something I could do."

"But?"

She laughed. "But sometimes widows have needs, and Eddie Echo's always been easy on the eyes." Grandma Maureen shot a speaking look my way. "Zion looks a lot like him."

"You knew?"

"That he was Zion's father? Before Zion was even born. There was another possibility or two, but Liz swore the baby was Eddie's before she took off." My grandmother gave me a sheepish smile. "I was probably a little soft on Zion because of it. By the time he was in elementary school, it was painfully obvious to anyone who took a good look, and if looks weren't enough, the boy's mind was plenty of proof. Seeing

Eddie with him was almost enough to make me forget my objections to giving us a chance, but even then, the club always came first for Eddie, and my family was first for me."

"And Zion?"

"If anything had happened to Eddie, I would've been raising a little hellion." Her smile turned sad. "Eddie wouldn't give him up while he was still alive, but he wasn't going to let him grow up parentless. If Eddie ended up dead or in jail, I would've had custody of Zion. As it was, the club raised him . . . but you knew that part."

I felt like my whole world had tilted. "So you really get it? This mess with . . ." I looked toward the living room.

"I do," she said. "And I stand by what I said before: if you think you're going to end up in the life, I'll buy you a ticket to Oregon right now. What Eddie and I had was a lousy excuse for a relationship, and if I can help it, I'll not see you do the same—*or* worse yet, truly commit yourself to a man who's going to end up dead or in jail."

I was silent. She wasn't telling me anything I didn't know.

"I'm going over to check in with the girls," Grandma Maureen told me after a few moments. She shot a look toward the front porch. "Talk to him before things fester." She took a steadying breath. "I don't approve of you getting involved with a Wolf, but from the looks between you last night, you're already involved enough that some serious conversation is in order. You need to find a solution or get quit of him."

I flushed bright red, but all my grandmother did was

shake her head. "No judgment, lovie. Just a plea for common sense."

Then she was gone, and I was left with an angry Wolf at my door. I wanted to try. I really did. I walked into the living room, watching him as he sat silently outside my home. He was there to keep us safe, and I *felt* safer because of it. For the first time in my life, I wanted to attempt a relationship.

I pushed open the door and stepped outside.

Zion looked over his shoulder at me. "Is this the part where you tell me we can't be together again?"

I sat down next to him, close enough that our knees touched. "I promised you a date, and I meant it, but that doesn't mean that your father was wrong."

He stared out at the street.

"I can't ask you to leave your family. I *can't*," I said. Zion opened his mouth to argue, but I held up my hand. "If you walk away from them and we . . . don't work, you'll resent me. I can't bear that."

"We have something here, Red."

I nodded. "We do."

He stared at me, waiting for me to continue.

"Thank you," I said. "For being here for me last night and for the first night at the fair and at the bar and . . ." I stopped, took a deep breath, and said, "You keep appearing when I need you."

At first he didn't answer, but after a moment he said, "If you let me, I'll be at your side so you don't need to wait for me to get to you."

I held out a hand to him.

Silently, he stood and took my hand. I didn't know how to fix the things that were wrong. All I knew was that I wanted to make him happy. Hesitantly, I asked, "Will you let me try something?"

I stood and started to walk, pulling him behind me. He followed me into the house, but when he realized we were headed to my room, he stopped.

"We're the only two people in the house," I assured him.

Zion studied me for a moment. "Tell me what's going on here, Red."

"I'm sober, and we're alone, and I want . . ." My words left me as we walked into my bedroom and closed the door behind us.

He raised one brow and looked at me. "You want what?"

"You." I walked to the nightstand, opened the drawer, and pulled out a small foil packet. I met his eyes as I placed it quite obviously in the center of my nightstand. "I just want to put all of this aside and . . . be with you."

His eyes darted to the condom and then to me. "Is that the proposition I've been waiting for, Red?"

"Not very sexy, but—"

"It is," he interrupted. "What I need is for you to be clear and direct."

I swallowed nervously. "I want you. Now."

Zion fixed his gaze on me but didn't speak. He withdrew his gun and put it and the holster on my dresser. That was it, though. He left his shirt on, and he stayed on the far side of the bedroom, just in front of the closed door . . . the same door he'd pinned me against last night.

"Do you w—"

"Let me see you," he ordered.

I was nervous as I let my shorts drop to the floor. I stepped out of them, kicked them to the side, and met his gaze.

"More."

I pulled off my shirt, leaving me in only my bra and underwear.

His eyes seared my body, but I couldn't look away from him. He took several steps closer, but I held up a hand. He stopped halfway across the room.

"Your turn," I said in a surprisingly steady voice. I gestured toward his shirt. "I want to see your skin. I've wanted to since you were on my porch without a shirt."

He didn't hesitate. He jerked his shirt over his head, leaving him in nothing but jeans. Then he advanced the rest of the way to me. He was so close that I *needed* to touch him. I leaned forward and kissed his bare chest.

"More," he repeated, sliding his hands over my stomach and up to the edge of my bra. "Take it off."

I tilted my head to look up at him, and then I reached back and unhooked my bra, letting it fall to the floor between us.

Zion cupped my breasts in his hands reverently. Slowly, he leaned down and brought his mouth to one breast while caressing the other.

"Perfect," he murmured.

Then his hand trailed down my stomach until he reached the top of my underwear. "More, Red. I need more."

I shivered at the hunger in his voice, but I did as he asked. I took his wrist in one hand and guided him lower. At the same time, I used my free hand to push my underwear down.

For several moments, I gave in to his caresses, trembling under his skillful fingers, and then I pushed him backward toward the bed.

He sat on the edge of my mattress, but when he reached for me, I shook my head. "Back up."

I pushed on his chest so he'd lie back and then climbed up after him.

"Red—" he started.

I ignored him and kissed my way down his chest, exploring the hard planes. It felt unbelievable to know that of all the women in the world, I was the one he wanted to have touching him.

He hissed when I paused to flick my tongue over his nipple, cussed when I repeated the action on the other side, and moaned when I grazed his collarbone with my teeth. Muscles tightened under my hands as I reached his flat stomach, and he drew a shaky breath as I unhooked his belt. "You don't have to—"

"I *want* to." I willed myself not to blush as I admitted, "I've never tried this, but I want to. With you, I want to."

He watched me intently as I slowly unbuttoned his jeans. His hand stroked over my hair and brushed it away from my face so he could see me.

"I've fantasized about this," I whispered between kisses on each bit of skin I exposed. When he made a growling noise in his throat, I licked as much of his skin as I'd bared.

His hand stilled in my hair. "More . . . please."

I freed him from his jeans and slid my hand over his length. Then, while he was arching up, I followed the motion of my hand with my mouth.

Zion said something, but it was unintelligible.

I might not have ever done this, but I'd watched a few movies and read more than a few sex scenes. So I experimented, letting his moans and arching hips guide me on what he liked.

And I discovered that what *I* liked was having him desperate for my touch. As I sucked and stroked him, his hand fisted in my hair.

I gave a hum of appreciation. My own reactions to the sheer power of having him on the edge were unexpected, and I wished he could touch me too.

When I reached down and cupped his sac as I swallowed around him, he took a shuddering breath and tensed.

"Fuck, Red. You're killing me," he muttered.

I repeated my actions, and after another groan, he ordered, "Stop."

Confused, I lifted my head, releasing him. I looked up

and met his eyes, but I couldn't resist flicking my tongue out to lick him when I saw how excited he was.

"Turn around and come up here," he demanded, moving me as he spoke.

It only took a moment to realize what he wanted. I flipped around, and he grabbed my hips, pulling my body up roughly. Before I had a chance to even speak, he had his face between my thighs and his tongue on me.

It wasn't slow, but I didn't want slow. I wanted the way his fingers dug into my skin, the way he feasted on my body. I'd done that, made him need me that much. It was a dizzying feeling.

I lowered my mouth to him again, wrapped my hand around the base of him, and met him moan for moan, thrust for thrust, until we were both shaking.

"Stop," he ordered. "Stop and . . . just let go for me, Red."

He moved me so I was facing him, looking down at him as his mouth made me whimper and his hands trailed up my chest. My whole body was trembling, and still he pushed me higher. Time ceased to exist. There was only skin and breath as he showed me joy I hadn't known was possible.

When I stopped writhing, he pushed me onto my back and said, "Tell me yes."

For a moment I was too dazed to answer, but then I felt him slide against me. My answer was more sigh than word: "Please."

He tore open the condom that I'd left on the nightstand, sheathed himself, and then he was inside me.

Nothing in my life had prepared me for this, for him. My entire body felt like it was burning, and the more he moved, the more I knew that the fire was going to consume me. As he moved, I understood how very, very wrong I'd been about sex. What I'd done before was a pale mockery of what sex was like with Zion.

There were no words for the feeling building inside me.

"Harder," I whimpered, feeling the edge of heaven just out of reach.

He jerked my legs up so they were straight in the air and he pressed deeper inside me.

The universe expanded, and I could swear there were stars exploding in my eyes. As soon as he felt me tightening around him and heard me cry out, he followed me into that impossible pleasure.

As aftershocks rippled through me, he rolled onto his back and pulled me onto his chest. Words were still out of reach, but in that moment, they were extraneous anyhow. Zion's hands traced over my body as I curled against him, and that was all the conversation we needed.

Chapter 25

THE PHONE'S BUZZING PULLED ZION OUT OF THE BEST sleep he'd had in ages. For a moment, he wasn't sure where he was. A warm body curled against him; soft hair spread over his chest. He didn't spend the night with women. Ever. It gave them the wrong idea.

Then he looked at the woman he had pulled tight to his side. *Red.* He ignored the phone call and looked at her. It was hard to believe she was there. That *he* was there next to her. It was what he'd wanted since the night they'd met.

He'd gone from furious that she wasn't truly willing to give them a real shot to terrified that she was in danger to . . . this. He was holding her, in her bed, after finally being with her. He didn't think he'd ever been as content as he was right now.

The phone buzzed at him again.

He slipped out of the bed, pulled on his jeans, and stepped into the hall. Once he was out of earshot, he returned the call he'd ignored.

Echo answered, "You don't refuse my calls, boy."

"Sorry."

"If the girl can't handle hearing you talk to me—"

"She's asleep, Echo. I didn't want to wake her." Zion walked back to the living room and sat on the sofa that had been his bed the night before. "That's all. It was two fucking minutes, man. I called you as soon as I was out of the room."

Echo was silent for a fraction of a moment before he said, "You need to get your head on business, son. Lack of focus is dangerous."

Zion bit back a sigh. "Duty calls, then?"

"Meet me at the house in thirty. Someone should be there in ten to keep an eye on the women until one of us can go back over," Echo said, and then he disconnected.

When Zion looked up, Aubrey was standing in the doorway watching him. Her arms were folded over her chest, and all the boldness of this morning had vanished. There was no soft smile or inviting glance. She was so closed off he wasn't sure if he could even kiss her good-bye.

"I need to head out."

"For . . . work?" she asked quietly.

He nodded once.

"Right," she said. Her gaze dropped to the floor for a moment, but then she straightened her shoulders and looked at him. "I'll deal with it."

"Just for a few weeks longer," he reminded her.

She nodded.

"I'll be back as soon as I can," he added.

She gave him a watery smile. "Can you . . . *not* wear the gun next time? I know you're still *theirs* right now, but . . . here with me, could you—"

"Yes." He hadn't thought about it, but he could see how uncomfortable it might make her. He beckoned her to him, and she stepped forward. He pulled her into his arms and held her. "One month. Then I'll figure out something new to do, and we'll keep figuring us out."

She tilted her head up, and he kissed her, feeling the stress melt out of her by the moment. When he pulled back, she said, "Be safe."

"Always," he promised, grateful that she hadn't taken the time to ask about any of the scars he wore from too-close encounters. Hopefully he wouldn't need to answer any questions about the past until he was no longer doing things that could result in getting injured.

WHEN ZION GOT to Echo's house, he didn't bother knocking. They were far past that sort of nicety. Maybe they'd never been there in the first place. He opened the door and keyed in the alarm code. If Echo hadn't expected him, Zion would've needed his key too, but he had long since learned that Echo would unlock the door if he knew Zion was visiting. It had always felt a little like coming home, not that either of them acknowledged it. No one ever had until Aubrey did so last night. It felt strange to have had his first ever conversation where someone came right out and called Echo his dad.

Zion tossed the lock and called out, "Echo?"

"In here."

Zion walked farther into the house and found Echo standing in the dining room staring at a map. His table had long since been turned into a giant desk of sorts. He glanced at Zion and asked, "What are you grinning at?"

"How awkward everyone is about me being your kid, even though it's the worst-kept secret in the club," Zion said with a shrug.

Echo stared at him for a moment before tossing a beer his way. "Your old lady mentioned it, I gather."

"Seems someone tried to warn her off me because of it." Zion twisted the top off the bottle.

"Don't look at me, boy. I didn't own up to you being mine. Figured I wasn't going to do that until you got the balls to call me out on it." Echo set his own beer down and pulled out a half-crumpled pack of cigarettes. "Took you long enough. Thought I'd be having this talk on one of our deathbeds at the rate you were moving."

Zion looked at the pack of smokes and grinned. "First

time you caught me having a post-sex smoke, I thought you were going to say something."

Echo pulled out a cigarette and slid the rest of the pack toward him. "You looked like a cocky little bastard. I wasn't sure whether to be proud or cuff you for it." He packed his cigarette. "You look about the same right now."

"Christ, Echo, you want to give me a birds-and-bees talk now that I admitted to knowing you're my old man?" Zion held a hand out for the lighter.

Once Echo lit his, he tossed the lighter toward Zion's head.

Zion snatched it out of the air and lit his cigarette. "I'm not going to call you Dad or some shit."

"That's your business. I wasn't a great example of a father. Don't imagine I earned the word," Echo said.

And for the first time, it occurred to Zion that he wasn't the only one their silence had hurt. He'd never really thought of Echo as a father. He hadn't thought of anyone that way. He had a lot of uncles and one boss. It wasn't the most traditional family, but they'd done okay.

Zion stood there awkwardly with Echo. "You've been good to me."

Echo snorted. "So good you want to leave."

"If Mrs. E. had asked *you* to give up the life . . ."

"You go from ignoring everything to putting everything out on the table, don't you?" Echo stared at him for several moments. "I don't know. Thought about it when you came along, but . . . I didn't have anything to offer her. We had what we had. I spent a lot of nights slipping into that house after her kid was asleep. I did what I could to be there when she let me." He took a drink, looked at the table, took another drink. "Maybe I would've left. She didn't ask, though."

"Neither did Aubrey," Zion said. He paused, smoking in silence for a moment before adding, "You didn't need to talk to her."

Echo lifted his cigarette, took a drag, stared at him, and then when he exhaled, he said, "I simply pointed out that she was asking you to give up a lot. I might not call you my kid, but I don't want to see you throw everything away over a girl."

"Not your call," Zion said. "Not as my boss *or* as my father. I'll go through whatever it takes to walk away from the club if that's what I have to do to be with her."

"It's like that, then?"

Zion nodded.

For a moment, the only sounds were the ticking of the clock on the wall and the nearly silent sizzle of burning tobacco as they smoked. Finally, Echo sighed. "You two better be sure you know what you're doing. I don't want to get caught between you and Maureen." He lifted his bottle and took a drink. "And just so you know, Aubrey's father hates me, so there's that too."

"Great," Zion muttered.

Echo grinned then. "If there's kids, I expect they'll call me Grandpa."

Zion let out a groan, and his father laughed. It was good,

and Zion was increasingly sure they could work it all out. Cautiously, though, he said, "If it stops being such a secret that I'm your kid, I could still come around to see everyone, just not for work."

The look Echo gave him was appraising. "You've thought this out."

Zion shrugged. He'd been pondering possibilities the past week. He'd even looked into a few things.

"Out with it," Echo said. "I know there's more."

Zion held Echo's gaze as he asked, "What do you think of me enlisting?"

"You could, or you could go to school. You're smart enough, and your art's good."

It was foolish to be happy to hear Echo admit to noticing either detail, but it still made Zion smile. He shook his head, though. "Thanks, but I'm not sure I'm cut out for that. I can't see being in an office eventually or a classroom now—and being a student doesn't exactly pay."

"You should have enough money tucked away. You don't spend anything." Echo watched him, studying his face the way he had when Zion was a teenager. "So enlisting . . ."

"I'm good with guns, planning, take orders well. My record's clean."

Echo nodded. "All right, then."

"I'm going to go over and tell her tonight," Zion said.

"Tomorrow. I need you to come with me to talk to some people tonight," Echo said.

Zion nodded. Talking at night probably meant they were

meeting someone who either would rather not be seen meeting Wolves or wasn't expecting their visit. Either way, Zion was the one who enforced Echo's words. That was his job, the violent act to back up his father's authority.

"We need to get this business with the trouble over at Maureen and . . . Aubrey's place squared away before you sign up for boot camp." Echo pointed at the map. "This is all the area they've bought up so far . . ."

Chapter 26

I FELT EVEN MORE CONFUSED AFTER THE THINGS I'D SHARED
with Zion. I wasn't going to say that I was in love simply
because he'd proven me so very wrong about sex, but
I couldn't pretend my feelings were simple lust—or mere
friendship. I thought about him constantly, and I had done
so since the night we'd met.

The sound of motorcycles led me to the front porch.
When I stepped out of the house, I saw two Wolves on
Harleys that they parked in the street. They didn't get off
the bikes. Instead they waved and stayed where they were.
I realized they were guards sent over by Echo. I lifted my
hand in greeting and went back inside. Maybe straightening
up would help me clear my mind.

After a few hours, the house was completely clean, but my mind was no more settled than it had been. I was forced to admit that I needed a better distraction than reorganizing my grandmother's pantry, which was about all I had left to do.

I'd just decided to call Ellen when the doorbell drew my attention. Standing on my porch was a Wolf. Two more men stood outside. One wore a Wolves vest, and the other had no insignia. There weren't any more Harleys, though. Instead, there were a couple pickup trucks.

"Echo says the window needs fixing," said the biker on my porch. He was young, maybe a year older than Zion, but he looked a lot less comfortable than the guys I'd seen at the bar with Zion. He shuffled his feet and muttered, "You can call him or Killer if—"

"You're wearing club colors," I interrupted. "And I've seen you around the bar, *and* he said he was sending people."

The biker lifted his gaze from his boots and smiled. "I'm Phillip."

"Hi, Phillip." I stepped to the side and motioned him inside. "We put up plywood, but . . ." I shrugged. I wasn't sure what the protocol was. I stood with the door half-open, looking between Phillip and the two men outside.

One of the guards from earlier was talking to the biker who had club colors on his vest. After a moment, he nodded at me, and the two bikers who'd been there rode off. I didn't feel uncomfortable with them at the house, but having them around made it harder to avoid thinking about how much the Wolves were in my life.

When I thought about asking if it was okay to go out, I realized it was ridiculous. I didn't need to check with Echo *or* Zion. I wasn't a Wolf or someone's property. They hadn't even suggested that I needed to check in. I was just trying to figure out what was normal.

I walked to my room and called Ellen. When she picked up, I asked, "Do you want to catch a movie?"

"Only if you tell me you really had Bobbie tossed out of the bar last night."

"She threw a drink at me," I started to explain.

"Because Killer turned her down for you," Ellen added.

I closed my eyes. "How do you know that already?"

Ellen laughed. "Doll, these are my *people*, my home. Mama got a call, and a bunch of them were toasting your curvy badass self for standing up for 'sweet little Killer' like they forget who he is or what he's done." She paused before adding in a softer voice, "Don't you forget. He's not one of your uppity college boys."

"I know."

"Just . . . watch yourself," she said.

I sighed. "He spent the night. We had a break-in and—"

"Are you okay?" she interrupted.

"We are. Echo and Zion came over and—"

"Jesus, girl! I'm getting in the car. I'll be there in twenty. I want to hear everything."

As she spoke, I could hear a door slam on the other end of the line. "You're coming now? I'll check what's playing at the theater."

She scoffed. "Skip the movie. We'll talk."

Briefly, I considered going along with what she said, but I wanted to let it all go for a little bit. "We can talk after. I need to shut my brain off for a while. Movie first."

Once Ellen agreed, I pulled up the listings. The next showings were a low-budget horror film and some sort of comedy. I couldn't decide which was more likely to make me laugh, but either would distract me. I got ready, and by the time Ellen picked me up, I'd settled on letting her pick.

The comedy was exactly what I needed, and Ellen was great at letting her curiosity go unanswered up until we were walking out to the parking lot.

"Okay, spill."

I laughed. There was nothing else to do. Ellen was a force of nature when she turned her attention to a subject, and I'd already learned that true resistance was pointless.

"Zion is leaving the Wolves for . . . us, me, however you say it," I told her.

"Seriously?" Her eyebrows darted up, and her voice went squeaky. "Killer? *That* Zion? I mean there's no other Zion—"

"Yes."

She whistled. "Damn. No wonder Bobbie was pissed. You tamed—"

"No. I didn't. We hung out and—"

"Hey," she interrupted in a gentle but firm voice. "Not a criticism. Like I said, he was bound to fall hard when he fell. I just underestimated how hard."

"I'm scared," I whispered, finally admitting aloud what I'd been thinking all day. "What if he's making a mistake? What if I'm not worth it?"

Ellen hugged me. "Sweetie, the fact that you're even worried about that instead of what if *he* hurts *you* is proof that he's not making a mistake."

I started to fill Ellen in on everything I was willing to share about things with Zion while we drove the ten minutes to the diner she wanted to go to. I felt guilty about keeping details back, but I'd feel guilty about sharing them too.

We got out at the oddly named Mama's Grub and Grill, and before we made it to the front door, we were stopped by the roar of a Harley. I couldn't say I was shocked to see a bike—the town was full of Wolves—but I *was* surprised when I realized that it was Noah's. He swerved to a stop in front of us and cut off the engine.

"Are you okay?" he asked me in lieu of a greeting.

"Yeah. How did you find us?"

Noah ignored my question and said, "I heard about the break-in. Last thing you needed after that mess at the bar and"—he glanced at Ellen—"the other stuff."

"She and Killer sorted 'the other stuff' out," Ellen said as she crossed her arms. "And *you* best not be stirring up trouble."

Then, with a protective attitude that I was coming to realize was her default way of being with me, Ellen linked her arm in mine and started toward the front door. She didn't bother to stop at the hostess stand, instead continuing to a booth.

It didn't take Noah long to catch up to us. He slid in beside Ellen as the waitress came and handed us two menus.

"Sorry, I can bring another one," she said.

"Nah, I'll share." Noah scooted closer to Ellen. "Ellie doesn't mind, do you?"

Once the waitress turned away, Ellen glared at Noah. "Here." She slid the menu toward him. "I don't need it."

He leaned back and draped his arm over her shoulder. "Me either." He grinned at her. "Burger, fries, strawberry shake . . . and onion rings, unless you're free for a ride."

Ellen flipped him off, rolled her eyes, and said nothing.

"How did you know where we were?" I asked again. "Or did you?"

Noah turned away from Ellen. "Miss Bitty."

"My mama," Ellen interjected.

"Right." I frowned. "But we just decided to come here."

Noah laughed. "You were upset. That means Ellie would bring you here. Comfort food. It's how the South works."

By the time we had ordered, it was as if we'd actually all been friends for a while. The discomfort I'd felt with Noah over our brief flirtation seemed to be completely forgotten, and Ellen brought up the subject of discussing more personal questions at a later time with a stern "There will be spilling of secrets. Don't think this reprieve means I'm letting it go."

"Yes, ma'am," I snarked.

Noah laughed. "Someone else unwilling to face your wrath, Ellie. Smart move, Aubrey. Smart move."

Ellen flipped him off again, and Noah hauled her closer and tried to kiss her cheek. She shoved him away so hard she almost slid out of the booth.

Noah scowled. "What the fuck was *that*?"

"You're pretty, but . . ." Ellen shrugged.

"I'm pretty but what?" He sounded genuinely hurt, and I wondered how much baggage they had behind them.

Ellen shrugged again, took a sip of her soda, and said lightly, "Let it go, Noah."

"Ellie—"

"Drop it." Ellen elbowed him. She looked at me. "He's just jealous because I'm not interested."

Noah's snort was his only reply, but his body grew tense.

"Poor babe's been pining for me since we were . . . what?" She glanced at Noah. "Ten years old?"

"Only because everyone else was afraid of your temper," he teased right back, seeming to shake whatever mood her pulling away had caused. "Seriously, Aubrey, she was the scariest kid ever. Even *Killer* was afraid of her."

"Respect, not fear," Ellen corrected. She took another drink and looked back at him. "Unless you want to start a fight, Noah Eli Dash, you best be minding that tongue of yours. I'm still in possession of that temper."

He stared at her for a long moment before saying, "I haven't forgot anything, Ellie Belly."

As Ellen looked at him, I realized that he was the boy—the one she'd talked about. I felt wretched realizing that I'd taken her with me to the races where she'd watched the man she loved flirt with me.

"Ellen . . ."

Something in my tone must've been revealing because she kicked me under the table and said, "Shall we tell Dash the big news?"

"Not my news to tell," I said lightly, "but we could tell him about the movie . . ."

Ellen laughed, and launched into a recounting of the ridiculously bad spoof we'd watched.

They were a lot more at ease than they'd been at the races, so much so that I realized that while I had noticed that they'd both been tense that night, I hadn't guessed why.

The rest of our extra-late lunch—or maybe early dinner—went by without any stressful or awkward moments. They were my friends, and despite my only knowing them a short while, they were in some ways closer than the people I'd left behind in Oregon. With both of them, I felt natural, like I didn't have to be anyone but myself. It was a rare gift.

When I got out of Ellen's car a couple of hours later

and walked into my house, I felt more together than I had in a while. Without meaning to, I had put down a few roots in Williamsville. I still wasn't staying here long term, but I was a lot less opposed to being here for the time being.

Chapter 27

GRANDMA MAUREEN AND I WERE FOLDING SOME OF THE tower of laundry that I'd washed and dried earlier in the day when we heard the sound of footsteps. She put a hand on my wrist and nodded toward the laundry room door.

"Where are the Wolves?" I whispered after I pulled it shut.

"Sent them home," she said quietly. "Eddie's coming over tonight, and it was just an hour or two and I thought Zion was still with you, so he'd be here when you got back."

We exchanged a tense look.

"Eddie would've called out. It's not him," she said, looking around the tiny laundry room for a weapon. I did the same. There wasn't anything other than bleach.

The phone in the kitchen rang.

I pulled the bottle of bleach down and stepped in front of her just as the laundry room door was jerked open.

There were two men; both had their faces hidden by balaclavas. One wore a lime-green knit balaclava that left only his eyes exposed. If it weren't for the fact that he also had a snub-nosed pistol in his hand, he would have looked ridiculous. Masks on intruders weren't odd, but garish green ones seemed more suited to children on skis or snowboards than armed intruders.

"Red?"

We didn't have more than a moment to get nervous before I heard Zion's voice.

"Where are you?" he called. "Mrs. E.?"

The man with the gun motioned for her to reply, using his pistol like a pointer. The other man looked at me and lifted a finger to his lips.

"Now's not a great time," my grandmother called out in a remarkably calm voice.

Zion laughed. "Echo's on his way over, so I know you're decent."

When neither of us answered his cheeky remark, Zion went silent. I wasn't foolish enough to think he'd left. He wasn't the sort of man to leave without answers, and we'd had enough trouble that no matter how calm my grandmother sounded, he'd know something was wrong.

A minute later, Zion came around the corner.

"Dumbass," the man without the gun rasped. The other one said nothing.

Zion didn't stop. He walked forward until he was between us and the two men. "Get the fuck out. Now."

The armed man shook his head. Whoever he was, he must know Zion or he wouldn't keep silent. That was the only thing I could think: Zion would recognize his voice. I heard the telephone ring again. I wished I could get to it, but there was no way to do that without getting past the intruders.

I realized then that Zion was unarmed—because of me, because I'd *asked* him to be. If he'd had his gun, he'd have drawn it by now. I did that. I asked him to come unarmed. There were two intruders, one with a gun, and Zion was unarmed.

"Zion, just . . . they can take whatever they want," I said.

"Of course they can, lovie," my grandmother added.

The green-masked intruder lifted his gun again and waggled it.

"Shoot me or get out," Zion taunted.

"Zion," I said, but my grandmother grabbed my hand and tugged me backward. I wasn't resisting enough to injure her, but I wasn't going as quickly as she wanted.

She jerked on my hand. "Come on, lovie."

I didn't have a solution. What was I going to do? Open the bleach and throw it at the robber? Charge him and try to get to our kitchen knives? They weren't even sharp enough to do much damage if I could get at him. Zion was better equipped and more experienced with violence.

My grandmother pulled me back, and much like he had the day I was hassled at the bar, Zion didn't look my way at all. His attention was solely on the man in front of him.

"You can walk away right now, but if you stay"—Zion shook his head—"bad things come to those who mess with the Wolves' families. Unless you're from out of town, you have to know that. There is no one more important to us than these two."

The man lowered his gun slightly, not all the way, but like he was considering it—or maybe his arm was aching from holding it out. I didn't know. I wanted to believe the best.

Maybe everything could still be okay.

Maybe this could end without trouble.

Then I heard Beau's voice from the front hallway. "I called the sheriff, Maureen." The door slammed behind him. "Should be here any minute. Dumb as a post, that one. Told me to wait."

I stepped closer to my grandmother.

"Call Echo," Zion yelled out to Beau. "Back out the door and call him."

Beau laughed. "Who you think sent me to check on the ladies, boy?"

The armed man turned to look at Beau as he came around the corner.

Beau held a shotgun in his hands, not aimed, but held

there ready to lift. For a moment, I wanted him to raise it, to shoot the stranger under the grotesque green balaclava. For all my discomfort with weapons, right now I was wishing Beau would use his gun.

"Put that peashooter down." Beau shook his head at the intruders. Like Zion, he didn't seem to take them very seriously. I was starting to think I was the odd one because I *was* alarmed, but a glance at my grandmother proved that theory wrong. She looked tenser than I could recall ever seeing her.

"So you're the jackasses been causing all our late-night troubles. You best hope the sheriff gets here before Mr. Echo," Beau taunted.

"Shut your mouth," Grandma Maureen snapped.

But it was too late—the man with the gun lifted it and aimed it at Beau.

Zion grabbed the gunman and knocked him to the ground as the weapon fired.

At first, I thought everything was okay. Zion had disarmed the man. Sheriff Patterson was right behind Echo, who had run into the house looking like the sheriff was actually in pursuit of him.

Beau cackled and aimed his shotgun at the other man. "Let's see who you are under your hoods."

Then I saw blood.

Zion wasn't moving.

My grandmother was jerked into Echo's arms. "Zion?"

My knees felt unsteady. I let go of my grandmother's hand and took two steps forward.

He wasn't moving. Zion was still on the floor, and blood was puddling around him.

I wasn't sure if I'd kneeled on purpose or if my knees gave out. All I knew was that I was crawling across the floor to Zion. He didn't move, didn't answer me.

The sheriff said something. I had no idea what, though. I couldn't focus on anything but Zion.

The man under him, the one with the gun, squirmed out from beneath him.

"Quincy!" The deputy snatched the first man, the one who hadn't shot Zion.

Meanwhile, the sheriff grabbed the man who *had* shot Zion and shoved him toward another deputy who had apparently arrived at some point.

Echo squatted down and put his hand on Zion's throat, checking for a pulse. "He's alive."

He rolled Zion to his back. Blood had soaked his shirt. I couldn't even tell where the bullet had entered. It was all blood.

Echo ripped Zion's shirt off. The bullet had entered near Zion's left shoulder, near his collarbone.

My grandmother's voice broke through the roar in my head. "Lovie, help is coming."

Echo took one of my hands and put it on a shirt he'd shed and balled up against Zion's shredded skin. "Hold this. Tight."

Mutely, I did as I was told.

I was vaguely aware that the sheriff and his deputies had

escorted the shooter and Quincy out of the house. I noticed my grandmother walking away. It all felt like it was in a haze, though.

My grandmother came back and put a towel under Zion's head. The pale yellow cotton turned red.

"He's hurt," I said stupidly. "His head. There's something there too."

"He hit it," Echo said.

And I nodded. I wasn't sure what else to say or do. There was nothing in my life that had prepared me for kneeling in blood next to my boyfriend's father. The best I could say was "I'm sorry. This is because of us and—"

"He'll be fine," Echo interrupted.

I nodded again, trying not to sob or pass out, wishing this weren't real. I'm not sure how long we stayed like that; it felt like a minute and an hour all at once. But then the paramedics were there, and in what felt like mere moments, they were taking Zion out to an ambulance.

When I looked around, I realized that several other Wolves were there in my house now. Noah was one of them. I hadn't noticed any of them arriving.

"Dash will bring you to the hospital," Echo said.

A biker I didn't know handed Echo a shirt.

Echo jerked it on and looked at my grandmother. "I need to go with him."

She kissed Echo's cheek. "We'll meet you there."

Once the paramedics left with Zion, my grandmother

walked me to the bathroom and helped me wash the blood from my hands.

"What you need is a shower, but I know you want to follow him. This will get us through for the time being," she announced in the same no-nonsense tone she'd once used when I broke my wrist trying to do tricks on my bicycle.

Once the blood was gone, she ushered me to the bedroom. "Get changed while I deal with the sheriff. Then we'll go to the hospital."

By the time we got to the ER, it was a sea of black leather. That sea parted as Noah escorted us to Echo.

My grandmother met his eyes, and whatever she read there was enough for her own expression to relax a bit.

"He's in surgery," Echo told us.

"And?" I asked.

He shook his head. "You know what I know."

"Sit down, Eddie," my grandmother ordered gently. "You need to sit before you fall."

He did so. I stood silently at her side as my grandmother looked around the room, and in that moment, I could see that she was now the one in charge of this assorted group of worried bikers. "You, there. Come here."

A biker walked over to her. "Ma'am."

"Echo needs his jacket," she ordered. She reached into her bag and dug around until she found her keys. She held one out. "Take this off my ring and go to his house. It's too damn cold in here to not have his coat."

It wasn't that cold, but no one was fool enough to suggest that Eddie Echo's comfort wasn't important, especially to the face of the woman my grandmother had suddenly become.

"And you, Mike, isn't it?"

Mike stood and came to receive his orders.

"This"—she held out a grocery sack with Echo's vest—"needs to be cleaned. Albert's over on East Main does a fine job with blood. Go get it in before they're closed."

I sank into a seat and looked over at Echo. My grandmother stood in front of the empty seat between us and continued to survey the crowd. "Who hasn't had dinner?"

Several men raised their hands.

"Well, go on." She made a shooing gesture at them. "Bring something back for Echo too. And you, Alamo, the coffee here is—"

"Maureen," Echo interrupted.

She looked down at him and tilted her head.

"I'm okay," he said in a level voice. "Zion's going to be okay too."

My grandmother put her hands on her hips. "Well, I know that, but I figured I might as well get things sorted out while we wait." She lowered herself into the empty seat, and then she reached over and patted my hand. "Plus, we don't need to take up all the chairs."

" 'We'?" he repeated.

She shook her head. "The boy got shot protecting us. If I wasn't already his legal guardian if something happened to you, that would certainly *make* him my boy too." Her voice grew a little louder. "He's been all but my son, and if you're going to keep being too damn idiotic to own up to being his dad—"

"We talked earlier today."

She stopped, nodded her head once. "It's about time."

Echo took her hand into his. "Hush, woman. I'm going to hold you a minute." His voice grew so low that I only heard him because I was beside her. "I love you. If something had happened to you . . ."

"It didn't," she said just as quietly. Then she looked at me. "Zion made sure we were both safe. He's a good boy."

They talked, filling in gaps in what had happened and sipping the coffee one of the bikers brought us. Several covered plates of food were brought too, but all anyone did was pick at them. The waiting room was a rotating crowd of men and women in leather. They alternated between talking to us and keeping a respectful distance. The only one who stayed near us was Noah, who had arrived and positioned himself at Echo's side like a sentinel.

I didn't need to ask to know that there were bikers seated so they could watch the door and others positioned between us and the door for our safety.

We sat there for at least an hour before a surgeon came out. "Is one of you Edward Echo or Maureen Evans?"

"Yes," they answered in tandem.

Echo came to his feet and held a hand out to my grandmother. She took it and stood. I wasn't invited, but there was no way I was waiting here. I jumped up and went over to the surgeon with them.

"Your son will be fine, Mr. Echo," the surgeon said. "He'll be in recovery soon, and once he's settled in the room, he can have . . . more visitors. The nurses will go over all that, but the critical news is that he's going to be just fine."

"No permanent damage?"

"No," said the surgeon. "He's very lucky." The man paused and cleared his throat before saying, "It is, however, hospital policy that the police are called for any gunshot victims. There's nothing I can do about that, but if any of your"—he glanced at the crowd—"*family* members need to leave, now's the time."

"The police arrived when my son was shot," Echo said, not unkindly.

"He was shot protecting us from a home invasion," I snapped. "This was heroism, not a crime, you—"

"Thank you, Doctor," Echo interrupted. He pulled me into an unexpected hug. When he leaned back, he looked down at me. "Thank you for standing up for him."

Then he walked away and went to talk to the Wolves.

I watched him for a moment. Various bikers nodded at me, including both Noah and Alamo, but they were all around Echo. A few were still obviously guarding the door, but the mood had lightened considerably.

My grandmother reached out and took my hand. Her attention was still on Echo, though.

"It's going to be weird if I have to call him Grandpa and I'm dating his son," I teased her.

She *tsk*ed at me, but she couldn't stop the smile that followed. "A little less sass, lovie."

Then we settled in to wait until the surgery was finished and Zion was in a room where I would be able to see him.

Chapter 28

Z ION OPENED HIS EYES TO FIND ECHO, MRS. E., AND
Aubrey watching him. Aubrey sat beside his bed,
her hand on his. Mrs. E. sat in a chair a little farther
away, and Echo was looming over everyone like he was too
tense to sit. They were all safe. Whatever happened after
he got shot must've worked out okay because they were all
here and safe. Zion felt like his pulse slowed down signifi-
cantly at the sight of them.

"Everyone okay?"

Echo nodded.

"Beau?"

"He's fine," Mrs. E. said, coming to her feet and stepping closer to the bed. "I thought he was going to get him-

self arrested, but Eddie pointed out that a lawsuit would be messy. Sheriff Patterson shut up pretty quickly at that. He was more concerned about Quincy."

"Quincy?"

"How about you keep quiet, and we'll fill you in?" Aubrey said. Her fingers entwined with his. She squeezed his hand. "You need to rest and be calm. You were . . ." Her words faded, like saying the word was too much.

He looked at her. "Sorry about getting shot. I didn't have my gun, and I wasn't going to let any of you—"

Her sob cut him off, but she didn't say anything. No one else spoke either, and Zion wasn't sure what to say. "I didn't mean to," he added, trying again to make her feel better. "Beau was—"

"Shut up, son," Echo said. "Poor Aubrey's just finally stopped sniffling on me, and now you've got her crying again."

Mrs. Evans sighed and came to stand beside the bed. She put her hand on Zion's shoulder. "You did a brave thing. Aubrey's just been worried. So was your father." She glanced at Echo and scowled. "We're going to start you in some remedial parenting classes as soon as he's out of here, Edward."

Tears still slid down Aubrey's cheeks, but she flashed a smile at her grandmother and Echo. Whatever issues she'd had with Echo seemed to have vanished.

"'Edward'?" Zion repeated, happy to encourage whatever was making Aubrey smile.

Echo gave him a look that wasn't as intimidating as his

usual glares. "Stick with Echo or Dad, son. Only person that gets away with calling me *that* is Maureen."

Mrs. Evans stepped back from the bed and took Echo's hand in hers. "We're going for a walk, *Edward*. Leave the children to talk."

Then she tugged Echo from the room, and Zion was left alone with Aubrey.

"Are you okay?"

Aubrey looked at him and shook her head. "I was so scared. You were bleeding, and I . . . I . . . It was *awful*."

"I'm sorry." He wasn't entirely sure what he was apologizing for, scaring her or getting shot or probably both, but he *was* sorry that she was upset.

After a few minutes, she started to fill him in on the fact that the sheriff hadn't been involved in the break-ins after all, he was just covering because Quincy got mixed up with some unsavory characters at his job. "Quincy made a promise to the contractors, but then the senior citizens refused to be intimidated, so he hired some people to help him make people nervous . . . I guess he didn't know what else to do or have money to pay them off."

"So he shot me?"

"No." Aubrey squeezed his hand. "He paid a few guys to help intimidate people, stir up trouble, and it got out of hand. Quincy wasn't the one to shoot you."

"But it was him organizing everything?"

Aubrey shook her head. "Organizing? No. Setting into motion? Yes. He was an idiot, and he'll end up either doing time or, if he's lucky, with a suspended sentence. All he wanted was a way to make some easy money, and I guess he thought that making deals with shady contractors was safe or something. He explained over and over that he didn't mean for anyone to get hurt."

They sat there for a few minutes before Zion said, "I talked to . . . Dad. That's what I was coming to tell you. I'm going to enlist. I can still *see* the Wolves because, well, they're family, but I wouldn't *work* for them anymore."

"He said you finally asked him about being his son," Aubrey interjected.

"Right." Zion shifted, and then promptly winced as the movement pulled on the still-tender stitches. "So, what do you think . . . about me enlisting?"

Aubrey was crying again, but she was smiling too. "That's what he wouldn't tell me. He said you had a plan, and you would tell me yourself when you woke."

Zion waited. He wanted her to reach out again, to do *something* to clue him in. Instead, she asked, "Are you sure? About us and—"

"Yes."

She took a deep breath. "Well, I sort of promised your dad that if there were grandkids, we'd name one after him. He wanted two—Echo for a girl and Eddie for a boy—but I only agreed to one," she said.

For a moment, Zion was speechless. "We're having kids?"

Aubrey ducked her head for a moment. "No. I tried to tell him that we weren't planning any longer than this month, but he patted my knee and said, 'Echo is a beautiful name for a girl.'" She smiled. "He was really sweet. He apologized, and . . ."

"Careful there, Red. I might start thinking you've got a crush on the old man."

She laughed for a moment before taking Zion's hand in hers. "No, but I think I'm falling in love with his son."

He stared at her. "Say that again. I want to be sure I heard it right."

"I'm falling," she whispered. "Maybe I already fell. I just . . . when I saw you there . . . I can't imagine my life without you. I don't *want* to either."

Without thinking of the consequences, Zion reached up to pull her down for a kiss. He let out a grunt of pain, and the heart monitor started beeping. He ignored both and said, "Come here."

She leaned down, so he could kiss her.

When she pulled back, he said, "I love you."

Aubrey let out a sob, a happy one this time, and kissed him again.

They were still kissing when they heard "Well, that explains the alarm."

"Zion," Aubrey scolded as she pulled back again. Her face was bright red, and the nurse was shaking her head at them.

"She loves me," Zion said.

"Fabulous," the nurse replied in a tone that made it quite clear that she didn't care. "Perhaps she could love you after you've recovered."

"I will," Aubrey murmured.

"Great, then." The nurse came over to the bed. "Let's check your vitals, since you're awake and I'm here." She glanced at Aubrey and chastised, "You were supposed to tell us when he woke."

Zion cut in, "We figured my father had told you on the way out."

"Your father?"

"Eddie Echo," Aubrey clarified.

The nurse straightened. "Of course. I thought you were . . ."

"A Wolf?" Zion finished. "No, I'm just his son."

Aubrey squeezed his hand, and he looked at her. "I'm enlisting once I'm recovered. Marine."

The nurse gave him a kinder smile, but Zion's attention was all on Aubrey, who was looking at him proudly.

Chapter 29

I WAS AT ZION'S BEDSIDE SO OFTEN THE NEXT WEEK THAT I thought he was going to get tired of me. Instead, we spent a lot of time talking—and I was forced to admit that what we had was inevitable. The break-in sped things up, but that was it. We would've ended up together one way or another. Admittedly, it was easier now that he wasn't off doing jobs for Echo, but even if he had been, I knew I wouldn't have been able to walk away from him. Zion was it, the man for me, and we were at the start of a forever kind of love.

By the time he was due to be discharged, I was a little resentful that Echo was insisting Zion stay at his place. I didn't want to be apart from Zion, and I wasn't sure I was going to be able to cope with the separation. The nurses hadn't enforced visiting hours, so I'd pretty much lived at the hospital. I still left to go to classes and work, and I slept at home, but that was it. Every free hour was spent right at Zion's side, even to the point that I did my homework there.

And now Echo had dropped this bomb on me. It wasn't something I was going to accept gracefully.

"I can stay at his apartment and look after him," I argued. "Or maybe he can stay at the house with me. You're there every day to see my grandmother. You'd see him plenty."

Zion looked vaguely amused as I faced off with the older biker.

"No," Echo said.

"You're being unreasonable." I glared at him.

"I'm not going to have Maureen upset with me because you're shacking up with my son," he said, as if admitting to being cowed by a woman was not the least bit shameful.

I had to give him credit for that. They seemed to have a tentative peace between them, not officially a couple, but Echo was at my house often enough that seeing him walk in for breakfast most mornings was normal now. He didn't sleep there, but he was at the door bright and early.

"I'd be out of your way," I pointed out. "Maybe she'd let you stay over . . ."

Zion snorted.

Echo looked at Zion, who held up his hands. Then the older biker crossed his arms, looked back at me, and said,

"You're not in the way. If I agree to you staying with him, Maureen would be angry *and* she'd miss you. I'll give you a key to my place to come and go as you want, but Killer is staying with me. That's final."

Zion laughed and then let out a pained noise.

"What?" we both asked in tandem.

"I would've gotten shot earlier if I knew it would make both of you want me around so much," he teased.

Echo glared at him. "Idiot."

"It's genetic," I muttered.

When they both turned to look at me, I realized what I'd said and winced. I had just called the president of the Southern Wolves and his enforcer idiots.

"It's true." I straightened my shoulders. "You"—I pointed at Echo—"are afraid of my grandmother, and you"—I glared at Zion—"ever joke about getting shot again and I'll . . . I don't know what I'll do, but you *won't like it*."

Echo looked at Zion and said, "And that is why I'm *respectful* of Maureen." He glanced at me. "Not afraid, mind you, but well aware that she's not one to trifle with."

Then he leaned down and kissed the top of my head. "Maureen and I will be at my place getting things sorted out for Zion. You're on your own for dinner." He nodded at Zion. "We'll be here tomorrow to pick you up when they discharge you."

And then he was gone.

After he left, I went over and sat on the edge of Zion's bed. "I was looking forward to being alone with you."

At his wicked smile, I added, "Not for *that*. You're not up for that yet."

"Says who?"

"The doctor."

"What does she know?" Zion muttered.

I kissed him. More and more, I thought he complained just because it made me kiss him. It had become almost a joke between us over the past week.

"Come here." He held out an arm, and I snuggled up against him carefully. I didn't mean to, but I dozed off like that until the nurse came in to check on him.

It was late afternoon by then, but I didn't have work. At some point, I'd need to go to the hospital cafeteria for food, but for now, cuddling with Zion was too perfect to stop. We stayed that way for a while until he asked, "What are you going to do about school? I know you weren't ready to go back to Oregon, but . . ."

"I'm not going back to Oregon."

"Really?"

"Really. *You* aren't in Oregon."

He smiled and lapsed into silence again. He didn't push me on a lot of things, letting me have space to figure out my thoughts before talking. I realized that part of why I felt so at ease with him was because of that. He let me be *me*.

I started to tell him what I'd researched: "If you get stationed at Camp Lejeune, there's UNC-W about an hour away or North Carolina State about two hours away. If we lived midway, I could commute, or I could live in Raleigh and see you on weekends. It probably depends. I think you *have* to live in the barracks unless you're married."

"We could—"

"I'm not ready for that," I said firmly. "I *love* you, but going from I-don't-date to thinking about marriage is already pretty huge and terrifying for me."

"You're thinking about marriage?"

"I am, but . . . *thinking* about it, not ready to do more than that." I kissed him, feeling giddy that I could. He was alive, *and* he was mine. It was enough that I wanted to say *yes yes yes* to the idea of marriage, but I wanted to wait to be sure that we weren't going to move too fast and mess this up. He was changing his entire life, and mine had already been in flux when we'd met.

"Boot camp is about three months," Zion said after I stopped kissing him. "Once I'm all healed, I'll ship out, and then you can finish your semester here."

"I know," I said, feeling a little sheepish still. "I've done a lot of reading while you've napped."

"Yeah?"

"And I called my parents." I was proud of that, of standing up to them and letting them know that I was done letting their drama impact my life. It wasn't easy, but I wanted to get my degree. That meant being able to afford tuition, and *that* meant they couldn't claim me as a dependent on taxes this coming year. They shouldn't anyhow, since I wasn't their dependent. Grandma Maureen had already said she certainly wasn't going to. That should mean I could get financial aid for college. I'd already explained how that all worked to Zion, so he understood what it meant when I added, "I will be filing taxes independently this year."

"What if I'm not sent to Camp Lejeune?"

"Camp Pendleton has great options too. That and Miramar are in San Diego. There are plenty of school options. Plus, I'm over halfway done with my degree, so I can finish it wherever we're stationed."

"We?"

I blushed at my slip. That *was* how I'd been thinking of it, though. "I might not be ready to get married this week, but that doesn't mean that I'm not ever going to be ready," I admitted.

Zion pulled me closer. "Good."

I had thought I'd lost everything by having to move to Tennessee. I'd thought that following The Plan would make me happy. I'd been wrong. Happiness was letting myself feel, finding a way to trust my heart, and still looking to the future. I could get my degree, teach, or even go on to law school or grad school, but I'd be doing it with a man I loved at my side.

Coming to Williamsville hadn't been the end of my possibilities; it had been the beginning of a better future and an amazing right now. By losing everything, I'd found a home, friends, and Zion. And because of him, I was undaunted by the challenges still ahead of me.

Acknowledgments

A S ALWAYS, THERE IS A LIST OF GUILTY PARTIES TO BLAME/ to whom I owe gratitude. In no particular order, I want to thank the following:

My longtime crit partner, Jeaniene Frost, for years of saying "When are you going to finish one of those romance novels you started?" and for guessing that the first one I pubbed as Ronnie was mine *even with a pseudonym on it*.

My mother, who stood in my kitchen and recommended my indie-published book to me, upon which the following was said:

Me: Does the author's name seem familiar?

Her: Well, it's *my* last name, but Douglas is a
common . . . Hey! Wait a minute.

Me: What was my confirmation name, Mum?

Her: You wrote a romance and didn't tell me?
Finally! When will there be more?

Acknowledgments

My father, who instilled a love of motorcycles, classic cars, and good whiskey in me—and taught me that hardworking, motorcycle-riding, truck-driving, gun-toting, whiskey-drinking, rock-listening, blue-collar workingmen are often the best sort.

My agent, Merrilee Heifetz, for never being put off by my random moments, including the ones that led to writing and self-pubbing the Unfiltered series with a bunch of friends.

The friends (collectively called "Payge Galvin") who plotted, wrote, published, and promoted twelve short novels with me under pseudonyms in 2014. In particular, C. J. Omolulu (a.k.a. Cynthia, a.k.a. Lynn Jaymes), Jeanette Battista (a.k.a. Jane Lukas), Rachel Vincent (a.k.a. Katy West), and Jenna Black (a.k.a. Abby Lombard), who also "came out" as part of Payge . . . I adore you *and* the other parts of Payge (who are *not* coming out, but are still in the shadows with support and drinks). It was not only fun to write together, but it was awesome to have our Secret Identity.

The men on whose Harleys I've ridden, in whose arms I've danced, and for whom there aren't words enough to describe both the fun and the trouble. It was a truth then and is now that no one knows passion like rabble-rousers.

Excerpt from
UNRULY

By Ronnie Douglas

Chapter 1

ALAMO STOOD IN THE MIDDLE OF A SEA OF BOXES THAT filled his new house. He was no stranger to moving. Growing up, he'd been rousted from his bed more times than he could count to move to a new place in the middle of the night. His mother would let the back rent build up as far as she could, and then they'd skip out. Mix in a few turns in foster care over the years when she was arrested, and he'd become something of a pro at quick moves—and a light sleeper. This wasn't a quick move, though. It was everything he owned and most everything his sister owned, and he had absolutely no desire to put it to rights.

Truth be told, this new house was the nicest place he'd ever lived. It wasn't *home,* though. Home was a modest-size apartment in Durham, North Carolina. Home was having his sister, Zoe, in the house, badly imitating his Spanish cusswords and singing like a cat in a surly mood—and he missed it.

If not for some jerk hurting Zoe's best friend, Alamo

would still have his sister in his home. He'd lost that right when he'd lost his temper. He knew it, but that didn't make it any less frustrating. He'd done the right thing, and there wasn't a minute of it that he regretted. The man deserved every punch, but that was neither here nor there. Truth didn't change facts, and the facts were that Alamo was a big man, and his long-gone father wasn't as white as his mama had been. Race shouldn't matter, but sometimes, having darker skin still did, especially in a city where drug traffic was as common as it was in Durham. The police tended to blame it on one segment of the population: those with darker skin. To them, it didn't matter whether he was Latino or black. To add to that, once the police saw the motorcycle club patches on his jacket, Alamo had far too much of a likelihood of ending up in jail because he'd put that *pendejo* in the hospital—despite the fact that the white boy in his expensive clothes and fussy car had hurt a defenseless girl. Men like him could afford the sort of lawyers who twisted the truth until it looked nothing like reality. Alamo knew it, had known it before he'd taken the first swing. Sometimes, though, a man had to stand up for a woman regardless of the cost. Zoe's friend had no one else to stand up for her, so Alamo did what needed doing. It was that simple.

"You can't just do that!" Zoe snapped at him when he'd *walked into the little apartment they shared. "I might not be a kid, but I still don't need my brother in the lockup."*

"He hurt Ana."

"You are not the law, Alejandro. You wear that jacket"—

she pointed at the vest with the Southern Wolves patches prominently displayed—"and you forget that you're not above the law."

"Lobita," he started.

"Don't you 'little wolf' me, mister!" His sister's hands landed on their customary position on her hips. She was a tiny little thing, but she had the attitude of a dozen girls. "If you end up in jail, I'll . . . I'll find someone big enough to kick your ass. Then where will you be, eh?"

Alamo bowed his head, as much to hide his smile as to let her know he was listening to her chastisement.

"You call Nicky, you hear me? You find out where you can move because you're not staying here. That boy . . . he has friends. I don't want this to get worse."

"Lobita . . ."

"No! You call your Wolves, and you move. We talked about it for next year anyhow. Clean start." Zoe took a shaky breath, let it out, and looked at him. "Ana says thank you and that she's okay. She's . . . sorry."

"Don't need to be sorry. She did nothing wrong, Zoe. You make sure she gets that." His hands fisted despite his intention to keep calm, and the already bloodied knuckles smarted.

Alamo might not have had a father most of his life, but he knew what a man was supposed to be like just the same. Growing up, he'd just studied what his mother's long list of lovers did. Whatever they did, he did the opposite. That was all the guidance he'd needed. That *was* why Alamo went *after the buttoned-up man-boy who'd gotten Ana drunk and taken what wasn't his right to take.*

"Call Nicky," *Zoe said, and then she turned away.* "And put ointment on those cuts."

She was right. Being the stand-in parent with Zoe had always been hard because she was right more often than not. Her excesses of common sense made her awfully hard to handle. Of course, it also meant that she was less worrisome to leave behind with Ana. She'd be okay; he knew that. Both of the Díaz siblings were survivors.

So far there hadn't been any charges filed, and the jackass who hurt Ana claimed never to have seen Alamo's face. He *did* see Alamo's jacket, though, and it was best for everyone if there was no reason for the police to be looking too close at the Wolves. The local chapter president, Nicky, agreed with Zoe, so he'd made a call to another chapter. Within forty-eight hours, Alamo's things had been packed, and he was in Tennessee. With his life in a pile of boxes. Between a move and a stay in jail, moving was a better choice—but that still didn't mean Alamo was happy with it.

He looked around the cluttered house. Boxes and furniture sat in a jumble, but he needed to get out. Being here, being alone with his thoughts, wasn't going to do anything but make him think about the mess he'd gotten mixed up in. He didn't regret it. He didn't think he was wrong to defend Ana. That didn't mean the consequences were easy to take.

He walked outside, pulled the door shut behind him, and

headed to the bar that the Tennessee chapter frequented. Getting to know his new brothers was the best thing he could do now. The Southern Wolves were the only family he had other than Zoe, and while Zoe would visit, she was still in North Carolina while she finished up her college degree.

By the time he'd pulled his Harley into the parking lot of Wolves & Whiskey, he felt more like himself. All he needed was to stay focused. No distractions. No trouble. No fights unless they were ordered by the club. All he had to do was focus on his job and the Wolves, and not let himself get invested in anyone else's life. He could keep his distance from everyone. That was the one surefire way to keep his temper under control.

No more bad habits. No more mistakes—regardless of how good the reason for them was. Tennessee was going to be the beginning of a new lifestyle, one that would keep him out of trouble and enable him to build a stable home for his sister.

"Ellie?"

Noah reached out, fingers catching a lock of hair and tugging like we were the kids we hadn't been in years. Noah was turning twenty-four this year, old enough to have more of a plan for his life, old enough to stop running from anything that had even the shadow of commitment to it.

Somehow, I was the one who had it more together. I was

only two years younger than him, but sometimes I felt older. He was a mistake I kept making and had been making since not long after I was old enough to get a driver's license. Noah helped me learn, and we celebrated with what had turned into a decidedly unhealthy relationship. I wasn't ever going to get my life together if I didn't figure out how to change my bad habits, and Noah Dash was a bad habit. We were never going to be anything but friends who were naked together sometimes.

He was propped up on one arm in his bed, looking like we'd been doing exactly what we had been.

"Do you want a ride to the bar tonight?"

"I thought you didn't want me on your bike where we might be seen," I replied, my voice sounding a little more upset than I wanted to admit. He'd given me a lift to his apartment, but that wasn't quite the same.

"What's between us is between *us*," he said, as if that answer was going to sound less irritating with repetition. It didn't.

I rolled onto my side so I was facing him. "I'm going to drive myself."

"Come on, Ellie, don't be like that."

"Leave it alone." I folded my arms, feeling silly as I did so. It was hard to look stern while we were both naked.

"You know people would misunderstand if you were on my bike regularly." Noah's fingers trailed up my thigh. "Showing up at Wolves is like a statement."

"Well, we wouldn't want them to *misunderstand*."

"There's no one else on the bike." Noah sat up and eased closer. "You know that, don't you? I might go on a date or whatever, but that's not anything. I just like a little strange, you know?"

"I know, Noah." I'd known that he wasn't particularly *celibate* before we were together, and that hadn't ever changed. It was his way of making quite clear that he wasn't in a relationship. He got his "strange"—sex with other women—and we agreed not to discuss it. I went on dates too, but rarely did those dates even make it as far as a kiss. I let Noah believe otherwise, but that didn't make it true. The only rule I'd insisted on was no dating each other's friends . . . and Noah quickly agreed to it after I'd gone out with his cousin.

I wasn't sure whether I was more embarrassed that I'd wasted years in and out of Noah's bed or that I'd resorted to manipulation to try to get him to see that we *were* having a relationship. Either way, the truth of the matter was that Noah Dash wasn't going to change—and neither was I. I didn't want forever, but I was over being someone's secret. He wouldn't carry me on his Harley more than once in a while because people might think I mattered. God forbid, they might even think I was his old lady. The truth was that I was his best friend and had been his regular bedmate since we were old enough to start exploring. That was it, though.

I used to think it was enough.

I used to think it would change, that he would change.

I even used to think *I* might change.

"Do you think you'll ever let people know about us?" I asked, even now hoping that he'd tell me I was wrong, even now hoping that there was an answer he could offer that would let us keep this messed up thing that we had. Neither one of us had ever tried dating anyone else. We'd settled for this, and it was no good. Not for me. Not for him.

"What if people *did* know?" I asked, pushing a little harder for the answer I hoped to hear.

Instead, he looked like I'd just told him I loved him. Sheer terror was written on his face. "Ellie . . . come on. People know we're friends. All they don't know is that we do *this*." He gestured between us at the bed. "Why would we need to tell anyone our business?"

That's all this was to him: friends who sometimes had sex. That was the bald truth. We were friends, so we talked, and if we were in a bad way about anything, we knew that we could call at any hour of the day or night. And if we had a need for something other than talk, we had that too. It looked a lot like a relationship, and maybe it was. It wasn't one that worked for me, though. I wasn't ready for a husband or kids or any of that forever stuff, but I was ready to *matter.* I was ready to not be a dirty secret.

And I was ready for someone who *knew* why I was in a lousy mood this week, who cared enough to remember what week it was, who understood why I needed reassurance. I didn't want to have to tell Noah to be kind to me because I needed a little extra *this week*.

Noah wouldn't change, and I couldn't. What we had

wasn't enough. I was done with that, with *him*, with being the girl who didn't deserve more.

I started to climb out of bed to grab my clothes.

"Where are *you* going?" Noah tugged me back onto the bed and rolled me under him. "I just got you here, El."

"You got me here six years ago, Noah."

"I did, didn't I?" He grinned down at me. "Beautiful Miss Ellen, all naked and in my sheets . . . so why can't I take you to the bar tonight? It's been a while. No one would think anything."

"Just let it go. Please?" I asked, hating that he thought that my worry was being found out. I'd all but asked him to be open about us, and he still couldn't hear what I was telling him.

"I'll take you home later if you still want to get your car." He was curled behind me, holding me to him as he only ever did when he was too exhausted to remember that friends don't cuddle. He kissed my shoulder and murmured, "I hate when we fight, Ellie. Just think about it."

And then he slept . . . and I slid out of his bed for the last time. I felt like a thief as I tiptoed over to gather my clothes, shoes, and books, but better a thief than a fool. Maybe there wasn't anyone out there who would be happy to be with me. Maybe I was an idiot for caring that Noah didn't want more. I didn't mean to care, but I had enough of my heart in the mix that I couldn't stay with what we were doing, not if I wanted to respect myself at all. The next time I let a man into my bed, he sure as hell wasn't getting into my heart.

Keeping sex and love in separate rooms was a safer plan. Regardless of which it was, though, I wouldn't be hidden away.

"Never again," I promised myself as I went downstairs.

At the bottom of the steps, I pulled the building door closed behind me. Not for the first time, I was left stranded because of Noah Dash.

I could call my mother—who was more of a roommate than a parent—but I didn't know if I was in the mood for her counseling me on patience. For reasons I wouldn't even try to fathom, she thought Noah could do no wrong. That left me with calling my friends who didn't know about Noah, calling Noah's cousin Killer, or calling the bar.

I called the bar.

"What's up, Little Bit?" Mike asked.

"I need a ride. No questions, and no one who'd tell tales about . . . anything." I walked farther from the building where Noah lived. I felt like a vagabond holding my boots, bag, and helmet, but I was afraid I'd wake Noah if I tried to put my boots on inside.

Mike sighed. "I can call a taxicab. Depending on who's working, they might not tell Miss Bitty."

"Ugh." I sat on the curb and shoved my feet into my boots. "Mama's got everyone in her damn pocket. I swear she'd put a tracking chip in my ass if the veterinarian would do it."

Mike snorted. "Don't go giving her ideas."

It was one of the mysteries of my life. My mother never put any restrictions on me, but she kept awfully close tabs on my comings and goings. There was no way that the local drivers wouldn't tell her where I was.

"I can send the new guy to fetch you," Mike said. "He just walked in. Seems a good sort. Wouldn't tell . . . either of the young'uns."

"That works."

Mike paused and cleared his throat before asking, "Do I need to guess where you are or do I just assume you're *with* one of the young'uns?"

"Got it in one." That was the thing. People *did* know, maybe not everything, but enough for me to be embarrassed by the fact that Noah treated me like I was a secret.

"Do I need to send a helmet?"

"I have mine," I said, glancing at it, trying not to think of going shopping for it with Noah and Killer. "I just need a ride . . . and if you can avoid mentioning it to Echo or Uncle Karl."

Mike's tone shifted. "You know better than that, Ellen."

I nodded even though he couldn't see me. Everything to do with Noah or Killer was reported to the Wolves' president *and* to the biker who'd raised both boys. It was simply the way of it. Hell, I'd been the one reporting things in over the years. Everyone did it. Echo cared about every little detail of their lives. Nothing was considered too insignificant to mention. Killer had coped by devoting himself to Echo, becoming Echo's right hand. Noah had done the opposite—refusing to even be patched in to the Wolves.

"What's the new guy's name?" I asked.

"Alamo."

"Okay." It was a little bit of a silly question. I'd know him when he arrived because he'd be wearing club colors, their insignia clearly marked on either a black leather vest or black leather jacket. Plus, there weren't any Wolves I didn't know *other* than the new guy, so a biker who arrived with club colors was obviously my ride. That said, I wasn't going to be rude and not know his name.

I disconnected and sat on the curb. I wondered if anyone else realized that this week was the anniversary of my father's death. Noah certainly hadn't, and that told me more than anything else. A man who wasn't there for me wasn't what I needed. A woman didn't *need* a man at all. Mama had been telling me that since my father died . . . but sometimes I wanted one, not just in my sheets but in my life. I wanted someone who cared about me, who remembered to hold me, who treated me like I was special. Instead, I was waiting for a stranger.

Chapter 2

TEARS WERE STARTING TO STREAK DOWN MY CHEEKS when I heard the gorgeous growl of a Harley headed my way. There weren't a lot of Harleys in Williamsville that weren't ridden by Southern Wolves. It was almost an unwritten law that if you were going to ride for pleasure but *not* be a Wolf, you rode something else. It was odd to me, but folks seemed to think it was a sign of respect to the club.

Regardless of what I thought of the town logic, the result was that I knew that the sound of a Harley likely meant that I'd know the rider. Noah didn't like drop-by visitors either. It was just another way to keep me hidden. Well, it *had* been. No more. I wasn't anyone's dirty secret as of the past hour.

"No one respects a woman who doesn't respect herself," I whispered.

Then I stood, wiped the tears from my face, and watched the arrival of my ride home. So far, Alamo had my respect.

Loud pipes were always something I could appreciate. Good pipes meant I could hear him well before I saw him. People who didn't ride thought pipes like that were about arrogance or intimidation, but after you'd seen a biker laid up in the hospital because someone had plowed into him claiming, "I didn't see him!" you realized exactly why a Harley roared.

No one was going to miss Alamo. I was fairly sure that his pipes were only just this side of legal. As he cruised up the alley, I took a breath. I wasn't looking for anyone to distract me from what I'd just lost, but if I were, I'd be glad my gaze fell on the man who'd just ridden up to me on a cherry-red Wide Glide. Alamo was tall; I'd guess he was over six foot. He had on a black leather vest that revealed broad shoulders and muscles that made him look like he should've been on a football field.

"Ellen?" he asked as he stopped beside me. Even with that one word, I heard a pleasant drawl. He'd obviously *not* moved to Tennessee from up north or out west. He was a Southern man.

I nodded, feeling oddly self-conscious. I'd heard that the new guy was from another chapter, but that was all. I hadn't seen him, and no one had described him to me. I didn't expect Mike to tell me that Alamo had almond eyes I could get lost in. Mike was as rough and blunt as most of the club.

"Climb on, darlin'. Bartender says I'm to carry you wherever you want to be."

"Is that so?" I asked. "What if I want to go over to Wilmington and see the ocean?"

Alamo looked at me and grinned before replying, "Well, then, I'd hope you're going to want to stop for a meal along the way because that's . . . what? Nine or ten hours easy?"

I laughed, pleasantly surprised by Alamo's relaxed attitude. Bikers, as a rule, were either wired too tight or mellow. Of course, I'd seen even the calmest of them turn from chilled to ready to throw down in a blink, so I wasn't so naive as to think that what I was seeing was the all of it. A man as tall and built as Alamo had undoubtedly needed to have fighting skills because wannabe badasses would've tried him.

"So the beach is a little too far," I said.

"It is."

"Any other restrictions?" I prompted.

Alamo shook his head. "Barman said you were in need of a ride, no questions and no trouble."

"Mike's good people," I said. "The Wolves don't put up with folks who aren't, though." Despite everything, I looked back in the direction of Noah's apartment. Noah *was* a good guy, just not good for me.

Alamo looked at my tear-wet face and added softly, "Let's say we get going?"

I nodded and took a step toward Alamo. This was it, the start of a life without Noah. For years, he'd been tangled up in my life, and I'd been waiting for magic to happen. Sometimes you just gotta cut bait and go. The magic I wanted wasn't going to happen for me—*or for Noah*—if neither of us was willing to move on.

"Do you have anywhere you need to be?" I asked impulsively.

"There's a mountain of boxes over at my house that needs unpacking, but . . ." He shrugged. "They'll still be there later."

"Have you ever been to Memphis?"

"Not yet."

"I'll treat if you want to go," I offered. "I could go for a little music."

I knew that music wouldn't fix everything that ailed me, but it would go a long ways toward making me feel better. My father had played, so I grew up with music until he'd passed. It used to be a joke that the best way to tweak my mood was with music, but no one tried it anymore—not since Daddy died and I stopped singing. Today, though, I wanted to sing. I wasn't going to make a habit of it, but I could break my silence for a little while.

"I'm in," Alamo said.

"Perfect." I put on my helmet and climbed onto the bike behind Alamo, careful to keep some distance between us. He might be easy on the eyes, but this wasn't a date or an invitation for anything other than a meal. I didn't want either of us to get the wrong idea. He wasn't acting like he had, but the reputation bikers had for casual sex wasn't all lies and exaggerations. Most of them had no trouble getting regular loving, and only a few of them turned down a little strange if it was offered up. I wasn't offering.

"You good?" Alamo asked as I settled my feet on the pegs.

"I will be," I said, surprised that I wasn't lying.

He started the engine, filling the quiet street with the sound of his Harley. Briefly, I wondered if it would wake Noah. On the one hand, he hadn't come down when Alamo pulled up. On the other, the initial silence-shattering growl of the bike starting was a lot more noticeable than the sound of one passing by or stopping.

"Go," I urged, a little more forcefully than I might typically have done. I didn't want trouble, though, and seeing me ride away with a stranger wouldn't go over well with Noah. In a few days, he'd realize that we were done, but right now, it would be awkward if he came outside.

Alamo eased us into the street and headed out of town, and I let my mind go silent. All that mattered was the feel of the road. Every curve and dip resonated through the machine, and the rush of the wind—even at lower speeds—was tantalizing. There was no metal frame, no cage between us and the world. There was no radio to distract us. It was air and nature. It was speed and elegance. Alamo handled his bike like it was an extension of his body. There was no doubt in his management of the road. There was no hesitation in choosing the right speed for each twist or turn.

I gave him directions when needed, and an hour or so later, we were tooling down the streets of Memphis.

"Where to?" Alamo asked.

I directed him to B.B. King's Blues Club; it was a great

spot for everything I needed just then: blues, food, and a great atmosphere.

By the time we had placed our order, Alamo got a call. He frowned and said, "I need to grab this."

I nodded, but he was already gone. I wasn't particularly displeased by the timing. I'd never been much for small talk.

I sipped my drink and watched a couple of women dance. The beauty of blues bars was that there wasn't some sort of computer-made music. Here it was the traditional stuff—guitar, drums, bass, and voice. It was the sort of music that I still sang in the privacy of my house. Whether it was blues, rock, or country, the classics worked for me.

"Come on," a woman said as she shimmied past my table to the tiny dance floor. The band wasn't even on the schedule, and I wondered if they were just musicians passing through who felt like jamming for a few songs. They were all in the senior citizen range, which made me like them even more. They were still jamming at their age and obviously loving it.

"If you're going to dance in your seat, you ought to be willing to dance with us," the woman said with a wide smile.

I glanced in the direction Alamo had gone. He was nowhere in sight, and even if he was, I didn't owe him—and if he thought I looked the fool out on the floor, I didn't much care. I was sick of thinking about what other people thought. "What the hell."

"That's right," the woman said, and wriggled up to another three women who seemed to know her.

Two songs later, I was singing out loud as well as dancing. I hadn't realized that the singer had hopped down and was approaching me until he leaned in and, consequently, put the mic near enough to pick up my voice. I startled and stepped back.

He shrugged and finished the song from out there on the floor with us. He looked at me and frowned, and I met his gaze. I'm not sure which of us recognized the other first, but it was him that said, "Little Ellie, all grown up. Well, look at you."

"Mr. Lavon," I said with a smile. "Still looking spry and sounding damn fine."

The band was playing since we'd been chatting, and he looked up at them and said, "This here's Roger's little girl, Miss Ellie."

The drummer nodded at me. The other men might've too, but then Lavon asked, "Just sing us one song, Little Bit. Been a long time since I heard you sing."

I wanted to. I might've even needed to. That didn't mean it was easy. I'd not sung in public in years. People had finally stopped asking me to do so.

"I was sorry to hear about Roger," Lavon said quietly when I didn't reply. "I hope you and your mama been doing well."

The last words were lifted in that way that told a listener they could be a statement or a question. It was a courtesy I always appreciated, a Southern tendency to ask without outright asking. Today, I wasn't willing to dwell much on anything that could bring me down, and thinking about my father always did.

"We've been good," I said, being as truthful as anything I said could be when reducing a decade to only a couple words.

He nodded. "Good to hear . . . I've been down in New Orleans these last years. Moved away right before your daddy passed. I'd've been at the service elsewise. I didn't hear he was gone until a whole lot later."

I nodded. We didn't know each other in a talking way, and I suspected we were both near out of words already. "One song wouldn't be bad," I said softly.

"I could stand for hearing some Nina Simone. I remember you singing her with your daddy when you were just a wee little thing."

Briefly, I glanced around the bar. I didn't see anyone here who'd hear me and let the folks back in Williamsville know, and it wasn't like singing was off the table when I'd asked to come here.

"Anyone here play piano?"

"Charlie," Lavon called into the mic, "get yourself up on the stage for Miss Ellie." Then he looked at me expectantly and extended the microphone to me.

I took it, but I didn't climb up on the stage. Here, standing on the floor with a man I'd only ever met when I was with my father, I felt like I could sing. Here, where none of my family of Wolves would hear me, I could let myself get carried away by the music.

So I did.

I closed my eyes and sang the opening lines of "Feeling Good." After I'd finished the first verse, the band came in with me right where they should.

The waitress who had taken my order when I'd been seated leaned in and said something to Lavon. He nodded at her, and she walked away. I was curious, but I figured if it was any of my concern, I'd find out sooner or later. For now, I threw myself a little further into singing.

Even though I hadn't been feeling good when I'd arrived in the bar, I was starting to now that I was singing. Music healed. That was sheer truth.

I was *choosing* to feel good. I was choosing freedom. After today, I was free of the way Noah had made me feel, free of the humiliation of hiding our relationship, and this was the start of a new life. I was going to change things, and no man was ever going to make me feel like I was something to be ashamed of.

Never again.

I channeled all my feelings into the lyrics, and it felt like a weight was lifting from me. This was what music did. It was why I needed to sing, why I still did so when no one was listening.

Today, though, they *were* listening.

Lavon motioned to the stage, but I shook my head.

He pulled up a chair and nodded along with the song, as if it wasn't weird to sing from where we were.

When the song ended, he stood, and I handed him the microphone.

The band started playing "Baby, Please Don't Go." Lavon sang the first few lines to me, and I had to laugh. I danced with him as he sang to me. There was no way around it. He didn't go back onstage, and I didn't go back to my seat. He held the microphone out toward me several times so I could join him. I didn't sing much of the song, but I joined in enough that I was pretty sure we both knew I wasn't done singing just yet.

I danced and sang with a man old enough to be my grandfather, and as it almost always had, music erased any trace of stress for me. My upset over Noah wasn't completely gone, nor was the feeling of loss, but it was easier with every verse. I wasn't weak. I wasn't foolish. I was going to be just fine.

By the time Alamo returned to the table, I was singing the Stones' "Honky Tonk Woman" as a duet with Lavon.

I saw Alamo join the rest of the room in clapping their hands in time. Then he shook his head in wonder and sat down. It felt good to have him look at me, not that I was planning to do anything about it. I couldn't help preening just a little at being watched appreciatively, though.

I held up my hand in a "what can you do?" gesture and then leaned in to whisper to Lavon, "Just one more song."

He nodded, and when we finished "Honky Tonk Woman," he told the band, "Stones, 'Satisfaction.'"

We segued into the song, and he pointed at the stage.

Giving in, I gestured for him to precede me. He did so, and then he extended a hand down to me like any proper Southern man should.

With a nod, I took it and rejoined him to continue singing with him. We continued as we had been, taking turns with the lyrics as the mood struck us. There was something pure about singing like this: no grandstanding, no competition. It was about the joy and the music. Mama never understood why I couldn't sing for money. I knew I *could* do it. We both did. Maybe someday I'd think about it more seriously. So far, though, that wasn't what I wanted. I wanted this. I wanted to feel transported.

I let go of everything but the music.

By the end of the song, I'd all but forgotten the people watching us. Then they started applauding, and I glanced at them.

"Let's hear it for Miss Ellie," Lavon said. He grinned and bowed to me.

"And thank you, sir." I curtsied to him. Then I looked at the rest of the band and curtsied again. When I turned back to face the crowd, I waved and then made a sweeping gesture at the whole band and started to applaud. The listeners joined in. While they were doing so, I hopped down off the stage and walked over to my table.

I hadn't been seated but a couple moments when the waitress brought our food over and told us that the bar had comped our meal on account of my singing at Lavon's request.

I looked up at Lavon, and he tipped his hat at me.

I blew him a kiss and mouthed, "Thank you."

"You always sing for your supper?" Alamo asked lightly.

"Been a long time, actually," I admitted. "I needed to sing tonight, though. I won't ask you to keep a secret, but I *will* tell you nobody would believe you if you told them I did it."

"Why's that?"

I shrugged and set to eating my meal. I didn't know him, and I was already far more at ease with him than made sense. He wasn't making a big deal of it. He eyed me curiously, but that was it.

We ate our lunch without a lot of talk. That was something most people couldn't seem to do. I liked talking, but there were times that the only sound I wanted was music. When the band was decent, I saw no need to take away from it with a lot of words. Lavon's band wasn't going to break any new ground, but they were solid bluesmen.

When they took their break, Lavon stopped by the table, kissed my cheek, and told me, "You give us a shout you want to be up onstage where you ought to be, Miss Ellie. I suspect your daddy's old boss man would like you to do so too. Mr. Echo always did like your voice."

I promised I would, and he left us.

Alamo looked at me. "I feel like I'm missing enough things that I need to ask: Do I need to expect trouble from bringing you here?"

A wave of guilt washed over me. He was new in town, and here I was telling him secrets and dragging him halfway across the state. There wasn't any reason to think trouble would be coming from it, though, so I shook my head. "I used to sing all the time, but when my father died—ten years ago now—I stopped. Today, I ended things with the guy I've been . . ." I shook my head. I couldn't say dating and I wasn't going to say a vulgar word for what we'd been doing. Even if that's all it was to Noah, it had been more to me. "I realized I wasn't in love, and he's never pretended he was. We're friends who made a mistake, and now I'm done."

"A Wolf?" Alamo asked. "The guy was a Wolf?"

There wasn't a good answer to that either. Noah was the son of the late club president, Eli Dash, and while Noah might not be flying club colors, he was still an unofficial club member as a result of his father. "More or less."

"Prospect?"

"No," I said carefully. There was no real way around it, so I clarified. "Dash's dad was the president before Echo. Dash is . . . commitment shy."

Alamo nodded, and I could see by the way he looked at me that he understood the words I hadn't expressed as well as those I had. All he said, though, was "So you and Dash split up, and—"

"We weren't ever together," I corrected. "I was his dirty secret. I'm done with that."

"Right." Alamo looked past me, frowning now. "And Echo likes your singing, but you don't sing."

"Echo knows I'll sing if he tells me to. My father was one of Echo's friends. A Wolf for life."

"So let me see if I have this, darlin'. You're the daughter of a Wolf, regarded enough that Echo still cares about you—"

"Echo cares about *all* the Wolves' families," I interjected. "Echo's . . . there's nobody better for the club or club families."

Alamo nodded. "I heard plenty good about him. Not disparaging him. I wouldn't be here if I hadn't heard the right things." He caught my gaze before adding, "I'm just trying to see what I've walked into here."

I realized that he thought there was going to be fallout. There was no way to avoid saying the things I'd really rather not. I owed him the courtesy of a blunt answer, so he knew he wasn't going to have problems with the Wolves.

"Alamo?" I started. Once he met my gaze, I explained. "Dash doesn't care. All we ever were was friends who ended up naked sometimes. The only one who will admit he knows about us is his cousin Killer. As to the rest . . . Mike sent you to pick me up, and all we did was have lunch. I'm not anyone's old lady. There's no stepping out going on here."

He nodded, but I wasn't sure he completely believed me.

"No one will be angry that I sang," I added. "They might not believe it, but that's all. Echo knows that I sing at home still. My mama . . . well, let's just say that she's pretty sure the Good Lord himself made Echo personally and on a particularly good day. If Echo told her he was able to call God up on his cell phone, Mama would ask him to pass along a few notes. She probably reports exactly what I sing and how often—and how much she'd love it if he'd maybe tell me to do it more."

Alamo laughed. "Your mother sounds interesting."

This time I was the one laughing. "Oh, you'll meet her. Miss Bitty is like the local newsline when it comes to anything having to do with the Wolves. She'll be coming 'round to get the scoop on you."

We dropped into silence again for a few moments before Alamo said, "You don't owe me an explanation, but thanks all the same."

We were both quiet, but the ease that I'd been feeling had vanished. There was something else here, something I couldn't let happen. There wasn't any trouble coming right now, but I wasn't ready to start having an attraction to another man. I hadn't done anything wrong, and I wasn't looking to do anything, but I couldn't deny the spark I felt with Alamo—not if I kept sitting here with him.

"Are you ready to head back?"

For a moment Alamo looked at me like he was studying me, but then he nodded, and that was it. My escape ended. Now all that was left was putting together my life as a truly single woman, instead of one who was only pretending to be single. I could do it. I knew that.

It still hurt.